A Darker Light

A Darker Light

a novel

Heidi Priesnitz

THE DUNDURN GROUP
TORONTO

Editor: Barry Jowett
Copy-editor: Jennifer Bergeron
Design: Emma Kassirer
Printer: Transcontinental

National Library of Canada Cataloguing in Publication

Priesnitz, Heidi, 1972–
A darker light / Heidi Priesnitz.

ISBN 1-55002-459-0

1. Title.

PS8581.R469D37 2003   C813'.54   C2003-904050-X

1   2   3   4   5   07   06   05   04   03

Canada

THE CANADA COUNCIL | LE CONSEIL DES ARTS
FOR THE ARTS | DU CANADA
SINCE 1957 | DEPUIS 1957

ONTARIO ARTS COUNCIL
CONSEIL DES ARTS DE L'ONTARIO

We acknowledge the support of the Canada Council for the Arts and the Ontario Arts Council for our publishing program. We also acknowledge the financial support of the Government of Canada through the Book Publishing Industry Development Program and The Association for the Export of Canadian Books, and the Government of Ontario through the Ontario Book Publishers Tax Credit program, and the Ontario Media Development Corporation's Ontario Book Initiative.

Care has been taken to trace the ownership of copyright material used in this book. The author and the publisher welcome any information enabling them to rectify any references or credit in subsequent editions.

J. Kirk Howard, President

Printed and bound in Canada.⊕
Printed on recycled paper.
www.dundurn.com

Dundurn Press
8 Market Street
Suite 200
Toronto, Ontario, Canada
M5E 1M6

Dundurn Press
2250 Military Road
Tonawanda NY
U.S.A. 14150

acknowledgements

Thank you to Ken Shorley for hours of ideas, encouragement and love.

Thank you to the Nova Scotia Arts Council for a generous creation grant.

And thank you to everyone who has given me insight, energy and inspiration during the process of writing this book

I deeply appreciate all of it.

for Ken

book I

chapter 1

From the height of the terrace where she sat, Sara framed the city's rooftops against the mist of the morning sky.

click
Red tile hides beneath moist, swirling air. The hood-like dome of a mosque rises above the mist and shines in the early rays of sun. There is a shadow that might be a woman shaking out a rug through an open window. There is a hint of blue that might be the sea.

"That's not enough for a tip," a young British woman said, making Sara turn away from the view. "You've never waited tables, so you have no idea what it's like."

The woman's greying husband, with the vista of Tangier behind him, flicked a crumb off the white tablecloth and counted the foreign currency in his wallet. "I know you think I'm made of money, but my fortune has to last another two weeks."

"Just give him something reasonable. I can't stand looking cheap."

Sara turned away from the quibbling couple and tried to catch her waiter's eye. Lifting up her empty cup, she motioned for a refill. She always drank too much coffee while she was travelling. *I'll ease up when I get home,* she thought, but she was never there long enough for it to matter.

"Where will you go today?" the young waiter asked, as he cleared away her dirty plate.

"To take more photos," she said.

"You want a nice place to see? You go to supermall. Good deals. Brand names."

"I'm looking for something older, more historic." Her editor wanted a story about romantic getaways — quiet dining, gorgeous hotels, ancient mosques, exotic views. Something beautiful to look at, not something to take home.

"This is oldest restaurant in Morocco," he told her. "It has always been here."

"Can I take your photograph?" she asked, lifting her camera from her lap. "I work for an English-language magazine."

"Yes, yes. Wait please."

He rushed off into the kitchen, fixing his hair and checking his shirt for stains or spills. When he returned, he stood where she asked him. He smiled fully, his mouth curved, his eyes robust.

click
A young man dressed in good pants and a well-ironed shirt smiles too hard for the camera.

click
The young man blinks, although he tries not to.

click
He blinks again.

"Thank you — Shukran," Sara said, lowering her camera slightly. "Maybe one more coffee?"

"Na'am." He lifted her cup and began to pour.

click
A man, with his eyes lowered and his lips determined, pours coffee on a terrace in Tangier.

On the street, Sara chose to walk to her first destination. With the strong coffee still in her veins, she moved fast — her eyes darting from building to building, looking for images worthy of her camera. The air was already warming — she could feel the heat gathering on her skin. She stopped at an open door.

click
A swirl of cloth as a woman turns away.

Soon, the walls of the medina stood before her. Remaining in full sunlight, she shot a roll of thirty-six, capturing angles and arches and awkward corners. Kneeling down, with her body bent forward to create some shade, she changed films rapidly.

Once inside the medina, she photographed a series of decorated doorways. For some, she filled the frame with white plaster, for others she included bits of sky, or patches of the dry, caked earth. There were moments when the dust moved like a sparkling mist, but she avoided these, knowing her editor would not approve of flying dirt.

Pressing herself into a wall to get the distance she required, she waited for some young boys to pass by. At the last minute, the smallest boy changed direction and ran straight through an archway. Sara snapped quickly, following the boy's movement with the camera's eye. After he disappeared, she repositioned herself so that she could see down the full length of the street. A middle-aged man with crooked teeth and a white hat watched her from his idle newspaper stand as she shot another series of frames.

"Good holiday?" he called out, scratching an elbow with one of his dark, inky hands.

"Excuse me?"

"Good holiday?"

"Actually, I'm working."

"No!" He shook his head. "You are too happy to be working. Look at me, I am working!"

Sara smiled. She couldn't imagine doing anything else. "You're right," she said. "It's a great job."

"Maybe we trade?" the man offered. "I am free — you stand in hot sun until it is time to eat, sleep and start over again. Or maybe you come home with me? Bring your camera, take nice picture of us together in…"

His voice trailed off as Sara walked away. She was finished with mosques and archways and ready to move on. After walking back to her hotel, she ordered dinner and amused herself by critiquing the clumsy composition of a handful of shiny tourist brochures.

Waking before the alarm, Sara bought a banana at a stand near the hotel and ate it while walking. Then, taking a cab to speed up the process, she headed for a small Internet café that, for much of the day, lounged lazily in the shade of the university. Through the propped-open door she could see two computers, both occupied by silent, stone-faced students. Waiting her turn with a cup of coffee and a square of almond baklava, she sat down and organized her notes. She kept track of everything. For her editor, she noted where, when and what time of day. For herself, specific or unusual lens choices and camera settings. When a computer finally became available, she typed fast, double-checking place names but misspelling her own.

Leaving the café, Sara was ready to courier her rolls of film. She walked to a little shop she'd used once before and pleaded for rush service, but five days to America was the best they could do. Carefully she bundled the rolls in a protective box and began to negotiate her way through a courier form that was difficult to read. With a combination of blind guessing and explicit hand gestures from the clerk, Sara wrote something on every line. Her signature was a scribble in the lower left corner. The clerk smiled and placed the package, along with an overflowing pile of others, on a large central desk. Sara wondered how many slid unnoticed to the floor.

After a last stop at her hotel, she was ready to leave the country. Ordering a cab from the lobby, she began to prepare herself for the hassle of getting on the ferry.

click

An unveiled woman with curly dark hair and long thin limbs lifts her camera bags over a mob of hungry young boys. All eyes are focused on her as she plows through the crowd.

Surrounding every other foreigner on the way to the ferry there was a mirror image. Except some of the children were grown men and some of them wanted more than money.

Keeping her mouth set and her eyes firm, Sara pushed her way forward.

Once on board, she decided to stand outside. She loved watching the city disappear one frame at a time as the ferry chugged through the water.

After a two-hour wait in Algeciras, Sara caught an overcrowded bus to Malaga. When she arrived at the station, she grabbed her luggage and hailed a cab to her favourite hotel. The four-storey building with its clean, simple exterior looked as familiar as her own apartment. Gratefully, she smiled at the man who signed her into a room.

Once upstairs, she dropped her luggage and ran herself a hot bath. The splashing water erased the tension of the bus ride, and her stomach began to settle down. Moving slowly, she dried off, dressed in clean clothes and ran her hands through her mess of damp hair.

Relaxing into the comforting arms of the Costa del Sol, Sara indulged herself in the evening she had hungered for. The restaurant she chose was lit with a gentle glow that bounced off the whitewashed walls and illuminated her food. She ate slowly, sipping wine and watching the flickering shadows her candle made on the table. At the end of the large meal, she tipped her waitress generously and took one last gulp of strong, sobering coffee.

As she walked back to the hotel, she could still feel the wine buzzing slightly in her head. Squinting at the street's detail, her eyes were as full and sore as her belly. Silently she walked into the cool, formal lobby without noticing the ceiling fans twirling endlessly above. She kept her head down, imagining frame after frame of symmetrically patterned carpet.

"Señora?" a man's voice said.

"Hmm?" Sara paused but did not look up.

"My name is Alvaro."

"Yes?"

"I have often seen you walk this way — your eyes down around your ankles. Why not look up," he said, smiling, "when you have so many things to look up at?"

"You've seen me before?"

"Si. When you checked in, and also other times."

"I was," she brought her hand to her face and smiled, "I was looking at the carpet."

"So, you are not sad then?"

"No. Is that what you thought?"

"Beautiful woman, always alone, drowning her sorrow in her ankles…"

"I was thinking."

"I have been thinking too," the young man said, coming out from behind the counter. "I want to show you somewhere happy."

"I was just going to bed."

"Oh." The man's wild eyes flashed through a whole roll of possibility. "Maybe tomorrow then, unless you want… no. No, you must sleep. Good night, Señora. Sleep well. I will show you some other time."

"Si. Some other time."

As she climbed the stairs, she was thinking of the boyish man with his muscular arms and well-formed smile. In her room, she walked to the small basin and ran water from the tap. Her neck was tanned where it showed through her loosely buttoned shirt and there was more colour on her cheeks than she expected. Squinting into the large, square mirror, she framed herself against the room's soft texture. She fixed her hair before pressing the shutter.

click
A dark curl escapes the others.

With the imaginary photograph complete, she washed her hands and dried them on the bleached white towel. Walking quietly to the door, she eased it open and allowed her gaze to explore the empty hallway. She could imagine his arrival — a blur of black and white dancing through the glowing red. She would use a long exposure to capture him as he passed through her life. *C–l–i–c–k* and then *click, click.* Movement and a sudden goodbye.

When the streetlights outside the window blinked off one by one and the sun rose on the other side of the building, Sara's head was under a pillow. She surfaced briefly from a dream and then rolled back into sleep.

At noon, still lolling in the smoothness of the hotel sheets, she was reluctant to get up. Her mind was filled with images from other visits to Malaga.

click
The dripping foliage of freshly watered flowers on a third-storey balcony.

click
Through an iron gate, an abandoned wooden chair on the well-worn steps of a Gothic cathedral.

click
A scattering of birds as a young boy chases a dog through a half-forgotten street.

Sara enjoyed the visual luxury of the city — she could sit at a sidewalk café and take a handful of beautiful shots without leaving her chair.

When the phone rang, she was startled and forced to sit up. She reached over and answered, recognizing the silence immediately. It was her editor.

"Hello?"

"Sara, did I get you up?"

"No. I was just about to run out the door. What is it? Did you get the Portugal negatives?"

"Sara, I want to talk to you about your photos."

Pulling the sheet over her breasts, Sara listened. Joyce rarely called unless she wanted to change an assignment, and sometimes not even then. Email was cheaper and easier to use.

"I think I sent seven rolls," Sara said.

"Yes, I have them, but they're horrible. In fact, this is a terrible batch."

"I don't understand."

"Maybe you should check your camera."

"But —"

"These negatives are all trash. There's nothing here I can use."

"But, I thought you wanted shots of —"

"The subject matter is great," Joyce said. "I'm talking about the quality. They're all fuzzy. I think you should check your camera."

"I don't know what you're talking about. My camera's fine!"

"Well then check your head, because I can't use anything you sent."

The phone went dead in Sara's hand. Joyce gave no further instructions.

Unable to swallow, Sara got up and spit into the sink. Pulling her temples back to stretch her tired eyes, she glared at herself in the mirror. With an elastic band she pulled back her dirty hair and bent over to wash her face. She needed to test her camera.

Brushing off the woman at the reception desk, Sara rushed into the street. Adjusting her camera quickly, she took a series of frantic shots. Then, deciding she needed to match the conditions in Portugal, she hailed a cab.

Sitting in the back seat, her hand waiting to open the door, she rocked with the motion of the car. Reading her anxiety, the driver wove through the heavy traffic as quickly as he could. When they arrived, she thrust a bill at him without waiting for the change.

Standing on the beach, she squinted at the light reflecting off the water and the tiny speckles of sand. Pulling her camera out of the bag, she aimed low, just below the horizon. The intensity of the sun made it difficult to see.

click
Three-quarters water. One-quarter sky.

click
One-quarter water. Three-quarters sky.

click
Half water. Half sky.

click
A wave in transition.

Mechanically, everything about the camera seemed fine. Aim. Shoot. Advance. She had done this a thousand times. After shooting the rest of the roll, she walked back to the main road. This time she would develop the prints. She wanted something that she could study with her own eyes.

With twelve hours to wait for the film to be processed, Sara sat in a crowded sidewalk café drinking strong black coffee. Absently she stared at the texture of the table. When her eyes glazed over, she shifted to the dark green foliage dangling from the wall beside her. It moved from translucent to opaque as the wind blew it in and out of the dappled sun.

Jittery from the coffee and the anxiety of the wait, Sara walked down to the harbour. With the orange glow of the sky behind it, she chose a perfect angle to sit and watch the sun fall. In the distance, there were small boats returning, full of fish and tired men. The rusty hues of their bodies matched the sky. Out of habit, Sara lifted her camera and took a few shots. Then she waited for her subjects to draw nearer.

On the boat she chose, the fish shone silver and grey, their mouths pale against the black of the floor. Three men, with faces wrinkled from many seasons of sun, shouted with their arms — *move this way, more to the left, now tie her off.* Sara waited until their faces had turned away. She wanted hands and rope and squirming fish, not the eyes of tired fishermen. Although she tried to tighten the focus of her telephoto lens, she couldn't get a clear view. She shook it, shielded her face, wiped the lens clean. But there was no change.

Kicking up stones, she started walking the short distance back to the hotel.

Taking a shortcut down a quiet, narrow street, she watched a man come out of his repair shop. As he turned to lock the door, she saw "Fuji" and "Kodak" on large plastic signs posted in the window.

"Perdón, Señor! Habla inglés?"

Looking her up and down, he answered suspiciously, "Si. Un poco."

"Do you repair cameras?"

"Si."

"Please," she started to dig hers out of the bag, "the focus is blurry."

"No. Today I am closed."

"It's an emergency," Sara pleaded.

"Five minutes." He held up his hand, displaying each finger in case she didn't understand.

While Sara waited in the cramped space of the storefront, the repairman took out his tools and looked closely at the camera.

Returning to the counter, the man spoke carefully, exaggerating each syllable. "Camera no problem," he said. "No problem."

"I'm a professional photographer," she told him. "PHOTOGRAPHER. I *know* my lens has a mechanical problem. My photos are BLURRY."

"No, Señora." He shook his head.

"Have you worked on Nikons before?"

"Camera no problem!" the grey-haired man repeated.

"But close-up shots come out fuzzy — FUZZY!" Sara explained again, wondering how much English he really understood. "The lens won't focus. NO FOCUS."

"Si. But CAMERA NO PROBLEM!" the man shouted. He put the Nikon on the counter, but she wouldn't take it. "Por favor, Señora. Por favor." He pulled keys out of his pocket, as if ready to lock up the store.

"Please, just look at it again," she said. "This is IMPORTANT!"

"¡Basta! Camera is good."

Slamming the door, she slung the camera bag over her shoulder and started walking. She would look for another repair shop tomorrow.

Pulling open the hotel's heavy lobby doors gave her a rush of comfort. Soon she would throw herself into the tub.

"Señora!" the woman at the front desk called. "Señora, I have an envelope for you."

Sara stopped and turned.

"It has been here all day," the woman said. "And this too." She held up a fax.

In the elevator, Sara scanned the page. It was an apology from her editor.

Look, I didn't mean to come down so hard on you. I've been thinking, maybe you should go home for awhile. You've been away a long time. Do what you have to do to change your ticket.

She crushed the paper with her right hand. She would think about it in the morning — after her trial photos had been developed. Opening the envelope she read, *Meet me at four. Bring your camera. — Alvaro.*

It was already after five.

chapter 2

With the window and the early-morning rush of Halifax traffic at her back, Sitara raised her hands from prayer to temple — elbows pointed down, palms pressed hard together. Balancing on one leg with the other tucked into half-lotus against her supporting thigh, her belly-expanding breath was deep and even. Standing in a self-made temple did more than calm her mind and regulate her breathing, it connected her consciousness with her body — something she needed now more than usual.

After moving through a flow of postures, she rested for a moment before sitting on a small Persian rug. With her pelvic bones balanced evenly on the ground and her hands upturned on her knees, she let her eyes softly close. The emptiness she searched for was beginning to fill her head.

Following a long period of meditation, Sitara stood up. In the bedroom, she slid off her black drawstring pants and looked for some jeans. After finding a pair that was fading from black to grey, she pulled a small black t-shirt from her drawer and slipped it on.

For breakfast she sliced an apple that was past its prime and dipped it in almond butter straight from the jar. To lift the sticky residue of the nuts and rinse away the mushiness of the fruit, she chased the meal with a glass of grapefruit juice.

Stepping into the bathroom she brushed her teeth with cinnamon and baking soda. It was dry and gritty and didn't leave her mouth feeling clean. Spitting it out, she decided to use the remainder of the jar on the grimy scum around the drain.

As she cast a quick glance at a belly-high mirror, she grabbed a book she had been reading the night before, and let herself out the door.

On the bike ride to her clinic, she cut off several cars and almost hit a pedestrian waiting at a crosswalk. Sighing, she thought, *Maybe meditation doesn't work.*

The sun flashed through twenty-four empty bottles before disappearing again behind a cloud. Jasmine, cinnamon, ylang ylang, cedar. The lavender was in her hand.

Three drops of oil fell into a shell.

There were two patients waiting in the lobby. Sitara was more than an hour behind. She set the shell on the windowsill next to the row of coloured glass and inhaled deeply from the bottle that was still in her hand.

Her father had bad timing. She'd always known that — her mother had reminded her every day. Parvati was forty-one when her husband made her pregnant. That was her opinion — that he'd made her pregnant, as if it was fully his fault. She'd married him on the condition that he wouldn't and, of course, he hadn't intended to. Even as the years went by, she accepted no responsibility for her baby's birth. Sitara was ill-conceived, and her mother never let her forget it.

Hearing the restless shuffle of clothing in her waiting room, she put the bottle down, smoothed the white sheet of her examination table and checked the bedside drawer for cotton swabs and needles. Then, opening her office door, she smiled intentionally and motioned for her next patient to come in.

Patrick sat down in the chair across from her, barely touching the wood. Like a bird, he fluttered every extremity. His eyes darted and fled. Every time he entered her clinic, he brought a wave of motion with him, but today it made her queasy.

Forgoing her usual pleasantries, she invited him to lie down. Glancing up at the *Meridians of Chinese Medicine* poster framed above the bed, she listened to the flow of blood through the veins on his wrist and legs and asked him a series of questions.

"How have you been sleeping?"

"So-so."

"How are your bowels?"

"Fine."

"What about headaches?"

"Same as usual."

"Why did my father choose today?"

Patrick started to fidget and Sitara looked away.

Sarasvati beckons to me with three of her four arms. I crawl into the kitchen cupboards to see her. She hides next to the sink, where my parents keep the spices. When I close the door I am surrounded by a darkness that is rich and raw with scent. I reach for the cardamom pods, thinking they are her favourite because they are mine. I try to crush them with my fingers, but they are awkward and tough. Instead I use my foot. Finally the papery shells burst open, and the strangely shaped seeds dig into my heel. When I find her, Sarasvati is warm and aromatic. She speaks to me in Sanskrit and I understand. It is our secret code. Holding the cardamom jar tightly in my hand, I ask

her to sing. Parvati, my mother, has been gone for hours and I
am alone.

Sitara rolled her shoulders back and straightened her spine.
After she turned eleven she no longer fit into that cupboard,
although she tried, by not eating, to stay small. For the next few
years she hid in her room or locked herself in the bathroom.
But her father always caught on. By age thirteen, her hiding
places were no longer in the apartment — she slept in parks or
on other people's floors. An old woman at the temple sometimes "forgot" to lock the door.

"Do you not care where she has been?" Bapa asks.
Parvati stares at him. "Has she been somewhere?"
I cringe, thinking that she notices him only because they share
a bed.
"She has been gone three nights."
"Oh." My mother shifts back to her book.
"Parvati, Sitara would like to speak with you."
I try to broaden my shoulders, lengthen my spine, make myself
large enough for her to see. She lifts an eyebrow but does not raise
her eyes.

With too much force, Sitara pushed a needle into Patrick's
leg. He winced and clenched his fists. She'd missed. Slowly,
without looking at his face, she withdrew the needle and rein-
serted it into the proper place.

Slinking off to my room, I hear Bapa say, "You should pay
some attention to her. She needs a mother."
"She has you."
"Parvati." He lowers his voice. "She is a woman now. There is
only so much I can do."

Ashamed, I close the door, knowing that he has seen the blood stains on my bed.

"I'm sorry," Patrick said, pounding his chest and trying to swallow a cough.

Sitara smiled. "Let it go, if you want to. A trapped cough is like a caged animal. The more you hold it back, the more angry it gets. There's a reason it wants out."

Eagerly, Patrick sat up and coughed and coughed and coughed.

"Maybe save a little for later," Sitara added, as his throat went dry.

He stopped.

"Lie down again. There's one more thing I want to do."

Using her dark, slender hand, Sitara pulled a new needle from its plastic sheath and positioned it at the midpoint of Patrick's collarbone. She had been treating him for depression, but all she could think of was releasing the phlegm that was clouding his heart.

Just after dinner someone knocks on the door. Standing up, Parvati coughs loudly and Bapa escorts me out of the room. I know the cough is a signal, because my bapa always responds the same way. After closing the door of my room, he sits down next to me on the bed and places his favourite book gently on his lap. The cover is stained with oil — "pakora pee" he calls it — and the binding is coming undone. He tells me he has had it since childhood — the one treasure he was allowed to take with him when he left home. Although I know this already, he reminds me that he is the eighth of nine children, and the only one who moved away from their province.

Proudly he lifts open the grease-marked cover and shows me the inscription inside. He reads it in Hindi before he says it in

English. Then he takes my hand and helps me run my fingers over the tiny letters. I try but, unlike him, I cannot feel the surface of the ink. I think maybe it has worn down and that all he feels is a memory. Impatiently, I beg him to move on. Smiling, he does. On the first page there are a lot of words that I cannot read. He translates some, with embellishments I think, because it's different every time. But it doesn't matter what he says — I'm busy feasting my eyes on the long hair, radiant skin and beautiful saris of the full-colour goddesses. In total, there are sixteen illustrations — nine gods, seven goddesses — and I have memorized them all. To me, Sarasvati is the most powerful because she is also on the front cover.

In the next room I can hear laughter. I ask Bapa, "Who is out there?"

"Some people from your mother's work."

"But who is laughing?"

"Your mother," he says.

I'm surprised because I've never heard her laugh like that before.

Repeating the same fast movement, Sitara removed each of the needles from her patient's skin. They were still humming as she dropped them into the sharps container next to the bed.

"We're done," she said. "When you're ready, you can get up."

Scratching his head, Patrick sat up and swung his legs several times before he jumped down. As Sitara wrote out a receipt, he shed more energy by unfastening and refastening his watch-strap. She could see that she was still running more than forty-five minutes behind.

"Shall we book another?" she asked.

"Yes, of course. Same time next week."

Like clockwork, she thought. *Something to write in his book.* "Try this," she said, handing him a bottle of herbs. "It will help to resolve your phlegm."

"I will, I will. Thank you." He jittered out the door.

Sitting briefly before admitting her next patient, Sitara lifted the lid of her teacup. There was no steam, but still she took a sip. *Hot, green tea is bliss,* she thought, *cold, it is piss.* She could no longer recall his face, but a professor at college had spoken it repeatedly — his own personal mantra. Even with its lid, her thin porcelain mug couldn't keep things permanently warm.

Standing again, Sitara looked out the window. There was a breeze on Hollis Street — she could see the bare-branched trees swaying — although no air moved through the clinic. For months she had been meaning to buy a fan. Lifting the brown and white shell from its place on the windowsill, she took one last long breath before leaving her office. Cool lavender to soothe her childhood heat.

Her next patient was an eighteen-month-old baby who had been waiting, more or less quietly, on the lap of her frizzy-haired mother. The toddler suffered from severe allergies, and visits to the clinic were becoming routine.

"Come in, Liz. I'm sorry you had to wait so long."

The woman stood, brushed some of the crumbs off her warm, creased lap, and carried her daughter into Sitara's office.

"How are you, Bella?" Sitara asked.

"Her runny nose is still bad," Liz answered. "And the only thing she'll eat right now is banana."

"Actually, banana is another food you should try to avoid for awhile."

"I'll try," Liz said, putting her daughter down on the examination bed.

"Alright Bella," Sitara whispered, as she reached for the baby's small hand, "let's see if we can toughen you up some more. Show me your tongue."

Bella turned away and buried her face in her mother's shoulder.

Liz laughed. "I saw plenty of that tongue this morning, believe me — every time I tried to give her a spoonful of anything. She just doesn't want to eat."

"Is it still swollen?" Sitara asked.

"Yes."

"Do you think she'll lie down?"

"It's possible, but I wouldn't count on it." Liz turned to Bella. "Hey sweetie, it's sleepy time. Do you want to lie down and look at the stars?"

"Uh-uh." Bella shook her head.

"It would be a big help to Mommy."

"Ahhhhhhh." Bella grabbed her mother's hair.

"Alright, maybe we'll try it like this." Liz climbed onto the white-covered bed beside her daughter and, sitting cross-legged, lifted Bella into her arms.

Sitara opened the drawer and pulled out a fresh packet of needles. The baby's skin matched her mother's perfectly — identical texture, hue, freckledness. They looked like they belonged together, as if one would be incomplete without the other. Sitara swabbed at the spot where she wanted to place the first needle, while Liz sang quietly to her squirming daughter.

Sarasvati wraps two arms around me. With a third, she smoothes my licorice hair, and with a fourth, she draws spirals like smoke rings on my cheeks. I hold her sari in my hands. It is burgundy and green — smooth and silky as coconut milk. There are old Sanskrit lullabies embroidered with gold thread in rows along the border. She sings them for me as she rocks me to sleep, her breath sweet with the smell of halvah.

As Sitara placed the first needle, the baby began to scream. Bella's pale skin was irritated and impressionable. Every time Sitara held her, she made a red blotch with her thumb.

"I'm sorry, little one," she said, trying to make her work as gentle as possible. "This won't take long." Still trying to clear the baby's congestion, Sitara inserted another needle.

I take a deep breath in, although only one of my nostrils is clear, and then breathe out fast and hard trying to flap the white paper tissue that hangs over my nose. Unsatisfied, I try again. I want to make the bird fly. The tissue is a white swan and I know that if I try hard enough, it will fly back to Sarasvati, with me tucked safely under its wings. I have been sniffing for as long as I can remember. Today is the first day I can breathe without having my mouth hang open. Bapa has just given me a steam bath because in the night I kept him awake with my snoring.

"Sitara is sick," I hear him say to Parvati.

"What do you mean?"

"She has a sniffle."

"She's a child," Parvati says. "They all get sniffles. Tell her to go to bed."

And so my bapa leads me back to bed. I complain because it's Saturday and he promised to take me to the park. But he is afraid of my mother and says that we can't go out. He offers to show me his book, but I dive under the blankets and hide there until he is gone. Then I slink over to the window and, using my dresser as a chair, I look out and watch other kids playing on the street.

Sitara removed the needles from the baby's small body. Bella was tense from screaming and Sitara wondered if any of her treatment would actually help.

"Let me know what happens," she told Liz. "And call me if you need anything. My answering machine is always on even if I'm not here."

"I thank you, even if Bella doesn't," Liz replied.

"She'll be fine." Sitara smiled. "She's strong and she'll find more strength in how much you love her."

"I can only keep trying."

"You're doing great, Liz." Sitara put her hand on the woman's burdened shoulder. "Goodbye Bella."

Liz smiled but Bella hid her face again and played at being coy.

"She really does like you. She sits by the door waiting when she knows it's time to come here."

"It's alright," Sitara said, laughing. "I've always been someone people love to hate."

"Thanks again," Liz said. She and Bella slipped out the door.

Following their path to the waiting room, Sitara prepared to accept her next patient, but there was no one there. She double-checked her calendar and confirmed that Rafqa had a three o'clock appointment. It wasn't often that her patients were late, especially when she herself was running behind. Distractedly, she went back into her office and sat down. The wind whipped a maze of brown leaves past her window — they tumbled like the half-digested chunks of almonds in the pit of her stomach. She stood up and plugged the kettle in to make more tea.

I am dressed in a silky black sari that shines as much as my hair, which is pulled back softly with a gold-coloured clip. On my left wrist I have twenty-seven glass and metal bangles — almost two for every year. The high-heeled shoes I wear are borrowed from the woman across the hall and I have paper stuffed in the toes to make them fit. Bapa stands and admires me in the front hall. I think he is proud of me for graduating, but he says he simply wants to remember my beauty.

We are waiting for Parvati to finish on the telephone. She has been gabbing for over an hour. Finally I beg Bapa to rush her because I don't want to be late. He calls to me that they are com-

*ing, and says I should go down to the car and wait. Holding my
breath, I open the door and pretend to go out.*

*"She looks like an Indian peasant," I hear her say. "What hap-
pened to that pretty dress I bought for her?"*

*"She prefers the sari," Bapa answers. "Now hurry. She is wait-
ing in the car."*

"I can't," Parvati says. "My head hurts. I'm going to lie down."

As Bapa protests, I silently close the door.

*In the car, he says, "Your mother has a hole in her head, and
will not be coming."*

*Biting my tongue, I wonder if it's a mistake in his English, or
if he hates her as much as I do. On the drive to school, I manage
to bend each one of my twenty-seven bangles.*

Releasing the unconscious grip on her left wrist, Sitara
stretched out her arms. She focused her eyes on her fingernails
and then turned her hands over and made an offering with her
palms. She could feel the strain through the muscle just below
her left elbow. Pulling back with her right, as if tightening a
bow, she shot a burst of tension along her sore arm and out the
window. Unintentionally, she hit a twig as it whirled itself to the
ground. Sighing, she remembered that she'd always had good
aim. She'd learned early by practising on her mother. At first,
the things she flung at Parvati were made of stone. But later, as
her resentment grew, they were made of words, which stung
much harder.

"Sitara, I am here. In Halifax. At a hotel," her father had told
her during his early morning phone call. "There are many
things I want to tell you," he'd said with a crack in his voice that
reminded her of calling India — reminded her of Chacha, who
always told her that he loved her, even though as a child she
knew that adults only loved each other.

Startled by the telephone, she'd knocked a book off the

table beside her bed, tipping both a mug of cold tea and the iron candleholder Carrie had given her for late nights of reading in bed.

"Listen, I have to go," she'd said to her father, while kicking off the blankets to escape the heat.

"Sitara, I have come a long way." It had been four years since they'd spoken.

"I can meet you after work. Where are you staying?"

"The Westin on Hollis Street, by the train station," he'd said, in a voice that sounded as grey as his hair. "Is it far?"

"Yes, quite far," she'd told him, although it was only a few blocks away.

She dropped a handful of leaves into a bamboo strainer and filled her cup with hot water. Then, sitting full-lotus on a small woven rug, she deepened her breath and waited for the tea to steep. Slowly she lowered her gaze to the floor and tried to let the space between her eyebrows soften. Memories boiled like burned dahl inside her, turning over and over, releasing their potent juices. She swallowed to wash the taste away.

"Sitara," she told herself, "it is only dinner with your father. You've done it a million times before — almost once a day for eighteen years. How hard can it be?"

Feeling the rough wool of the rug beneath her toes, she rocked from side to side to reposition her weight and then let her back and neck curl slightly forward before straightening her spine again. After a deep breath, she heard the rustle of clothing in the waiting room. Standing abruptly, she grabbed the corner of her desk until the blood rebalanced itself in her brain. Rafqa was more than an hour late.

"Namaste, Sitara," a voice called to her. "Do not be afraid."

Sitara stepped into the waiting room.

The woman had four arms. "Your bapa waits for you," she said. She was holding a cell phone and a jar of cardamom.

Sitara pressed her hands into prayer and sank to the floor. She recognized the dark green choli and the rich burgundy sari with the lullabies embroidered in gold.

"You are not a little girl anymore," the woman said. "Do not play one for me, and do not play one for your bapa. When you go to him, show him who you *are*, not who you used to be. Accept him and he will accept you."

Still on the floor, Sitara reached out to touch the silky coconut milk of the woman's sari. "Sarasvati, I haven't seen you for so long. How are you?"

"It is not your worry."

A cloud passed between the sun and the two angled skylights in the ceiling of the clinic. The image of the deity paled.

"Sarasvati, please. Don't leave. I can treat you."

"I am not the one," her voice shimmered as she faded away, "who needs your attention, Sitara. It is you."

Closing her eyes, Sitara parted her lips and exhaled.

chapter 3

Flying over the tiny speck of a Portuguese island, Sara let her head fall back. The headrest smelled of cheap perfume. With her camera lying casually in her lap she closed her eyes. Her mind was focused on the water below.

click
Blue-green water spotted with small sandy islands, like the brown flecks in a blue eye.

"You see, the thing is," he had started talking at the airport, before the plane had even left the ground, "we sell them by the boxful — square boxful." He was laughing. "I sell *round* rubber rings in *square* boxes." More laughter. "Of course, everything is standardized, organized by size." His shoulder touched hers. His blue linen suit was too heavy for the heat of Spain. She could see the sweat stains around his cuffs. "Do you know how many rings fit in a box this big?" His pudgy white hands showed no sign of tan. "One hundred and fifty. And the market is expanding. Modeque has come out with a new design for their 'Elite' line of faucets that demands our product. Wherever one is installed, we gain a new customer. Our rings have revolutionized kitchen sinks. We've begun a whole new era of dripless faucets that truly don't drip. And it's all as simple as that." He pulled one out of his pocket to demonstrate.

Sara turned her head slightly and produced a small nod. Wisps of white cloud had formed so that she couldn't see the ocean. With her left hand, she pulled down the blind.

"These little devils are the reason I'm alive. They've given me the house, the pool, the tennis courts. Hell, I'm even build-ing a golf course out the back." His chest was shaking with the kind of exaggerated laugh that proud men show in public. Overrun with the momentum of his own sharing, he searched his breast pocket for a photo of his four-year-old boy. "Adorable, isn't he? And handsome." The boy's fingers were cov-ered in rings. "He plays with them like toys," the man said, "but someday they'll be made of gold." He put his photo away. "First time in Malaga?"

Sara shook her head. "No," she said.

"You know, Spain's rubber market is virtually untapped. It's a miracle, really. It was here all this time and we just didn't know about it. Of course, they don't know they need us yet, but I have a feeling that's all about to…"

Absently, Sara reached into the pocket of the seat in front of her and pulled out the in-flight magazine. She wanted to read, to ward off the suit with a mouth that she was stuck next to, but the print was small and, no matter how she angled the bulb, the overhead light was not bright enough. Flipping through the glossy pages, she found a photo of one of the mosques that had been part of her own recent assignment. This version was badly cropped — or perhaps badly photographed.

click
A mosque with half a minaret.

Sara closed the magazine.

"...he always says the same damn thing to me, but I still don't buy it! The last time I was in Missouri I didn't even bother to look him up. I just don't do business that way. Our base price is the best I can do. I offer the same deal to everyone. That's what makes it fair, and if he doesn't like it, he can..."

click
The insides of a man's mouth — three shiny fillings on the lower right side, a large dry tongue, slightly-chapped lips.

"...'That's just downright poor form,' I told him, 'I think you should retract that statement,' but he butted his cigarette out in my face and told me he'd already switched to my competitor. Some things aren't sacred like they used to be, I can tell you that, but to —"

"Please shut up," Sara said under her breath, keeping her face towards the window.

"— cut a man off in the middle of a business deal. There isn't any justice in that. Hey, you alright lady? You're awfully quiet over there!"

The plane hit an air pocket and the bump temporarily shut the salesman's mouth.

Sara sighed. She was thinking of an old boyfriend who had given her a small rubber ring to "keep her safe" on her journeys. At their final parting, he'd tied it to her camera bag with a thick black thread. She'd held it intermittently — smooth and soothing between her fingers — for almost a year before it was torn off in a small skirmish with a conveyor belt. She began drawing a mental map of his face just as the salesman next to her cleared his throat as if to speak again.

Sara closed her eyes and pretended to sleep.

After a short cab ride from her apartment in Halifax's south end, Sara stood at the understated front doors of the Nova Scotia College of Art and Design where, for four years, she had studied photography.

Walking up the familiar stairs, she half expected to recognize the people she passed. But, of course, her friends had graduated years before. She had lost touch with most of them, since she spent so little time in the city. Opening the door to the photography labs, she took a deep breath in — the smell hadn't changed. It was the same vile combination of chemicals mixed with hundred-year-old, over-exhaled air. The only fresh oxygen was at the bottom of the stairs where it blew in off Duke Street every time someone opened the door.

Evan's office door was closed, as always. He tried to hide from the incessant chatter of the nearby hallways and common rooms. He preferred to communicate with cameras.

Sara knocked quietly, not wanting to startle him or disturb his solitude.

"Hello?" he called with an air of irritation that made her smile.

They should stick him in the basement, she thought, *where no one would find him.*

"Hello?" he called again, before she pushed open the door. "Try advancing the film," he said. "It usually solves the problem."

"I tried that."

"Sara? I forgot you were coming!" He laid down the camera he was repairing. "My apologies. It's first-year trauma day. You would have been the fifth one. Come in." He wiped his hands on a fine flannel cloth and stood up to greet her. "Where's the invalid?"

"Here," she said, patting the bulging bag at her side. "I don't know what the problem is. I just can't get it to focus. I took it to a man in Spain, but either he didn't understand me, or didn't want to do the job. He brushed me off."

"Probably had to meet a woman," Evan said. "Well, let me have a look."

Sara passed him her camera. She trusted his steady hands as much as the precision of his eye.

"Meter working?"

"I think so. It's a focus problem. This is what the shots look like." She pulled a handful of photographs from her pocket and placed them on Evan's desk.

He glanced up and said, "There are quite a few like that posted in the hallway."

Sara smiled. She remembered the exercises — intentional lack of focus, capturing fast-moving objects, long handheld exposures in the blackness of night. In those days, she was proud of her blur.

"Is Marisa still here?" she asked. The wild-haired woman had been her favourite instructor in first year. She had flickered and flashed like a silent movie — bright, except for the odd dark frame.

"Yeah. She surfaces," Evan said. "Can I see your other friends?"

"What?"

"I mean, your other lenses."

"You still don't get out much, do you?" she asked, handing him a telephoto and a wide angle.

"You mean out there? No. I can't stand the romantic drivel. It starts on the other side of that door and drips its way through every street of this city."

Sara smiled. For four years she and a friend had tried tirelessly to bring him to dinner and a late-night movie, but he refused. He was comfortable with his own world and uncommonly afraid of theirs.

"I've seen your work," he said.

"You have?"

"Sure."

She stared at him with surprise.

"I do read magazines!"

"Of course," she said. "So, what do you think?"

"It's good." He turned his head to look at her. "There's nothing wrong with your lenses."

"What?"

"Your camera is fine, Sara. I don't know what to suggest."

"Well, my editor's rejecting photos. I have to do something!"

"Have you considered seeing an optometrist?"

"You think the problem is with my eyes?"

"It's possible. People wear glasses."

"Yeah, but I thought…" She stood and reached for the photos she'd put on his desk.

"You thought you could blame the camera."

"Yeah, that's what I wanted to think."

"It can't hurt to have someone take a look. Sara, it's a good camera. Be patient with yourself. It'll all work out."

"Thanks for your time," she said. "I appreciate it." She reached for the camera he was holding out to her. Its familiar body was warm to her touch, but as foreign as a lover who had betrayed her. She buried it in her bag and slowly opened the office door. With her head down, she walked out to the street, past the young, able-eyed students who filled the halls.

By afternoon, Sara was staring at eye charts in a darkened room. She could read most of what she was asked to, but still the optometrist kept working.

"Anyone in your family wear glasses?" he asked.

"My father."

"Mine too," he said, as if it was a rare coincidence. Aiming for the back of her head, he grazed the skin of her cheek and ear. He was trying to bring her face closer to the wheel of lenses. "Is it still cool out there? It was brisk this morning."

"It's cool," Sara said. *But not as cool as your hands.* She was already as far forward as she could go. Any further would break the bridge of her nose.

"Alright. I'm just going to slide in a little closer here." His rolling chair squeaked when he moved it. "Now..." he leaned away from his instruments and glanced at the clipboard lying beside him on the counter, "Sara, I'm going to ask you not to blink. This will only take a minute — I just want to have a good look inside your eyes."

The young optometrist's chair was pulled up so close that his knees were touching hers. She tried not to blink. As if the two organs were connected, she also forgot to breathe.

After an unnerving moment of stillness, he pushed his chair back and asked, "Tell me again what you're seeing?"

Sara sighed and her stale breath created a haze around her. This was the third time he'd asked her to describe the sensation she was experiencing.

After more examinations under maximum magnification, he pushed the equipment away and shook his head. "I've never seen anything like this," he said. "I'd like you to see a specialist. You may need surgery."

click
A nervous surgeon slips and plays soccer with her eyeball.

click
Like a sloppy tailor, the man with the needle runs out of thread.

click
Prepared in a spicy sauce, she is offered two steaming eyeballs advertised as the specialty of the house.

As she walked home the wind was cold and fierce. She had forgotten that in Halifax rain could be horizontal.

Stepping into her apartment, she heard the insistent ring of her telephone. With her boots and rain jacket still on, she walked over the hardwood floor to answer it.

"Hello?"

"Sara, I can't believe I'm hearing you!"

"Who is this?"

"You don't recognize me?"

"Kyle?"

click
A long wet kiss.

"I heard you were back in town. It's been ages — do you want to have dinner?"

click
A handful of wild roses, their thorns all carefully cut off.

"Sure. Of course. When?"

"How about in an hour?" he asked. "I'm off at five."

There was cold water running down her neck and face from her hair. "Alright."

"Should we meet at the Argyle?"

"Sure."

"Will I know you?"

"What?"

"Well," he said, "it's been awhile! Unless," he added quickly, "you haven't changed."

"I'll be the blind woman with a cane," she said. "See you soon."

Still holding the phone in her hand, she slid down the wall into the puddle she'd made. An hour with Kyle would be like an hour out of the rain.

We broke up a long time ago. She could hear the words in her head, but couldn't make her mouth say them. He was sweeping her hair aside, trying to reach her skin.

They were sitting on his parents' sofa, shoved as it was, in front of a half-empty bookcase in his small apartment. It was the item she associated with him the most, and the only thing she recognized in his new home. The curtains were drawn, making the room feel small. She stood and brushed them aside, asking, "You ever open these?"

"Sometimes," he said. "Sit down. I'll make you tea."

As Kyle disappeared into the kitchen, she sighed visibly for the first time since dinner. The corners of the room were all empty. She wondered if he was afraid of getting trapped there. His walls were bare too. *He needs some photographs,* she thought, *or at least some good posters.*

When he came out of the kitchen, he was smiling. He put a bowl of sugar and a jug of milk on a small table in the centre of the room. The way he placed the teaspoons made her think of his mother.

Together they sat down on the sofa again — he against the arm, and she somewhere in the middle.

"There," he said, "that's better."

His domestic skills had improved.

"Thank you," she said. "For the tea."

"Sara, you look tired."

She smiled mildly, suddenly unable to discern his politeness from his genuine concern. She knew he liked to feign weakness as a way of gaining sympathy and wondered if he assumed she did the same.

In one continuous movement, he poured tea, added milk, stirred and moved closer to her. "I'll take care of you," he said.

"Actually, I don't know if —"

"Sara, I've missed you."

"Hmm." She smiled. Until he called, she hadn't thought of him at all.

chapter 4

Although he had suggested a café, Sitara arranged to meet her father in the simple, unshaded park across from his hotel. At their first encounter, she wanted to be standing.

He looked small as she approached from a distance. He was walking slowly away from her with his hands stuffed into his pockets. She could see his cream-coloured kurta hanging down below his leather jacket, and could hear her mother's scolding. *"Raj, tuck that damn shirt in or take it off. You can't have both!"* By both, she meant the long Indian kurta and the short Canadian jacket. Parvati didn't have room for grey areas. She lived in a world of black and white. Sitara felt her fists tighten. Her arguments with her mother were old.

Cutting through the grass, she walked towards her father. She hadn't seen him for eleven years and might not have seen him for another eleven, if he hadn't suddenly arrived.

She was now just a few paces behind him — so close she could smell his woody cologne. She wanted to surprise him to give herself the upper hand.

"Bapa?" she called.

"Sitara, your hair has grown." He stopped but did not fully turn around.

"Did you wait long? I was busy at the office."

"I have waited long," he said, "but not so much today."

His hair was thin and grey and she could see that he was shaking.

"It is cold here, Sitara, but I can see why you like it. I walked along the waterfront today, while you were at your office, and three people offered me coffee. No one asked where I was from, or how long I was staying, or if I had any money. They simply responded to an old man pouring breath on his hands to keep them warm. They opened their hearts to me." He turned to face his daughter. "That would never happen at home."

I have already packed my bags. I will leave before anyone gets home. I want to tell Bapa, but I know he will tell Parvati. "Say goodbye," Sarasvati warns. "For even if your mother knows, she will not follow you. She does not care if you go." But I have been preparing for days — sneaking food from the kitchen, coins from Parvati's purse and bills from Bapa's wallet, and I will not risk it.

"Sitara, you are flushed."

"From the walk," she said, trying to be casual. "How was your flight?"

"Fine."

"I could have met you at the airport if I'd known you were coming. You could have called."

"I could have done a lot of things, Sitara. But I did not. And now, perhaps, it is enough that I am here." His voice was tired and more resigned than it had been on the telephone.

Sitara didn't say anything. She knew that she could have done a lot of things too.

"Your mother did not know I was coming either," he said. "And still does not. She thinks I am in Seattle."

Sitara eyed him carefully, trying to calculate how many other secrets he had.

"There are some things it is best she does not know," he added.

Like what? Sitara wanted to ask, but didn't.

Raj shuffled his feet on the pavement while she watched a gull pick at a scrap of bread. He lifted his arms, as if to embrace her, but put them down again.

"We should eat," he said finally, as if remembering that it's something people have to do. "I do not want Indian," he added, dismissing the choice that stood so obviously in front of them. "Where else can we go?"

"There's a Japanese restaurant nearby."

"No," he said.

"Or Vietnamese."

"No, I feel like pizza."

Sitara shook her head. She'd forgotten about his taste for fast food — something he had clearly acquired from her mother. "There are a couple of choices downtown by the library," she said. There were, of course, places to order a "better" pizza. *But at least this way,* she thought, *dinner won't last so long.* "I'll get a cab," she offered, thinking it might be too far for her father to walk.

"But you are old enough to drive," he said.

"Yes, but I don't have my car here." It was old and decrepit and she didn't want her father to see her in it. Besides, she usually rode her bike or walked, unless she was leaving the city.

I have eighty-one dollars in my pocket, plus the change I was saving for the payphone. I was going to call Bapa before I got on the bus. I wanted to. I wanted to hear him say, "Be careful, Sitara.

Come back soon." But I didn't. I couldn't dial it. And now he does-
n't know I'm leaving. No one knows.

Paying the cab driver before her father had a chance to,
she prayed silently that the small hemp shop on the right
would go unnoticed. It reminded her of an incident that
they'd never had the courage to resolve. Walking past it, however, Raj said nothing and she focused on the swirling smell of
the shop next door.

"You still like incense?" he asked.

"I do."

"Sandalwood purifies the mind."

"You think my mind needs purifying?"

"We all need purifying, Sitara. At least from time to time."

At the corner of Grafton and Blowers streets there were
three pizzerias, and Sitara let Raj decide. As they walked
through the chosen door, she had to admit that it didn't smell
bad. She ordered a Greek slice and ate it in silence while her
father ate only half of his.

"Something wrong with it?" she asked.

"No," he said, "but I cannot eat as much as I used to." Then
she watched him carefully fold his paper plate around the
remaining crust. "A little midnight snack." He smiled as he wiped
his mouth. "Come. I'll buy you coffee at my hotel." He stood,
holding his pizza in one hand, offering his other to Sitara.

She nodded, but did not take his hand.

Seated in the warm, dark embrace of the coffee shop window,
Sitara watched condensation clear vertical paths down the inside
of the glass. Raj sat across from her stirring milk into his coffee.

"Your mother says I drink too much of this," he said.

Sitara was drinking hot water.

"She says if it was thicker I would eat it for lunch."

"Some people make it thick," Sitara said.

"So, you are condoning it? You think I should eat coffee for lunch?"

"If it makes you happy." She was still watching water droplets collect and spill down the window. She was thinking about evaporation.

"How far is your apartment from here?" he asked.

"The other end of town."

"And your clinic?"

"About halfway in between."

"Not one above the other?"

"No."

"I suppose that would be too easy."

"It has to do with zoning." She turned to him, irritated. "Why does it matter to you?"

"It does not — but that is what I would do."

He added more sugar to his coffee and she took a breath of the steam pouring out of her mug.

It's dark and there is steam on the tall, tinted window of the bus. I reach up and try to clear it with my sleeve, but instead I make a mess of the moisture. Eventually the dry heat of the engine clears the window and I sit up, thinking I'll be able to see something of the view. But it is dark now and the cold glass reveals more of my own shy face than the mountains I know we must be driving through. The window plays tricks with me — making me look at myself.

"Bapa?" She spoke gently. "Why are you here?"

"To see you, Sitara… in case I run out of time." Before she could say anything, he added, "See how age has scared me? Today I feel old enough to be your tata. Do not wait too long to have children, Sitara. You will enjoy them more when you are young. You should have multiple children. Maybe not nine, like my family, but more than one. One is so lonely."

It's a long drive east and I have never been in motion for so long. At first, I don't know how far I will go. In some ways, it doesn't matter. Being gone is my only desire. In the hushed dark of the bus I ask the driver to list the next five stops. When we arrive at the one he emphasized the most, I step off. Looking for a sign, I see the word "Halifax" printed in dark, bold letters. As the bus doors close behind me, I shrink. There is something so final about an "x."

"Think about it, Sitara, when you start a family. Make sure you save time. It is not good to have your babies when you are too old."

"Or when you're too young," she said.

"You are not too young now."

"No, not now."

In her mind she could see a baby's face — thick black hair, moist suckling mouth, almond-shaped brown eyes. A face that knew nothing yet knew too much.

"Maybe you will get lucky and have twins. You know they run in our family… Beti, are you listening?"

Her hair had fallen in front of her face and her chin was below her shoulder. Lifting her head to her father, she asked, "Bapa, how do you feel?" Like always, she returned to the soothing subject of health when she was unnerved. "Headaches? Dizziness? Aching joints?"

"I do not need a doctor, Sitara."

"Of course not — I didn't mean to…"

"But if I did," a small cloud passed in front of his face, draining it of expression and colour, "I am sure I would come to you. I know you are good at what you do."

She shifted uncomfortably in her seat.

"Sitara, I am tired. I want to go up to bed. You will call a taxi, yes? I do not want you to walk home in the dark."

Sitara nodded. "Will I see you tomorrow?"

"If you want to." He smiled and rubbed her shoulder with his hand. "Good night, beti."

"Good night."

Outside, she decided to walk home. It was a warm evening and she couldn't bear the idle chatter of a lonely cab driver.

chapter 5

On Monday morning at ten to nine, Sara walked into the well-scrubbed lobby of a downtown medical building. She avoided her reflection in the shiny panels of marble surrounding the even shinier elevator doors and pressed the illuminated "up" button. When the doors opened, a woman spilled out with her two young children — one barely walking, the other in a stroller. Their screaming made Sara want to flee.

Forcing herself into the elevator, she closed her eyes. They were heavy with the burden of what awaited her. The office door was closed when she arrived, but the handle turned easily. When she stepped into the fluorescent room, a dozen greying heads turned to look at her. Feeling the scrutiny of their collective gaze, Sara inched her way to the reception desk.

"I'm here to see Dr. Porter."

"Yes, I know," the woman behind the counter said. "Judy will take you in a few minutes. Have a seat."

Sara had the unbearable feeling that the woman knew, that they all knew, every detail of her situation. *"There's the young one with the blurry eyes." "Oh yes, the photographer who can't see straight." "The poor little girl from Annapolis with the bad genes. She got a rush appointment, you know. Her sight won't last long."* Sara could hear the words in their minds. She sank into a chair and tried to keep her heart in her chest.

"Sara?" Judy's gruff voice asked. "Let's get you started with some drops."

Obediently, Sara stood. Walking stiffly, she felt a rush of air as people's heads turned to follow her. Through a maze of halls, Dr. Porter's assistant led her to a darkly lit room with a large, padded chair. Climbing into it, Sara felt small. Sitting back, as the woman instructed, her feet fought to find the bottom rail.

With an eyedropper in her hand, the woman leaned over Sara's frozen body and barked, "Open wide." Sara opened her mouth before she remembered to open her eyes.

With the drops inserted, Sara was ordered back to the waiting room. When she returned, the only seat remaining was between two elderly men whose pupils were perversely dilated. On a younger man she might have found the effect alluring, but in the shrivelled sockets of the sunken faces, it made her shudder.

Unable to look at magazines and unwilling to look at the faces of the other patients, Sara turned inward. She would have to call her editor tomorrow with a decision. Joyce still expected her to finish in Europe and then take a three-week assignment in South America.

An hour later, she was convinced she'd been forgotten. The distracting voices around her were loud and rough — the hoarse prattle of a woman sitting next to her half-deaf husband, the overly chipper voice of a young man with his grandmother, the drone of people talking about the weather.

She was thinking about sneaking out the door when Judy came looking for her.

"Let me see those eyes. Yes, looks like you need another set of drops. Here, tilt back." She opened a bottle with her tightly gripped fist and landed one drop in each of Sara's eyes. "The doctor will be right with you. We'll just have to let those drops sink in."

For the next while, Sara sat trying to drain her mind. It was better if she concentrated on nothing. No words. No feelings. No fear. She tried counting sheep like her father had taught her to do when she couldn't fall asleep. The rhythmic certainty of numbers jumping a fence lulled her into a little bit of comfort.

"Alright," Judy said, "come with me."

With her hand dragging along the wall to guide her, Sara followed the woman back through the maze.

Dr. Porter was an older man with fine white hair and glasses. He smiled condescendingly as Sara climbed into his examination chair.

"Are you a student, dear?" he asked.

"A photographer."

"For the newspaper?"

"I work for a travel magazine."

He waved to his assistant. "Thank you, Judy. That's all." She nodded and closed the door. "Well," the doctor said, as he pulled his rolling chair up to Sara, "let's have a look." His hand was rough as he placed it on her chin. He moved her face for her, twisting and straining her neck, so that she found it difficult to swallow. "Yes, just as I thought," he said, squeezing her chin further. "Do you have a history of these symptoms in your family?"

"Ah-hun-no."

"Pardon?" He let go of her chin.

"I don't know."

He pulled her forward until her flesh met his equipment. "Put your chin there." He narrowed the focus of his probe light and intensified the power of the magnification. Then he reached out and tilted her head so that its angle was more comfortable for him. "What I'm seeing here is quite developed."

Sara's head felt heavy on her neck. Although it was a struggle to keep it in place, she was afraid to move.

The doctor leaned back from the viewer. "What you have, dear, is an abnormal growth of blood vessels at the back of your eyes. Although it's very unusual in someone your age, it's quite common in the elderly. I'm going to send you down to the old hospital for dye tests. I'd like to know just where the blood is leaking from. Then we'll get you set up." He turned in his chair, as if finished and expecting her to leave.

Sara shifted her head slightly and forced a large gulp of saliva down her throat. "Wait, I… I don't think I understand."

The doctor turned back and let his tired face show.

"You're going to need surgery. What you have is called macular degeneration. I can't offer you a cure. The only thing I can do is to try and prevent it from getting worse. There are two options, depending upon the results of the dye test. The simpler procedure is laser — it's painless and most people are up and running right away. But if it's as serious as I suspect, then we're going to have to consider incisional surgery."

Sara pictured the hot liquid of a soft-cooked yolk.

"Judy will take care of you." This time Dr. Porter stood to punctuate the end of the appointment.

Sara released herself from the chair and walked to the door, struggling to remember the details of the doctor's prognosis. As she stumbled into the hall, Judy spoke to her in a hushed tone.

"Are you here alone, dear?"

"Yes."

"Oh." She sighed and shifted her weight. "Well, you shouldn't be. Is there anyone who can pick you up?"

"No."

"Are you sure? Think about it."

Kyle. He loved coming to her rescue. "I can make a call."

"Perfect. Come with me."

Judy led her by the arm as if she was already blind. She asked for Kyle's number, dialled and then handed the phone to Sara. "Ask him to pick you up. He'll need to spend the afternoon with you at the hospital. It's going to be a long day, and you're not going to be able to see."

Kyle was delighted and arrived with a warm muffin and a cup of tea. He guided Sara into his car and opened his arms for her as if expecting a watery torrent, but her eyes were strangely dry.

They were silent as they waited in the cold, bright corridor of the old hospital. They sat next to each other in a long row of plastic chairs that were fastened to the wall.

"Kyle?" she asked. "Why did you come for me?"

He used his hand to smooth her soft brown hair. "I couldn't very well have said no."

"I suppose."

Sinking into the ease of his care, Sara scorned herself for ignoring his phone calls, for never leaving a forwarding address, for not sending greeting cards. Even though she knew it was a trap, she sank comfortably back into the mould he had designed for her. She wondered if one day she would have the courage to finally break it.

"Sara?" he said, gently rubbing her back. "I think the nurse is looking for you."

"What?" For a moment she'd been dreaming.

"It's your turn." He stood to help her up. "I'll wait here for you."

She nodded and followed the nurse.

It was the same small-nosed nurse who had, half an hour earlier, dug around in her arm, trying to find a vein big enough for the large injection of dye. In times of distress, Sara's veins hid below the surface. Now, as she walked, yellow liquid seeped into the puff of cotton taped to her arm.

As she entered the dark lab room, she was greeted by a technician who wore jeans beneath her hospital whites. Seeing the camera that was mounted on a stand and affixed to a long table, Sara took one calm breath.

"Alright. I need you to hold still. This might be a little bright." The woman pointed a beam of light at Sara's eyes. "I'm going to take a series of photographs over the next five minutes to chart the progress of the dye. It's important that you try not to move."

Sara's mouth watered at the first shutter click. She hadn't taken a photo in days.

Against the drone of the stopwatch, the nurse chatted idly. "Is it still windy out there? There was quite a chill this morning. My sister says it's colder than seasonal, but isn't April always like this? I try to not get my hopes up until May. Even then, we've had snow, although not for a few years now. It's the way the wind comes off the water. I keep telling my husband, we need to get away from the dreaded ocean. Of course, I love this city. But you know the feeling — months and months of the same cold weather. Makes you want to go south, doesn't it? Maybe even Florida?"

No one answered her. Sara was on a boat taking photos of the approaching shore. The technician was counting seconds.

"Are you alright there?" The nurse took Sara's limp hand. "We had quite a time with the needle earlier, didn't we? I'm still sorry about that. Her veins," she said to her co-worker, "are buried so deep."

The feel of the nurse's hospital-clean hands made Sara shiver. She was tired of the sterile world of doctors and medicine.

She wanted the dirt of villages, or the blowing sand of the desert. She blinked as if to clear something out of her eyes just as the photographer closed the shutter.

"I know it's hard, but try not to blink."

When the photos were done, Sara let the nurse shuttle her into the hallway where Kyle was waiting to take her home.

It took twenty-four hours for the yellow dye to work through Sara's system. In the meantime, she sat alone in the dark of her apartment, waiting. When the phone finally rang, the receptionist at Dr. Porter's office said, "I've scheduled you for surgery a week from Friday."

"Already?" Sara asked. "Does this mean the test results were negative?"

"Listen, dear, it's not negotiable. It's the only time I can fit you in. Be early and don't come alone. Understand?"

"Yes," Sara stammered, "but what about the test results? I had injections at the hospital... a big camera... yellow dye... Dr. Porter said —"

"He'll need you here by three o'clock. For goodness sake, don't be late."

"Fine. Three o'clock." Sara hung up the phone. She was so stunned she didn't ask what type of surgery the doctor had in mind.

chapter 6

Walking back from a lunch-hour trip to the grocery store, Sitara was swinging her bags — not a fast, happy swinging, but rather a slow, solemn swinging brought on by deep thought.

"Bapa, why are you here?"

"To see you, Sitara… in case it is the last time."

The words kept swimming through her head. And each time she replayed them, they sounded more alarmingly final.

For many years, she had intended to repair relations with her parents — eventually. She thought the six thousand kilometres separating the two coasts would make picking up the phone easier, since she was safe from the obligation of dropping by. But the distance only made it easier to forget.

On her walk back to the clinic, she passed a used bookstore. There was a paperback in the window that caught her eye: *Misplaced Indians*, it was called. Only after reading the subtitle did she realize that it was written about Native Americans and not her parents.

"Are your parents still in India?" a classmate asks.

"No, they live in Canada."

"Are you going home for the break?"

"Probably not. I'd like to catch up on my reading — I feel a little out of breath."

"Won't you be lonely, since everyone else goes away?"

"Not everyone," I say. "Hannah and Devora are staying, and Paul can't afford to fly home this year. I'll manage."

I don't want to go home, but I no longer bother to say it. For others, I've discovered, Christmas is a week out of time, affected by neither the past nor the present. It's an island of forgiveness and pretending in the name of religion and tradition and gift-giving. Although smiles and feasting seem to come easily to my classmates, I don't have the heart or the stomach for either.

Walking up the stairs to her clinic, Sitara wondered what had happened to Hannah and Devora. In the six years since they'd graduated from college she'd lost track of them.

Leaving her groceries in a pile beside the desk, she checked her phone messages and then prepared her office for an afternoon of patients.

Slowly, her father's words were subsiding, but not without leaving a sticky trace.

After her last patient left the clinic, Sitara met her father again in the park near his hotel. He was sitting on a bench with an open magazine, watching some kids as they performed tricks on their scooters.

"Wow, this bench is cold," Sitara said, sitting down next to him.

"That is why I wear a kurta." He smiled.

"Well, perhaps I should too."

"No, women should wear saris."

"I know, Bapa. I know."

The children with the scooters — two boys and a girl — were jumping off a tall stone ledge and trying to land on both wheels. One of them had almost mastered it and the other two were trying desperately to follow.

"I have been watching them for over an hour," Raj said. "The little one is very agile, and most comfortable, I think, when he is in the air. Perhaps for some, the ground is too hard. Do you think about these kinds of things, Sitara, or is it a sure sign that I am getting old?"

"I can't picture you getting old, Bapa. Age is in the mind."

"And sometimes in the body," he added.

"Sometimes, but you seem strong. Maybe I should buy you a scooter!"

"It makes me think of something I had when I was young. Of course, the roads were dirt where we lived, so we needed bigger tires. It is not easy being the second youngest of nine. There is a lot of catching up to do, and I tried many things, including some questionable self-propelled automobiles!" He laughed.

Sitara could feel the energy between them healing. She was happy to hear her father's voice again, and to be surrounded by the generosity of his laughter. *There are some holes,* she thought, *that we're not even aware of until they've been filled again.*

"I have tea," she offered. "And some rather crumbly cookies."

"Yes, I would like some."

After pulling a Thermos out of her worn Guatemalan bag, she handed her father a porcelain mug.

"This is nice," he said.

"It's made by a woman who lives here in town."

"Town?" Raj asked. "I thought Halifax was a city."

"It is, of course, you're right. I suppose 'town' is just an expression." She filled his cup. "Chai," she said, "with soy milk."

Looking doubtful, Raj took a sip and then considered it carefully. "It does not taste like chai. But," he said, after taking another sip, "I do not dislike it."

"I'm glad." She handed him a paper bag full of cookies.

Taking one, he said, "I think your hand slipped when you added the cinnamon. Chai should be heavy on the black pepper, cardamom and cloves, and more moderate with the cinnamon. Of course, many people will tell you differently, but that is because they do not come from my village. People from my village, they know about tea."

Sitara nodded in agreement. Her father's village was famous for many things — as he was very fond of explaining. Parvati, of course, believed none of it. Sitara, too, was skeptical, but she respected his need for roots and ancestry. *It's hard to know who you are,* she reasoned, *without knowing who your people are.*

The sun that had poured over the park, bathing everything in a forgiving light, was starting to set. Raj shivered first, but Sitara soon followed.

"Shall we get some dinner?" he asked.

"What do you feel like?"

"The one here is okay — I looked over their menu — and I am feeling rather Indian today."

Climbing the steps to the second-floor restaurant, Sitara noticed how much her father depended on the railing to pull him up. Walking slowly behind him, she resisted the temptation to help. Inside, they chose a table by the window so they could look out over the park.

"I like to watch the sun go down," he said. Sitara did too, but she gave her father the better seat. Poring over the menu, he asked, "What do you recommend?"

"I don't know. I've only been here once."

"Because you do not like it?"

"No, I just don't eat out very often."

"Then here is what we will have: one order of dahl, one order of aloo gobi, one steamed basmati rice, four chapati, two puri, two lassi — unsweetened, of course — and a basket of samosas to start. The pappadam is overpriced. A good restaurant brings it for free."

"But Bapa, what if —"

The waitress came and took his order before Sitara had a chance to say anything. She liked dahl, but was in the mood for chickpeas instead.

When the puri and samosas came to the table, he asked, "Do you like these, Sitara? Try some. These are potato with carrot and peas, and these ones —"

"I know what they are, Bapa. I've had them before. Actually, I thought you would have ordered pakoras."

"Why? I have no taste for them. Too hard and greasy. Especially the way Canadians make them."

"This restaurant has Indian cooks!"

"Yes, but something changes when they cross the sea. Or perhaps it is the climate here — it is too cold for good deep-frying. Why does it matter to you?"

"Samosas and puri are deep-fried too."

"Yes?"

"Then it can't be the oil, can it?" Sitara smeared a samosa in chutney and took a bite. "Blaming the oil is not logical."

"Sitara, what are you talking about? You sound like Parvati."

Poking at a pea with her finger, Sitara tried to formulate her thoughts. Her father's domination and insensitivity angered her. The man she remembered was more open-minded and fair. The man she remembered liked pakoras.

"Bapa, I can't believe you ordered for me. I'm thirty years old. I can read menus."

"Yes, of course. But do you know about Indian food?"

"I've cooked my share of biryani."

"Yes, but you practise Chinese medicine. We have a medical tradition too, Sitara."

"I know. I've studied the Ayurvedic approach. It is very powerful. But there are other valuable traditions too." She licked chutney off her thumb. "I went to college for this. I *am* certified."

"Yes, of course you are, Sitara. You are a good doctor, I am sure."

"A healer."

"It is the same thing, whatever you call it."

She resented being linked with medical doctors when she had, very intentionally, taken a different approach. "That's not true," she said.

"Health is life, Sitara. It is not something to take lightly. I wish you people could see that."

As Sitara held back the things she wanted to say, the waitress came with their main dishes. She laid them out in front of Raj as if he had ordered them all for himself. Sitara watched as she did this, but said nothing. Although the food smelled good, arguing had left her with very little appetite.

Without ceremony, Raj ripped apart a chapati and, using his right hand, shovelled a scoop of dahl into his mouth.

Looking down at the dark green tablecloth, Sitara thought, *At least he can't talk while he's chewing.* She needed a gap in the fighting to prepare her line of fire.

When my parents get home I am in the cupboard playing singing games with Sarasvati. I can hear them yelling even as they come down the hall. There is a high-pitched shout followed by a low-pitched rumble, then another high-pitched shout. As they come through the door, their voices get clearer.

"I want Sitara to go to an Indian school."

"There are no Indian schools in Vancouver. We've talked about this before."

"I am not talking about Vancouver. I am talking about India."

"I'm not going back, if that's what you're thinking! Not on your life, Raj. I am successful here. I have a career."

"I am not saying you should go to India — just Sitara. I have already spoken to my sister, Usha. She is willing to take her. She has a daughter the same age. They can be friends. Sitara needs friends."

"Perhaps, but why Indian friends?"

"Stubborn woman! I thought you would be happy to get rid of her!"

"Raj, you say too much and understand too little!"

"Tell me of one day when you have not complained about her? 'The child is too demanding. Tell her no, she cannot have whatever it is she is asking for.' Or 'Your daughter has taken my pens again. What is wrong with her? I have already given her four pencils this week.' Parvati, you say these things every day! If I send her to live with Usha, she will not bother you anymore."

"No."

"Why not?"

"In India she will learn Indian ways. And then what hope will she have? No. She was born Canadian, and in Canada she will stay. This is final, Raj. There is no room for negotiation."

Hearing Parvati stomp off, I breathe out a little sigh. I don't want to leave here, and I am worried that at my aunt's house there will be no spice cupboard.

"I can't believe you wanted to send me away," Sitara said.

"Away where?"

"To live with Usha."

"How do you know about that?" Raj talked with his mouth full, allowing Sitara to see the dark brown dahl being crushed and mixed with the pale white chapati.

"I know about more than you think."

Raj wiped out one of the curry bowls with his last piece of chapati. He had eaten the whole meal while Sitara sipped from a glass of water. "You should eat. Do you not tell your patients that?"

"It depends what their imbalance is. Sometimes I do, sometimes I don't." She was staring out the window, watching the street lights come on. Now, for every person who passed on the sidewalk below, there was also a shadow. "I'm leaving," she said. She couldn't imagine the four of them walking back to his hotel.

"Sitara... We have not had dessert!"

"I'm not hungry, and I think you've already had enough!"

Before Raj could stand up she was outside, hiding from the light on the darker side of the street.

chapter 7

Sara buried her camera in the back of the closet with the high-heeled shoes she bought but never wore. *I should have a yard sale*, she thought, *to get rid of this junk. Then at least I could pay my phone bill.*

Trying on a pair of pointe shoes that were stiff from layers of encrusted sweat, she remembered how, at one time, her plan had been to be a dancer first, then a photographer when she retired from the stage at age thirty or thirty-five.

She threw the ballet slippers back into the closet and closed the door. She hadn't expected to feel old at twenty-nine.

As she sat on the floor next to her bed, staring at the blur that was her bulletin board full of photos, her suffering sank into her stomach. She was hungry for the flavours trapped in her camera bag, the ones she'd been forced — by her eyes — to leave behind. From where she sat, she imagined the contents of her kitchen cupboards: a few half-empty jars of herbs, a bag of old fusilli, a can of tomatoes with the label torn so that she could no longer tell if they were whole or crushed. She knew without looking that the fridge was worse than the cupboards

— there was little more than a rousing combination of butter, baking soda and mustard.

With her mouth watering for ginger-glazed chicken, spicy bean burritos smothered in melted cheese, or dahl and egg-plant curry over fragrant basmati rice, she fumbled with her coat and cursed her buttons for being difficult. Although Halifax had plenty of good restaurants, she didn't have the money or the confidence to face young healthy waiters or the bright-eyed customers they served. Instead, she decided to walk to the grocery store, buy some ingredients and cook for herself. Bracing for an onslaught of people, she pulled on her shades and stepped outside.

The sidewalk, of course, was empty. Crossing the tree-lined street, she had to remind herself that she was only min-utes from the university in one direction, and from the har-bour and downtown in the other. She was accustomed to streets so crowded that she had to use her elbows to protect her breasts and camera, and squares so full that people breathed in the air she'd just breathed out. Feeling as though her defect was visible to anyone who looked at her, she was grateful for the luxury of living in a small city on the outer edge of a sparsely populated country.

Walking past the Commons, with its wide-open ball fields and concrete skateboard park, her body yearned for spices — the dark, sensual spices of India. She could smell the onions fry-ing, the garlic sizzling in ghee, the almost black cloves mixing with the cardamom and mustard seeds. She was drunk on the thought of it, her head swirling with the aroma.

Inside the Indian grocery store on Robie Street, the warm, humid air wrapped itself around her. She ignored the bags of chips, the silver-coated chocolate bars, and the flashy red and white advertisements on the sides of the refrigerators. Heading to the back of the store where the real food was nearly hidden, she filled her arms with oil-stained bottles, bags of ground spices, and the grains and legumes that would bulk up her meal.

At the cash, she bought a samosa to eat while walking. As she stepped out into the natural air of the city, she pulled her coat closer. Knowing it was warm in Spain and France, she sighed and bit into her snack.

With her head down, and her mind drifting through the barrage of fried finger food she'd eaten over the years while on assignment, she was oblivious to the fast-moving vehicle coming at her.

"Watch out!"

"Aaron?" she said. She hadn't seen him since college.

"Hey!" He stopped, flipped up his skateboard, and smiled at her. "What's going on?"

"Nothing," she said, swallowing the last bits of spiced potato and pea.

"Same here. I'm just out for some air." His jacket was open, his neck crowded with a stream of beaded necklaces intertwined with a cluster of metal pendants. "I didn't mean to scream, man, but I didn't know if you'd see me!"

"Probably not. I'm having issues with my eyes."

"Oh yeah?"

"Yeah." She tried to laugh. "Maybe I'm just getting old."

"Hey, you know, you should see someone," Aaron said. "I know a woman who has a clinic down on Hollis with the most amazing atmosphere!"

"What kind of clinic?" Sara asked. In college, she remembered, he'd often had ideas that made her squirm.

"Acupuncture, man!"

"I don't know."

"You don't know about what?"

"About all those needles sticking into me."

"You've got to take care of yourself, Sara. Really, it doesn't hurt." He pulled a crumpled red and gold card from his back pocket and offered it to her. "The dragon knows best," he said.

Her face went pale at the thought of it — another hospital-white waiting room, the hum of the lights eating away at her, the doctor's large, probing hand... "Thanks, but I think I'll pass." She dug her free hand into the pocket of her coat.

"Suit yourself, man, but you're missing out on a great trip." He smiled and dropped his board on the ground. "See ya around."

As he pushed off, she thought, *In ten years, he hasn't changed at all.*

The next morning, after cleaning up the disaster of her burned and overspiced meal, Sara waited for her mother to arrive. In the blackness of the night before, while her kitchen was filled with smoke and frustration, she had finally called her parents to announce that she was home.

It was a three-hour drive from Annapolis Royal, and her mother had errands to run along the way. When she arrived, Sara was waiting by the door.

"You look good, hon. Healthy," Peggy said.

"Thanks." She was surprised at how easily her mother was fooled. After stuffing her arms into the sleeves of her long spring coat, she grabbed her black vinyl luggage and thought bitterly of her idle camera bags full of gear.

In the car Sara wanted to say things to her mother that made her fingers twitch. But instead she drew her lips in tightly and kept them there — a gesture she'd used in childhood.

"Any big plans now that you're home?" Peggy asked to break the silence.

"I won't be here long," Sara said.

"I've set you up in the newest suite. Everything has been replaced except the bed. It looks out the side — I hope you don't mind."

"That's fine."

For more than four years, Sara's parents had run a bed and breakfast. Although Lauren, their younger daughter, always complained about being treated like a guest in her family's own home, Sara was not uncomfortable. She spent a lot of time in hotels. "Is business good?" she asked.

"No, it's still the slow season. I mean, look around. It's ugly here in April!"

Sara squinted out the window. The melted snow had left fields of brown and yellow, and trees as bare as skeletons. "I kind of like it this way," she said.

Peggy laughed. "You would."

"There is as much beauty in the starkness as in the lush green fields."

"You're the only one who seems to think so."

Sara sighed, carefully, under her coat. She wondered if Peggy thought both of her daughters were strange, or if Lauren was somehow considered "normal." Before allowing the question to burrow too deeply, she pulled her thoughts out of herself and let them drift freely alongside the car.

The sky was getting dark as they climbed the hill at the start of the valley. She gasped at the beauty of the basin full of water and the dying embers of sun burning out behind the mountain. Every time she saw it, her reaction was the same — she reached for her camera.

click
A blur of sky and mountain taken from the 101.

Sara used her hands to cover her eyes.

"Tired, hon?" her mother asked.

"Yeah. It's been a long couple of days."

Slowly, the last bits of light faded from the sky and Sara had to strain to identify things. Testing herself from the passenger's seat, she tried to read road signs. They were a smear of white and green, the words barely becoming clear before they were gone. In the brief second of clarity, she could catch only the first line — the town name but not the exit number, the destination but not the kilometres.

In the hollow body of the car, she clenched her fists tightly. *Damn it, I am not afraid. I am not afraid.*

Finally, Peggy pulled into the driveway and Sara was able to flee the claustrophobic darkness of the car.

As she walked up the stone path, the house looked round. Through the distortion of her eyes, its tall, proud lines took on a softness of shape — a curving — like the subtle bending of a spine.

The porch, she noticed, had recently been painted green. She pictured her mother sprawled out on the wooden boards, her brush quick and exact. She knew Peggy painted like she mothered — with certainty and a strong hand.

Inside, the house smelled of cloves. She found her father baking in the kitchen. The centre island he'd recently rebuilt was covered in a fine layer of flour dust and scattered with metal tools. He was scalloping the edges of a pie.

"Isn't it a little off season for mincemeat?" she asked.

Her father dropped his pastry knife and looked up. It had been four months since he'd seen his daughter. He stepped towards her and wrapped her in an embrace full of spices.

"How's my little onion?"

"Better," Sara whispered into the muffling fabric of his shirt. "Better and better."

Ron pulled back, but kept his daughter within arm's length, his hands still on her shoulders. "Look at that," he said. "You're making my eyes water."

"Dad, that's what little onion sprouts do."

"You're not a sprout anymore, Sara. You have too many layers for that. But I see the sun's been good to you."

"Yeah." She smiled. "It was warm in the Mediterranean."

"Why don't you help me with these pies, and then we'll put the kettle on for tea, unless you'd rather have a *coffee*."

Sara started a guilty grin, then said, "There's nothing wrong with coffee!"

"Not unless you drink it!" Ron picked up his pastry knife and finished the edges of the second pie. "Did you lose Peggy on the way in?"

"Yeah. I don't know. You have guests tonight?"

"No, my darling, all these pies are for you!"

Sara laughed and felt her shoulders relax. There was something predictably amusing about her father that she adored. "Thanks, Dad," she said. "You shouldn't have."

"Ron? Why didn't you tell me those Americans had cancelled? When did this call come?" Peggy was yelling to him from the alcove in the hallway where they kept the phone and reception desk for the business.

"This morning, after you left." He winked at Sara, who stood motionless, trying to melt away.

"I wouldn't have rushed back if I'd known," Peggy said. "I would have gone shopping."

"Precisely! We need to make money, not spend it!"

Sara stifled a laugh. Ron was mocking his wife — giving her back one of her own famous lines.

"Jesus Christ, Ron, if you knew what we spent on groceries!"

"I have a pretty good idea." He winked again at Sara and slid the first pie into the oven.

"Anyway, I wish you'd told me."

"Of course, dear," he whispered under his breath, making Sara smile.

She hadn't missed anything.

Later, when Sara stepped into the light of the smallest guest room, the rug was the only thing she recognized. For years it had been at the end of her parents' bed. She had walked on it, her bare feet sinking into the luxury of its fibres, each time she'd crept into the comforting warmth of their room. Now she noticed its colour, faded by sun and time and memory. Her mother's hair had seemed more vibrant in those days too — when red was really red, not just brown with a hint of auburn.

Gently, she put her bag down by the window. In the brightness of the room she saw more of herself reflected in the glass than she did of the neighbours' house or the herb gardens down below. She moved closer to the window and put her hands to her face to block the light. Along the base of the fence she could make out the shape of long garden beds. Her father worked hard on his plants, coaxing, nurturing, willing them to grow. She knew in the morning she'd be asked to approve, to nod pleasantly while he knelt on the ground, describing every newborn leaf.

Pulling her socks and jeans to the floor, Sara climbed into the queen-sized bed that was waiting for her. It seemed huge and half-empty and, feeling cold, she switched off the lamp.

In the car her mother had asked, "Sara, are you squinting?"

"Yeah," she'd said. "I'm really tired."

"Maybe you need glasses. I'm surprised no one has suggested it. You get used to them after a while, or you get contacts. It's no big deal."

Sara hadn't argued. *No, of course not. No big deal.*
She was still hoping for sympathy from her father.

At breakfast Sara cleared her throat more than she needed to
and fidgeted with her napkin ring.

"Sleep well?" Ron asked. "Or did your mother's snoring
keep you up?"

"Ron! You're the one who snores!"

"Really?"

"I slept fine." Sara said. "The bed's great."

Peggy was picking at a cream-coloured lump on her plate.
"Ron, what is this?"

"Scrambled tofu. I'm experimenting with vegan dishes."

"It's disgusting."

"How do you know that? You haven't even tried it."

"I just know." She turned her plate around so that the pile
of tofu was further away from her fork.

"What do you think, Sara? Could I impress a robust young
vegan?"

"Are all vegans *robust*?" Peggy asked. She didn't try to hide
the cynicism in her voice.

"It's not bad," Sara said. "I'd eat it. More garlic maybe, or
some hot sauce." She looked down at her plate and saw that it
was empty, but she had virtually no memory of the taste.

"So, how come you're on holidays?" Peggy asked. "Is it just
as ugly everywhere else in the spring too?"

"In Australia, it's fall," Ron said. "Hey Sara, have you been
there yet?"

"I have."

"So why the holiday?" Peggy still wanted to know.

"Actually…" Sara started to feel an uncomfortable pressure

in her gut. "I'm having some problems with my eyes."

"You need glasses, you mean. We talked about this yesterday. But couldn't you get those in London or Milan? I'm sure they'd be way more chic!"

"Fashion is hardly the point, Mom!"

"Sara…" Peggy lowered her voice. "Lots of people wear glasses. It's no big deal. Even your father managed to find a nice pair!"

"Notice how she said that, Sara? 'Even your father!' The poor old slob!"

"I don't need glasses!" Sara yelled, with an unexpected hint of adolescent whine. "I need surgery."

"Oh." Ron and Peggy both put their forks down.

"Since when?" Peggy asked.

"I found out on Monday."

"But how long have your eyes been bothering you? Was it sudden? Some kind of accident?"

"Two weeks ago my boss rejected a batch of bad photos. The surgeon says I need immediate treatment. He wants to operate next week. It's a simple procedure," she said, choosing her words carefully. "They just have to remove some extra blood vessels from the back of my eyes."

"Sara! That doesn't sound simple to me." Ron's hands were shaking and his face was pale. "There must be another option — something else they can do. How many people have you been to?"

"Two. The optometrist and the surgeon. Dad, surgery is the only option."

"Wait a minute," Peggy said. "What are we talking about here? Knives and stitches or a quick fix with a laser?"

"I don't know," she said.

"Well, if it's laser, that doesn't sound so bad. Karen's sister had it last winter. It was fast and painless and she hasn't worn glasses since."

"But this sounds a lot more serious than curing near-sightedness," Ron said.

"It is serious. I can't even work right now."

"Are you still on contract, or have they finally put you on salary?" Peggy asked.

"Contract."

"So, you're on an unpaid holiday. How are you for money?"

"It would be great if I could borrow some."

"Of course," Peggy said. "I'm sure we can help. How much do you —"

"Wait a minute." Ron raised his hand to interrupt. "This is happening too fast."

"Of course it's happening fast," Peggy said. "The doctor said she needs immediate surgery."

"No."

"No what?"

"No. We won't loan her money."

"Ron, you're being unreasonable. I'm sure we can pull something out of our savings!"

"That's not the point!" he argued.

Sara winced. Her father was a man of alternatives. She knew he didn't like making decisions before examining and re-examining all of the details.

"There must be other options. We just need some time. We need to learn more about this condition. Have you read anything about it?"

"Ron! If she said she can't see," Peggy leaned forward and dug her elbows into the table, "how can she possibly read?"

"I can read a little bit."

"Well, have you?"

"No."

"Sara," Ron took a deep breath, "you're not alone. We'll help you with this."

"But you won't loan me money?"

"Not until you've looked into some other options."

"For once, why can't you give me the kind of support I need? I still have to pay my bills." She was tipping her chair away from the table, balancing belligerently on two legs. "I am trying to be responsible. I can't just walk out on my commitments!" Sara knew this would impress her mother — she'd been drilling her daughters on the ethics of responsibility for years.

"What about the responsibility of looking after your eyes?" Ron snapped.

"Oh, please!" Peggy dropped her forehead into her hands. "It's not as if she *tried* to develop this condition. She's just asking for money — a loan — until she gets back to work."

"That is, if I can go back to work. The doctor said surgery won't repair the damage that's already been done. It will only prevent it from getting worse."

"Worse, meaning?" Peggy asked.

"Total blindness, I guess."

"All I'm suggesting," Ron's voice became gentle and soft, "is that you take some time to explore the alternatives. Naturopathy, for instance, or acupuncture. There are other methods of health care. You don't have to overreact."

"Dad, I hardly think that taking care of myself is overreacting! Acupuncture might cure a headache, but we're talking about something a lot more serious. We're talking about my eyes!"

"All I'm asking is that you consider the options."

"I have considered my options! But if you don't want to help me, that's fine." Sara stood up. "Thanks for breakfast." In the front hall, she jammed on her shoes, grabbed her coat and tried not to slam the front door.

After refusing a ride from her father, she caught the eleven o'clock bus and was back at her apartment by four. Immediately she turned off the furnace, realizing that anger made her warm.

click

There is liquid running down her face that tastes like egg. She swirls it in her mouth and it begins to thicken. Soon she has to make a decision — spit or swallow. She suspects both will make her gag.

chapter 8

It was five o'clock in the morning — hours before Sitara usually rose. She had slept badly and was tired of being in bed. In the night, she had woken twice with the taste of cardamom on her tongue. Her entire being was humming and she was looking for a way to make it stop.

Sitting on the lip of the tub, she ran her fingers through the rushing water. Although the heat was tolerable on her hand, she knew it would be painful for the rest of her body. She enjoyed extreme heat — like the first sips of tea — but wasn't in the mood to risk burning her skin. Turning the old ceramic handle, she increased the amount of cold in the blend. Satisfied with the temperature, she added seven drops of lavender oil and breathed deeply as the essence evaporated into the air.

As she entered the water her muscles tightened before they started to give way. Toes, calves, knees — she stood for a moment before sitting down. A sharp pain hit her as hot water penetrated between her legs. She sighed, thinking, *Why does the tension of protection so often precede the pleasure of release?*

Submerged in the water, she tried to lose herself in the steam.

"You were such an ugly baby," Parvati says to me. "Frowning, impatient, already set in your ways. 'Parvati, push!' the nurse said. But she did not need to. You came all at once on your own. Plop. A screaming baby girl."

Sitting up, Sitara reached for her bottle of lavender and added a few more drops. Swirling the oil with her hand made her think of stirring soup. Lavender soup in a yogurt container bowl, or bubble bath tea in a shampoo bottle glass. As a child it had occupied her for hours.

Absently, she reached for a sea sponge and tried to push it under. It was light and buoyant and wanted to float. Finally, when it was full and heavy, she squeezed it and let the hot water fall over her face and neck.

I am in the tub and Parvati is hurting me. She says she's trying to make me clean. White clean. Bleached clean. Sanitary, disinfectant clean. But I think she is trying to rub my skin off. Yanking the facecloth from her hand, I beg her to let me do it myself. She is reluctant and doesn't trust me. I tell her I have to learn sometime and she relents.

After she has backed away from the tub, I dunk the facecloth into the water. Then, fascinated by the drippy squelching noises made by ringing out the cloth, I dunk it again without touching it to my skin.

"Scrub!" she yells, and I try to because otherwise she will do it for me.

She waits at the door and makes me submit to inspection. She is surprised when she sees my blotchy red face and realizes that she has hurt me. "Here," she says, handing me some cream. "This will make it better."

Wrapped in a towel, I slink off to bed. With the help of the cream, my skin heals quickly, but the other things take much longer.

Sitara let the water drain. Instead of a bath, she would try to meditate.

Moving slowly out of the heat of the bathroom, covered in a camisole and a dark-coloured sarong, she sat cross-legged on her woollen rug and tried to focus her mind. With her eyes closed, she followed each breath as it made her chest rise and fall. In her distraction, she forgot that strength comes from filling the belly.

"Namaste, Sitara. Your skin is red."

Sitara's eyes fluttered open.

Sarasvati was brushing dust off the stereo with one hand and fixing the folds of her sari with another. "Do not be too hard on your bapa. Like water, he finds you impossible to hold. You are always slipping through his fingers or falling like rain from his eyes."

Sitara changed the crossing of her legs and took another deep breath — this one into her belly.

Slipping away, Sarasvati added, "He tries to love you, Sitara, even though he thinks Parvati will not approve. But he is scared of you too."

By eight o'clock, Sitara was at the clinic making tea. Ever since her father had arrived, she'd been craving the flushing power of liquid.

Sweating heavily from her brisk bike ride, she pulled off her wool sweater. The air in the waiting room was unbearably warm. Standing on a stool, she cranked open both skylights. She needed to keep things flowing.

After making a pot of ginger-green tea, she pulled *Acupuncture for Modern Ailments* off the bookshelf, flipped to the introduction and sat down by the open window, intending to read.

My heart is still smarting from where Parvati's words have hit me. I watch, concealed within the saris hanging from the ceiling above my bed, as she leaves the apartment and rushes off to work. When Bapa is in the bathroom and I hear him start the shower, I leave my disguise and creep into their bedroom. Heading straight for Parvati's dresser, I open the drawer where she keeps her nylons. I dig my hands right to the bottom and lift everything onto the floor. They are all the same colour — skin tone, she calls it — but they aren't the colour of my skin. Quickly, because I know my bapa's shower will soon end, I make holes with my paper scissors in the toes of each pair — holes so tiny they will be hard to detect, but will make yell-out-loud runs when she puts them on. Creeping back to my room, I hide the scissors beneath my bed and open a colouring book. I am using red when Bapa tells me it's time to go.

Reaching up, Sitara replaced *Modern Ailments* and ran her finger over the library of spines. She stopped at a slim volume called *The Seven Emotions of Disease.* Leafing through the pages, she read from the sixth chapter.

The tongue will have a red tip and the eyes will look unstable and often flap shut while talking. In order to stimulate the healing process, blockages must be removed. Qi must be allowed to move freely.

Sitara stood and checked her tongue in the mirror. It had an unmistakably red tip. She remembered a phrase her mother was fond of snapping. *"Just say it, or your tongue will go red from biting it."* Most of the time Sitara had wanted to say it, whatever it was, but in the instant before the words left her mouth, she lost the courage required.

Communication with her mother had never been easy. Neither of them was able to read the signals the other tried to transmit. *"Why can you not just talk about it?"* Raj would say, pleading. *"It is not as if you speak different languages!"* But Sitara often wondered if they did.

Sitting down again, she closed her thumb in the book. Communication was not the only problem, but it made the others difficult to resolve. She remembered times when her voice had gone shrill from trying. She had yelled and cried and kicked the walls. But Parvati never flinched. She just pretended not to hear.

The ear is the organ of fear, Sitara thought. *What we hear and what we don't hear.*

The door opened and closed in the waiting room. She heard the silver chimes ring. Confused, she looked up at the clock. Her first appointment wasn't until eleven.

Walking out to the waiting room, she saw her father sitting in one of the armchairs. "Bapa? What are you doing here?"

"I tried to call you at home, but you had already gone. So, I used the phonebook to find your clinic." He was examining a small rake that he'd taken from the Zen garden coffee table. "I could have called, but I decided to come here instead." He put the rake down without drawing a path in the sand. "It was not as far as you said."

Sitara was fidgeting, shifting, trying to block the doorway to her office. "There's tea," she said.

"I have already had coffee, thank you."

"It was warm here this morning, so I opened the skylights." To show him, she started to raise her arm, but then let it drop back to her side.

He looked up and saw three variations of grey. "I see," he said, pulling his jacket closed. "Do you have good neighbours?"

"They're quiet, if that's what you mean. And respectful."

Sitara's father nodded.

"Bapa?" She pressed one hand into each side of the door-frame as if the walls might otherwise close in around her. She was wearing twenty-seven slightly bent bangles that clanked each time she moved her arm.

"Yes, Sitara? What do you want to ask me?"

"Do you —" she paused, thought about what she really wanted to say, and decided to say something else instead. "Do you still have trouble falling asleep at night?"

"I do not have trouble sleeping!"

Sitara was still holding the walls apart. "I'm not accusing you of anything."

"Perhaps not," he said, "but I do not intend to get old arguing about it. I am tired of arguing, Sitara. For once, I wish everyone could just get along."

"Do you really mean *everyone*, or do you mean Parvati and I?"

Raj stared at his shoes.

Then, without knowing why, Sitara let her arms down. *Clank.* One after another, her bracelets fell to her wrist.

She didn't want to talk about her mother, she wanted to talk about him. She wanted to see his book of Indian deities — the one with the grease-stained cover and the illustrations of Sarasvati.

"Your patients must like it here," he said. "It is comfortable and tranquil."

"I try to put people at ease."

"It must help with the healing process."

"Yes," Sitara said. She used two fingers to check her pulse. *In order to stimulate the healing process, blockages must be removed.* "I have an appointment soon," she said. "We could meet again later — perhaps at four."

"Four is fine," he replied. "Not good, but fine."

Goodbye, she wanted to say, but again her tongue trapped the words in her mouth.

After breaking the seal on a bottle of herbs, Sitara took two tablets. They were strong and bitter on her tongue, but she chose not to swallow. She wanted to restore her mouth — to make up for the words she'd spoken, and not spoken, to her father.

Standing in the darkness of her herb cupboard, with only a sliver of light seeping in around the edges of the door, she tried to conjure an image of Parvati. It was hard, since she'd tried for so many years to forget. All she could remember were the furrowed lines of her forehead, not quite hidden behind the bangs of her dark hair, which was cut business-woman short and raked with a pick until it was fluffy and light. Parvati always wore her hair that way — she was fond of permanent solutions. When it was hot, she would blow a strong wind up past her nose to ruffle her bangs and loosen them from her sweaty skin. The way this gesture forced out her lower jaw and bottom lip made it look like she was pouting. But Sitara knew better. Her father was the only one weak enough to pout.

She crunched the remains of the herb tablets and pushed her way out of the cupboard. Even after swallowing, she thought she could taste cardamom.

Walking to the coffee shop where she'd agreed to meet her father, Sitara was conscious of her breathing. She wanted to be calm when she greeted him. *Bapa, I'd like to cook for you,* she was going to tell him. He had never eaten her version of spinach curry, or had her pasta with black olive tapenade. At first she had fought the idea of inviting him to her apartment, but as she walked and the spring air strengthened her lungs, she became more convinced that it was a good thing to do.

Even before she opened the heavy door of the coffee shop, she could see her father sitting on one of the high stools at the counter. He had a newspaper spread out in front of him and a coffee cup at his side.

"Hello, Bapa," she said.

"Sitara, you are late."

She glanced up at the clock mounted crookedly above the espresso machine. It was ten after four.

"I'm sorry. It's the best I could do. Are you hungry? I'd like to —"

"I am not hungry," he said. "I have been sitting here all day eating muffins and drinking coffee. And now I think I am quite full." He closed the paper.

"Would you like to go for a walk?"

"No, Sitara. I am going home."

"Today?"

"You are obviously too busy to have me here, so I have changed my ticket. A cab is coming at quarter after four."

"Bapa, that's now!"

"Yes."

"But I'd like to talk, cook for you, show you some of the city."

"Perhaps, Sitara, it is best if we are separate. I will not trouble you any more."

As he left she thought, *with four arms I could hug him better.* But, of course, she hadn't even tried with two.

chapter 9

Wandering through the Public Gardens, Sara was commiserating with the hemmed-in ducks. She wondered if any of them had been abroad, or if they'd always lived off other people's charity in a stagnant Halifax pond. *Even dried bread tastes better in Paris,* she thought. *Intentionally crusty, not just old and hard.*

She was watching a large mallard when a security guard walked by to announce that in a few minutes he'd be locking the gates. *Poor ducks,* she thought, *locked up for the night.* In her present mood, she had forgotten that they could fly.

Escaping to the sidewalk, Sara dug her hands into her coat. Halfway home, she decided to stop at a coffee shop.

In a small town in Turkey, she had discovered real coffee. It was rich and thick and everything else paled in comparison. To salvage the present experience, she ordered an oat-cake dipped in chocolate with spikes of almond slivers. Chocolate had a way of saving everything — even a poorly made espresso.

Sitting down at a large, round table, Sara felt suddenly alone. In Turkey, men had told her that a proper kafe should be accompanied by conversation. She wondered if they believed that, or if it was a line they saved for attractive female foreigners.

Kyle, of course, would have come out with her if she'd asked him to. But she'd been ignoring him — the way she'd been ignoring everyone. Since stomping out on her parents, she'd felt the dull ache of adolescence trying to reclaim her. She had behaved badly in front of them, and in front of Kyle.

Staring into her coffee, she was looking for something to calm the waves of panic that hit her like food poisoning from a Thanksgiving dinner. She decided to try a hot chocolate.

Waiting at the counter, she tried to make out the titles of the tea stacked in coloured boxes above the shelves of mugs. She could read EARL GREY because someone had written it on white paper with a heavy black marker. Presumably there was the usual selection of mints, fruits and zingers, but she couldn't read any of the small print.

Turning around with her mug of hot, frothy milk, she saw a man with a medium format camera. The disconnected components were spread out on the table in front of him like toys. Sara took a step closer. He was wiping a portrait lens with a yellow cloth. His hands were large and rough. She was worried he would scratch it.

"Can I help you with that?" she blurted loudly, moving towards him with so much force that she almost spilled her drink.

The man looked up, scanned her from face to foot, and then paused with a long, lingering gaze at her hot chocolate. "Sure," he said, "if you'll give me a sip."

"What?"

"You want to touch my camera and I want to taste your chocolate. I think it's a fair deal."

"I just thought maybe —"

"I've cleaned lenses before," he said. " I know what I'm doing."

Without seeing it printed, Sara knew it was a Hasselblad 500 series — something she could never afford, or was too afraid to have in her possession. She smiled weakly and tried to retreat. "It's a nice rig," she said.

"Yeah. It's not bad. A little temperamental at times, but not bad." He snapped the lens back into the comfort of its home on the body of the camera. "Your chocolate will get cold," he said, picking up a miniature screwdriver.

Horrified by the brutal act she suspected him of, Sara turned away. She listened for the smashing sound of plastic or glass, for the thwack of metal on metal as the screwdriver hit the vitals of the camera. She stood cringing with her shoulders raised, braced like her mother for the disaster of the car bumping over train tracks. When she heard nothing, her lungs released the air that had been trapped.

Sitting down so that she was safely at his back, she tried not to stare. He wore a white t-shirt that might have been a woman's or a boy's — his muscles exploded the arms of it. His dark hair was pulled back, revealing both the strength and vulnerability of his well-sculpted neck. He fidgeted, as if growing tired of his surroundings. She wondered why he remained when it was obvious he wanted to be outside. Absently, she took a gulp of her drink.

Entering loudly, a woman with flushed red cheeks caught everyone's eye. She had bundles of packages with her — on her back, in her hands, tucked underneath her arms. She laughed openly as she knocked the newspapers off their stand by the door. The man with the camera looked up.

"Maggie, you're making a mess again!"

She dropped her bags on the empty chair across from him and waited for him to stand up. "Jack, you look great," she said as they embraced.

"You're sticky," he told her. "And half an hour late."

"I'm warm. I've been all over the place. Is it possible to get a cold drink here?"

"Sure, what would you like? Water? Iced tea?"

"I don't care. Whatever." She fixed her lipstick and arranged herself in one of the big wooden armchairs.

Sara watched the man stand up — he was taller than she imagined him to be. His blue jeans were faded on the back of the thighs and his wallet was a thick bulge in his pocket. He ordered a water with ice and waited without turning around while the server poured it. Walking back to the woman with the parcels, he took a sip of her water and wiped his hand on the back of his right thigh.

"Thank you," the woman said, before he'd set it down. "I hope you remembered the book."

"I did," he said, moving his camera to keep it away from her glass. "I did everything you told me to." He dropped into his chair.

The woman sighed abruptly and tilted her head. It must have been a familiar point of contention. Sara sensed that they'd recited the lines before. Wiggling her cup to mix the remaining milk and chocolate, she realized that they'd dropped their voices and that she could no longer overhear.

The woman's face, though, was expressive. Even with her failing sight, Sara could read the well-known signs. They had been a couple, and were perhaps still in some state of love. Their lips had touched, as well as their bodies, but their minds moved in opposite directions. Sara could feel the dissonance bouncing off the table.

He was showing her some photos in a book and she was pointing, rearranging, creating in the air. She was excited, specific and full of demands. He was unable to understand — or unwilling. Finally, she put her feet up on the chair that held her packages and closed her eyes.

"Why are we having this meeting?" he asked loudly, as if with her eyes closed she wouldn't be able to hear.

"To make plans for my photos," she said.

"And?"

"To catch up… and talk."

"What's to catch up on?" he asked. "You're getting married."

Sara felt the sting. He was lost to her and she to him.

"Will you take the pictures or not?" She leaned forward as if to punctuate her question.

"You're paying me. Of course I will."

The woman shook her head, swirled the half-melted ice cubes in her glass and laughed. "That's what I like about you, Jack. You'll do anything for money."

As he lifted his camera and stroked the moulded plastic case, he said something low, almost under his breath.

The woman stood, gathered her bundles, and said, "We're counting on you, Jack. Please don't screw it up."

Reproachfully, he stood too. "I wouldn't miss the happy bells." He stepped towards her, kissed her blankly on the cheek and waited for her to disappear. When she'd gone, only slightly less awkwardly than she'd arrived, he nodded in Sara's direction and asked, "Watch my camera, will ya?"

He took his storm cloud to the bathroom and let it rain.

After he had packed up his camera and walked out, Sara licked the last drops of chocolate froth from her cup and stood up. Outside, it was already dark and cold. Walking home, she sank further into herself. Tucking her ears into her collar and stuffing her hands into her pockets, she twirled a collection of lip balm and quarters rhythmically, like a nun with a rosary.

Hers was an endless holding pattern — the fog so thick, it was impossible to land.

She was walking down a long hallway that led to the back of the building. Following the cracked and faded wallpaper, she moved past two heavily painted doors towards a flood of sunlight. She could smell the ink from the newspaper ad that was still in her hand. In the dream, she entered a brightly lit room and saw a bald man in a blue chair who said, "If the eye is the camera, the mind is the film. I remember everything."

"I've come about the Hasselblad," she said. "I want to buy it."

"It doesn't work," he answered, "and besides, it's not for sale."

"Please," she begged, as she walked around the side of his chair.

"The surgeon was nervous," he told her. "His knife slipped."

Standing in front of him she could see that he was blind.

In the morning, Sara decided not to get out of bed. She covered one eye with the cup of her hand, and tested the sight of the other. Shifting from the blanket to the dresser to the Indian frieze above her door, she could see none of it clearly. She sighed and then slowly, giving her eyes time to readjust, switched to the other eye. Nothing changed. The details of her world were just as blurry. She rolled over and closed her eyes.

For a while, she blocked out the ringing telephone. Finally, grabbing the receiver, her arm brushed a swath of dust off the alarm clock.

"Hello?"

"Sara, it's me. I'm in town today. I'm having lunch with Lauren. Do you want to come?"

No, a thousand times no, her head moaned, but her mouth betrayed her and said, "Sure, Mom."

After hanging up the phone, she placed a palm over each eye. Then, lifting them one at a time, she tested her sight again. There was more clarity in her right. Smiling sadly, she decided to look at them with her left — maybe it would make lunch more bearable.

As soon as she entered the restaurant, Sara knew she shouldn't have agreed to meet with them. Lauren and Peggy were early. They were already sitting down.

"Hey. I guess I'm late," she said.

"Sit down," her mother invited. "We haven't ordered yet."

Sara pulled out a chair. Her mother and sister were sitting comfortably across from one another. The table was small and square, and Sara had the feeling of disturbing the symmetry as she sat down. "What's that?" she asked.

Lauren stuffed a small white package of tissue paper into her bag. "Just something Mom's lending me," she said.

"Looks like a camera."

Peggy smiled. "She wants to take some pictures of the guys she rides with."

"Mom!" Lauren was obviously embarrassed. She let her hair fall in front of her face to obscure some of the blush. "I'll use it for other things too!"

"Of course you will."

Sara tried to force a smile. She'd wanted her mother's camera for years, but Peggy had always made some excuse not to give it to her.

"Excuse me." Sara raised her arm to flag down the waitress. "Can I get a menu?"

"Here," Peggy said. "You can use one of ours. I think we've both decided."

"Suggestions?" Sara asked.

"It's Lauren's restaurant," Peggy said, eyeing her youngest daughter.

"I don't know, it's all good." Lauren shrugged. "What do you feel like?"

"I'm having the smoked salmon baguette," Peggy offered. "Lauren says it comes with a great salad."

"All the sandwiches do, Mom."

"No," Sara said, "I'm not in the mood for fish."

"What about the pizzas, Sara? You eat cheese?"

"Yeah, but I don't know. None of them appeal to me."

"I guess this kind of place isn't exotic enough for you," Lauren said.

"Lauren!" Peggy snapped. "That's rude."

"No, it's fine. I've been here before. I just feel like a bowl of soup."

"The special is corn potato chowder!" Lauren said. "Not exactly ethnic!"

"I like corn… and potato." Looking around the room she noticed her sister's facial expression repeated on at least a dozen other young women. The mirrored walls, too, reflected Lauren's stylish distaste.

"Sara, did you have that meeting this morning?" Peggy asked.

"It was a phone call."

"And?"

"I've been excused from my next assignment. Joyce has replaced me."

"Who's Joyce?" Lauren asked.

"My boss."

"I'm surprised she didn't offer you a leave of absence, after how long you've worked there," Peggy said.

"Well, what could she do? Put me on maternity leave?"

"Something like that would —"

"I don't understand," Lauren interrupted. "Couldn't you take pictures even if you were pregnant? How hard is it to hold a camera?"

Sara cringed. Her sister had never taken the job seriously, and took every opportunity to belittle it.

"Let's not talk about babies," Peggy pleaded. "Remember, babies for you guys means grandchildren for me, and I'm not prepared to deal with that."

"Oh, Mom," Lauren said. "You like babies!"

"I do?"

"I wouldn't worry about it." Sara smiled. "It doesn't seem imminent."

"Well at least not for you!" Lauren lowered her eyes after she said it, as if she was thinking about something that could, but wouldn't, be added.

"Okay, so Joyce has replaced you for your next assignment, but what happens after that?"

"I don't know. I don't think anyone's going to buy my photos anymore."

"Oh, Sara. Don't be so dramatic."

"Well, if Joyce is any indication then —"

"Maybe you could be a translator," Lauren said. "Then you'd still get to travel."

"That would be a great idea, if I could speak more than one language!"

"You guys learned French," Peggy said.

"You're right. I can probably say 'yes,' 'no' and 'good night' in seven or eight languages. It doesn't exactly make me a translator."

"Well, what about a travel agent?" Lauren offered. "That way, you'd get lots of cheap tickets."

"Yeah, but I'd be stuck behind a desk five days a week."

As the main part of their meal was being devoured — slowly with a spoon for Sara, roughly with both hands for Peggy, and barely at all between words for Lauren — an awkwardness surrounded the table. Sara remembered how, after she reached the age of fifteen, Ron had laboured to get them to eat together. Sara, who had spent long hours watching him cook, had always nibbled too much in the kitchen. Peggy would stay late after work or schedule dinner-hour meetings, and Lauren preferred to eat out with her friends. Now, Sara looked up at the women of her family and saw two familiar sets of jaws distorted with chewing.

"Anyone want dessert?" the waitress asked.

"Just coffee," Sara said.

"For me too."

"I'll have an espresso," Lauren said. Then she paused, looked at her sister and added, "Make it a double."

Sara pretended to look at herself in the mirror.

"Mom, was Dad here on business recently?" Lauren asked.

"Yeah, he was checking out a new vehicle — which he didn't buy, as you might have noticed by the wreck I drove up in. Why?"

"I just thought," Lauren said, "that I saw him, that's all."

"Did he drive right by you or something? He can be in such a daze!"

"I was in a store, so he wouldn't have been able to see me."

"I suggested he call you, but I guess he didn't have a lot of time. Where's the bathroom, hon? There's no way I have room for coffee."

"At the back on your left. It's the one with the skirt!"

"Thanks." Peggy stood up and walked away.

"Do you know," Lauren leaned in close, making Sara wonder what kind of secret she was going to reveal, "if they have any friends in the city?"

"I presume so, why?"

"Well, I saw Dad walking with a woman."

"So," Sara said, "maybe she's in the hospitality industry."

"I don't think so — they were holding hands and laughing."

"Sounds hospitable to me!"

"Ugh!" Peggy exclaimed, as she walked towards them. "I hate lineups. I'll go back later."

Lauren straightened up at the sound of her mother's voice. "I was telling Sara about my plans for your birthday — you could have stayed away longer."

Sara shook her head at her sister's clumsy lie.

"We don't need to celebrate it," Peggy replied.

Lauren managed a weak smile. "We'll see." She wasn't used to such quick cover-ups. It was Sara who had used them many times before.

As Peggy sat down, the waitress arrived with a full tray.

The women drank their coffee the way they finished their conversation — in quiet little sips until there was nothing left in their cups. Lauren stood up first. She had a hair appointment. Looking at her bill she said, "Can I borrow eight bucks? I only have a five."

Peggy handed her some money across the table. Sara wondered how her sister was going to pay for the haircut but, as usual, decided not to ask.

"Have fun with the camera," Peggy said. "And don't get too much trimmed off the front — I think your bangs look great the way they are."

"Thanks, Mom." Lauren kissed her on the cheek. "See ya, Sis." She leaned into Sara's ear. "Parents are supposed to stay in love," she whispered. "I believe that."

Sara smiled at her sister's version of the world. "Use fast film if you're going to be outdoors," she said.

In a loud voice, Lauren responded with, "The guys are going to hate me for taking these."

"Just the guys?" Peggy asked. "Are there really no other girls that ride?"

"No, right now I'm the only one."

She's right, Sara thought. *She's the only one with enough belief to still be called a girl.*

"See ya," Lauren said, as she ran off with her helmet swinging from her hand.

"I still have to pee," Peggy mouthed to her remaining daughter and Sara was left alone at the table.

Strangers must think we see each other all the time, she thought. *It must seem so casual.* "See you tomorrow, hon." "*I'll drop by later.*" "*Don't wait up, I'll be home late.*" But in reality, the three of them hadn't been together in years.

When Peggy came back from the bathroom she was subdued. She leaned across the table and looked into Sara's eyes.

"You look okay. How do you feel?"

"Like shit," Sara said.

"You know your father was only trying to help you make an informed choice. He wants the best for you. We all want the best for —"

"Yeah, yeah. Spare me the sob story."

"I think you're the one who's sobbing, Sara. You're like a mopy three-year-old who didn't get her way. Do yourself a favour and get over it."

Sara was putting gloves on even though it was a warm day. "It was great having lunch with you. Say hi to Dad."

"I'm sorry you're not taking this well," Peggy said. "But really, Sara, it's not the end of the world. Maybe you should stick around for awhile, try to find another job. Lauren tells me there's an opening at her office. It's a permanent position and it pays well."

"Mom, I don't know anything about —"

"Listen, perfect eyesight isn't a prerequisite, and I'm sure with a little training, you'd be good at the job. Say you'll at least think about it, Sara. It makes so much sense."

She threw a scarf around her neck and stood up. "I'll think about it," she said.

"That's all I ask. Take care, hon."

"Goodbye."

After a brisk three blocks, Sara stopped and realized that she'd been walking the wrong way. Turning around, she bullied her way back along the street. With her head down, her arms crossed and her shoulders hunched forward, she felt more like a football player than a photographer. Crossing against the light, she forced two cars to slam on their brakes.

At her apartment, she fought with the front door key, nearly breaking it in the lock. Finally, after forcing the latch, she crumbled onto the seagrass mat and started to cry. They were hot, stale tears that she'd been saving for weeks. Like scratches from a manic cat, they stung her face and left her skin swollen and red.

Pacing her apartment with a runny nose and runny eyes, she felt sick. She wasn't used to crying and didn't know how to handle the flood. Spinning from room to room, she was battered by a hurricane of emotions — the strongest of which was fear.

click
From under a blood-soaked bandage, her left eye pops out.

click
With an enormous hole in her stomach, she stands in her parents' kitchen hoping for handouts.

click
Boxed in by beige dividers, she enters meaningless numbers into a droning computer.

Her lunchtime soup sputtered and fired inside her with a raging heat, but she didn't listen. Her entire mind was occupied by a newly obvious thought: *Life is about photography, not having a job.*

In a blooming of clarity, like radiant orange sun after a hard rain, Sara reached for the phonebook. She needed to save her photographer's eyes. Flipping through the Yellow Pages, she found the section for acupuncture. With her finger on the ad with the boldest type, she picked up the phone and dialled.

book II

chapter 10

When the cab stopped at the corner, Sara didn't want to get out. It had never happened before — not in Jakarta, Madrid, or Istanbul. She had always paid her fare, the strange foreign currency falling from her hands like water, and then rushed out onto the street, confident in her not knowing, calm. Now, in Halifax, the city where she went to college, she froze — her fingers awkward on the familiar paper bills.

The late April air swirled around her, lifting her long coat and penetrating areas she would rather have kept to herself. She pushed back the cuff of her left sleeve, although she knew she wouldn't find a watch there. "Doctors are always running late," she muttered to comfort herself, and walked faster. Turning off the main street, she walked down a stone pathway.

Placing her hand on the shiny gold handle, she felt her breasts turn cold. The sinking, churning turmoil of her mind had fallen into her body. Her stomach, too, sank hard against her bones. Lifting her feet over the threshold, she found herself in a small alcove — an uncertain pause on the way to other places. She shuddered and then, one step at a time, climbed the stairs.

Walking through the door at the top, she heard the sound of running water. The air, in contrast to the hallway, was warm and moist, and smelled of life and incense. Although there were no windows, the ceiling was filled with skylights and a breeze blew in from an open door. Sara took a deep breath.

There was music playing, although she didn't identify it as that at first. It filled the room — permeated the walls, the furniture, the basket of magazines. It seemed to come out of every pore in the building. Crowded with plants that thrived in the humid, living air, the room itself might have breathed, ate, slept. Sara was afraid to move — afraid of squishing some tiny, delicate life form.

The sound of running water stopped, and a young woman stepped out of her makeshift kitchen, drying her hands on the body of a soft, black towel.

"Hello," she said. "I'm Sitara."

Seeing and not seeing, Sara's eyes made her mind spin. This was the woman who had told her on the telephone, *"Bring your eyes to me, and we'll see."* She looked thirty, maybe younger, but her narrow face shone with knowing. Sara opened her mouth and waited, but nothing came out.

Finally the woman asked, "Sara, isn't it?"

"Yes."

"I'll be with you in a minute."

Following the woman's movements, Sara watched her lay the towel over the back of the chair. Behind the reception desk, she bent low and pulled something from a bottom drawer. She lifted the cap off a black fountain pen and wrote a short note. Then she licked her lower lip and replaced the cap.

"Okay," she said, gesturing for Sara to follow.

Floating — she was no longer aware of her feet touching the ground — Sara traced the steps of the woman in front of her and wiped the sweat from her palms onto the fabric of her jeans.

The room was large compared to the waiting area, with a four-paned window propped open to promote the flow of air. Next to a tall bookcase was an old wooden armchair. Sara sat down.

"So?" Sitara asked. "What do you see?"

"Things are blurry," she said. "I've had my camera checked, but…" She trailed off, knowing she'd said the same thing on the telephone.

"Have you been to anyone else?"

"Yes." The horror of it resurfaced and showed on her face.

"A medical doctor," Sitara said, "and the answer wasn't good."

"Right." Sara nodded, surprised.

"From over there, what do you see?"

Sitara was sitting in a similar wooden chair with black clogs dangling on the end of grey socks. Her fingers were unadorned, but there were strings of sandalwood beads on her wrist and at her neck, and a tiny gold stud in her nose. All of this Sara could see clearly, with the curved effect of her sight complimenting the woman's natural lines.

Sitara asked again, "Tell me what you see."

Sara shifted her eyes to the framed print above the woman's head. It was black and gold — an Indian deity holding a wheel of life.

"The frame bulges," Sara said. "It's warped in a way that a square frame could never be."

Sitara smiled. "Come and lie down." She stood and patted the white sheet.

Rising, Sara climbed onto the bed. Resting her head on the bean-filled pillow, she tried to not move.

"Any joint pain?" Sitara asked.

"No."

"Headaches or dizziness?"

"I don't know. Both sometimes, I guess. Headaches mostly." Sara's chest was tightening and she was finding it hard to breathe.

"Try to relax," Sitara said. "This works better if you're comfortable." She was testing Sara's pulse. "Do you mind?" She started to lift Sara's shirt.

"No." Sara was sinking inside.

As Sitara pressed her hand into the skin over Sara's liver she asked, "Are there times when your sight is better than others?"

"No," Sara felt guilty as she said it, "it's always bad."

"Are you sure?"

"Yes." In truth, she suspected it got worse around the time of her period.

"I'd like to try something," Sitara said. "Try to relax and lie still."

Sara turned to watch as Sitara opened a drawer and pulled out a handful of needles. After placing most of them in a porcelain bowl, she unwrapped one and dropped the packaging into a basket under the bed.

Horrified, Sara held her breath.

click

She tries to blink, but she cannot close her eyes. Like oranges stuck with cloves, they are full of needles that protrude in all directions and rattle when she shakes her head.

Carefully, Sitara tapped a needle into Sara's wrist.

Unable to control her panic, Sara sat up, removed the needle and bolted for the door. "I'm sorry," she said. "I shouldn't have come here." As she left, she threw a twenty on the floor.

chapter 11

Stunned, Sitara stood and watched as her patient disappeared. She'd never lost anyone mid-treatment before.

Walking back to her office, she took off her shoes and sat down at her desk. Staring at her appointment book with its cover of muted cherry blossoms, she took a deep breath. On the exhale, as she let her head roll forward to release her neck, warm air slid under her blouse and over her breasts. After the second breath, her vertebrae lengthened further and her chin rested on her chest.

"You have to make your patients feel comfortable," a second-year professor had told her in a class dedicated to patient comfort. *"To put people at ease, you have to be at ease. You have to learn to separate the personal from the professional. You have to leave your own problems at the door."*

Sitara had laughed, still believing that if she worked hard enough, she wouldn't *have* any problems to leave at the door. However, by the end of her fourth year, she realized with relief that enlightenment — like good tea — tastes better when it's not rushed. Now, just outside her clinic door she kept a tall clay urn where, before entering, she tried to empty herself of everything she didn't need.

Placing her hands in front of her on the desk, she lifted her head until it was in line again with her spine. Standing up quickly, she walked to the door, paused by the urn and slowly entered the clinic again. This time she was hoping to leave more behind.

When Norm arrived for his biweekly appointment, Sitara was raking sand. She usually ignored the Zen garden coffee table she and Carrie had built together, but for more than an hour she'd been making straight lines into spirals and spirals into straight lines. One, she knew, was reality, and the other, the chaos of her mind.

Leaving the miniature garden behind, she gestured Norm into her office. As he climbed onto the bed, she had to remind him about his suit jacket and tie. Ashamed, as if she'd asked him to undress completely, he hung the items over the arm of a chair.

"How are you feeling?" she asked, as she placed her hands at the base of his neck. "Did you try a long bath?"

Shifting his eyes from the ceiling to the poster at the foot of the bed, he answered quietly, "No."

"Heat relaxes muscles," Sitara said. "You could lose a lot of tension that way."

Norm suffered from debilitating headaches and erratic anxiety attacks. Secretly, Sitara thought he should quit his job — she was tired of seeing him in the same condition month after month — but instead, she facilitated another temporary solution and said nothing.

"I don't have time for baths. Ninety seconds in the shower is a luxury."

"When you come here, it takes most of an hour."

"Don't remind me, I already regret skipping my lunch."

"What you need is a few weeks off," Sitara said, inserting a needle into his hand.

"What I need is to get back to work." Norm sat up. "If you don't mind…" He raised his arm and motioned for her to remove the needle. Standing up, he armed himself with a fake smile. "Thanks," he said. "I feel a lot better." He put on his jacket and pocketed his tie. "And I'll try a bath. Maybe tomorrow. Heat and lavender. I remember." He bent over to buckle his shoes and then hurried out the door.

Sitara was still holding the needle that had barely been in his arm. "Shit," she said out loud, "I drove another one away." She chucked the needle in the sharps container, then pounded the bed with her open hand. "Shit. Shit!"

Leaving the clinic, she left a note on the door saying, *All remaining appointments for today are cancelled.*

Tracing the same steps her father had taken a few weeks earlier, Sitara was on a mission to buy coffee. At the café, she sat with her back to the window and drank an espresso in two gulps. Already she could feel the caffeine adding fire to the anger in her blood. With her lips curled from the bitterness, she stared at the table, fidgeting with the tiny cup.

"Tara," my friend says, refilling my mug, "let's work faster so this doesn't take all night."

It's late and already we feel like stowaways on an abandoned ship. We have an anatomy presentation in the morning, but Hannah wants to make love with her boyfriend and still have time to sleep.

"I think we're almost finished," I tell her, as I try to draw the digestive system from the inside out.

"What do you think this stuff does to our stomachs?" she asks, as she takes another sip.

Without saying anything, I use my pen to blacken my drawing.

"Great," she says, sarcastically. "Let's have another cup!"

Sitara ordered a second espresso and, sitting on the tall stool where her father had sat, she sipped this one slowly. She wanted to feel its dark power permeate her. She wanted her heart to pound fast enough to drown her. She wanted to feel something of what her father had felt when he decided to leave.

He always gives up, she thought, *conceding to the most popular idea. Usually Parvati's.*

"Raj, you are wrong," she could hear Parvati saying.

"Of course, I am wrong," he would answer. *"I am always wrong when you are right. All of the gods know this."* And then he would melt into the sofa, or the dining room curtains, or whatever was there to camouflage him. Growing up, Sitara had secretly scolded him for not being strong.

Pushing away her empty cup, she replayed again the appointments that had left her standing with a needle in her hand. *Perhaps,* she thought, *Bapa is right. Maybe I am no better than a medical doctor handing out prescriptions to mask symptoms while ignoring the deeper problems.*

Doubt had such a big mouth, and hope such a small one, that Sitara was afraid of being gobbled up. Raising her empty glass in defense, she realized she could use some air.

With blood racing through her veins, she started walking. Crossing against the light, she had to run between cars. Zigzagging through the back streets, trying to avoid the crowds of Spring Garden Road, she worked her way to the Public Gardens.

Taking the least direct path, and twice doubling back, her footsteps mirrored the pathways she was making in her mind.

I am standing in the cafeteria when I first hear someone speak my new name. For days I have been finding notes on my desk, tucked between the pages of my books, slipped into my shoes during yoga or meditation — all written in clear capital letters. I try to close my ears, but the calling is insistent.

"Hey, White Tara! Wait up."

We have been encouraged by one of our teachers to choose a new name, or even several, if we want. She hopes it will help us lose our attachment to things that are not important. But someone has chosen for me, and the name is larger than I can bear.

White Tara: Buddhist goddess of compassion and longevity, charged with health and healing, and blessed with seven eyes.

"Please," I say. "I am not white, and I'm not a deity."

Standing there, in line, I decide to add the Si back to my name. I have been Tara long enough.

Doubt was not new to her, but as she watched water spew from a grungy fountain, the foul juices of anxiety — mixed with too much coffee — started erupting in her gut. Opening her mouth, she hoped to let some of the gas escape, but the extra oxygen only added to the fire. Feeling her pulse, she decided to keep walking.

Sick to my stomach all night, I seek comfort in the spice section. I am supposed to be working cash, but Ruth has asked Adam to trade with me, allowing me instead to restock shelves. Breathing in the dust of cinnamon, coriander and cloves, I can almost feel Sarasvati beside me.

It is one year today since I left my parents' apartment. The date is forever burned into my memory.

Narrowly missing a collision with a woman and her baby carriage, Sitara moved onto the grass. The ducks, she noticed, were not threatened by her — they merely waddled out of the way. Running her hands over the bark of a tree, she had to submerge the temptation to climb it. She'd already been thrown out of the garden twice for reading in the upper branches.

"Tara!" Ruth says. "I've been trying to get your attention for five minutes. Didn't you hear me calling?"

"No," I tell her, quickly pushing a book back on the shelf by its spine. "I'm sorry. I lost track of the time." Looking up at her wild green eyes, I can see her compassion for me. Wringing my hands together, I scold myself for being sloppy. In the three weeks I've been here, she's already given me vitamins, bread and a box of organic apples.

"I need to leave early," she says. "Can you help Adam close up the store?"

"Sure," I say, grateful but undeserving of the confidence she so easily bestows upon me. "I'll start sweeping now."

"Thanks," she says, and then, just as she turns to go, she adds, "Take the book if you want, just bring it back tomorrow."

Though in my body I still feel a great loss, I smile, thankful for what I've gained.

Turning again, Sitara headed for the north-east exit. Swinging the heavy iron gate, she crossed the street and kept walking. Keeping her eyes lowered, she cut through the Commons and rushed towards Agricola Street. Like a salmon drawn to its spawning ground, she was looking for traces of spices that might still be lingering in the air.

When she arrived at the storefront where Ruth's Natural Foods used to be, she was surprised to see it occupied by a travel agency — it had been an antique dealer only weeks before.

Thrown off by the change, and no longer able to go in pretending to browse, she turned and started walking home.

"Well," Ruth says, "if you're serious about this, I can certainly find you some extra shifts. But why don't you consider the school in Vancouver? Going to the States must be a lot more expensive."

"Monetarily, yes. But not for my soul." I smile, hoping she won't ask me to explain. After a year and a half, she's learned not to.

"I'll miss you, Tara," she says. "It won't be the same without you!"

"I'm sure Adam will make up for my lack of chatter at the till."

"Perhaps." Ruth smiles. "But who will sing to the spices?"

Sitara reached around and unbraided her hair. Before she started working with patients, she'd always let it hang free. When she was young, her father had spent hours brushing it. One whole winter she'd been unable to sleep without the comfort of his brushing song.

Climbing up the steps to her apartment, she wrestled with the idea of calling him. Inside, she put her hand on the phone, but then walked into the bathroom instead. Washing the afternoon's sun and dirt from her face, she watched as her colour drained.

Slowly, the candle that lit her aching darkness flickered and went out. After sitting on the closed lid of the toilet for a long time, she decided to crawl into bed.

chapter 12

Sara was gasping from lack of air — or possibly from too much of it. Looking out from the top of the hill, she could see downtown as it fell towards the harbour. There were sailboats circling the island and the ferry was in mid-cross. As the wind flapped her loose pants and t-shirt, damp wisps of hair whipped across her face, irritating her eyes and getting caught in her mouth. She twisted them together and held them back with her hand. She'd never been to the top of the citadel before, although she'd often walked around it and looked up at it from below.

Turning slightly to the south, she tried to find her apartment building.

click
A white three-storey house with blue gabled windows and a tall pine tree.

Even with her hand raised above her eyes to block out the sun, she couldn't find it. She didn't have the height she needed and, despite all of her travelling, she didn't have a good sense of direction.

Bending over, she pulled at the heels of her new running shoes. With her fingers, she could feel the bubbly formation of blisters. Running was something she had first experienced in college when her roommates had dragged her out of bed at sunrise. Then, she had done it grudgingly because it was the only thing the three of them had in common. Now, she was trying to feel healthy.

She placed her hands on the white painted boards of the clock tower, stepped back until her body made a forty-five-degree angle and stretched her hamstrings carefully. Breathing hard, she could feel the tension in her muscles slowly giving way.

"Skydiving gives a better view."

Startled, Sara straightened up, looking for a face to go with the voice behind her. The man was wearing faded jeans and a weathered black shirt. He had a padded knapsack fastened to his back.

"You've never been up here before," he said.

"How do you know?"

"You're leaning."

"My feet are sore — from my new shoes." She pointed.

"To me, it looks like longing."

She stepped back to see him better. His brown hair was pulled into a ponytail, not unlike her own, but he was taller than she was, and broader. He filled the picture she was framing in her mind entirely.

"Do you have your camera?" she asked, remembering who he was.

"No," he said, and then, after taking a long, calculating look at her, he knelt down and opened the zipper on his pack. The camera he held out to her was the Hasselblad he'd had in the café — the one she'd been afraid he would scratch with his large, abrupt fingers.

She accepted the camera from him and tested it in her hands. The cold, black body was sleek and smooth, and polished to a shining perfection. Its weight and balance surprised her and she had to adjust her instinctive grip. Trying to be casual, she aimed the lens at its owner.

click
A man with a brash smile and a wind-ruffled shirt stares at the camera, while strands of the photographer's hair colour the view.

Frustrated, she handed the camera back to him.
"Take another one if you like."
Reluctantly, she returned the camera to her eye.

click
A man laughs when the photographer doesn't want him to.

"It's a portrait lens," he said, stepping towards her. "That's why things seem so much closer than they are."
She could feel his breath on the side of her neck, but his features were a blur. Taking his camera back from her, he touched her hands more than he needed to.
"You should continue your run," he said. "Your muscles will get cold."
She nodded and tried to stop her shiver.
He turned and started to walk away.

click
The trail of a man fleeing a photograph.

"When will I see you again?" she called.
"Tonight if you come to the gallery." He pulled a postcard from his bag and walked back to give it to her. "Free wine, stale

munchies, lots of posturing, pretending and primadonna-ing. The usual scene." He was already walking away.

She held the card without looking at it. "And if I don't come," she asked, "when will I see you again?"

"I don't know." He stopped, lifted the camera to his eye and snapped a shot of her. "But I'll see you when I develop these."

She watched him disappear over the bulge of her current horizon, taking a small piece of her with him.

Sara changed her clothes three times before finally settling on a long, black sundress. It was a cool May evening and, walking the few blocks to the gallery, she huddled under a belted cardigan that hung down to her knees.

Before approaching the last corner, she hesitated and tried to catch her reflection in a store window. What she saw was dark and vague and raised more questions than it answered. Feeling overly exposed, she undid her hair clip and let her curls fall over her shoulders and neck. Now, if necessary, she had somewhere to hide.

Nearing the sign for the FishHead Gallery, she took a deep breath and thought of its owners, Sally and Ru. They were a pleasant, if oddly matched, couple. She was a big business accountant with miniskirts and blazers and high-profile clients, and he was an eccentric little painter with continual smudges of colour on his hands and his shirts and all through his beard and moustache. He had good taste and she had good sense, and together they ran a modestly successful gallery.

The heavy glass door was propped open, and a crowd of smokers was gathered on the sidewalk, puffing secrets into each other's ears. Intensifying the effect of the toxic haze, something loud and indecipherable blared on the stereo. Sara had thoughts of walking past. She could get a coffee, stroll through the gardens, be home before dark...

"Sara?"

She was trapped.

"Hey, I figured you'd show up sooner or later, but I never guessed it would be here! I'm thinking about breaking the sound barrier and going in. Want to come?" Ru laughed. "It's way too loud, isn't it? I think it's the guy at the back. He has some kind of metalworking studio and he listens to Zappa all the time. But there's nothing I can do about it. So, instead of standing in this cloud, let's make a run for it." He grabbed Sara's hand and pulled her in. "Where have you been hiding, my little gem?" he yelled.

"In your backyard," she teased.

"Ahh, like a flower bulb. Hiding away underground all winter, only to burst forth when the weather tames and the temperature promises to behave itself. So what are you? Daffodil, tulip, some kind of hyacinth?" He was running his hands over her shoulders, threatening to reach for her breasts.

"I'm an onion," she said. "I make men cry."

"Is that right?" He pulled her into a hug so tight it made her spine straighten.

"Ru!"

Quickly he stepped back. "It's okay," he said, "I'm clean."

Winking at him, she was amazed at how easily they fell back into their familiar routine.

"Is Sally here tonight?" she asked. "I'd like to say hi."

"If she is, she'll be at the cash register, or in the back room making love to her computer. She's not like us, Sara. She doesn't understand about socializing and drinking wine. Come, I'll get you a glass. If we're lucky, what she bought isn't too cheap."

Sara followed him through the crowd to where he paused in front of a large framed photograph. "It's beautiful, don't you think?" A grandfather's bristled upper lip gave way to a slightly open mouth that was nipping his grandson's nose. With both hands, the baby was pulling on the old man's ears.

The music was still too loud, and Sara was having trouble concentrating. "It's interesting," she said. But in truth, she was confused. The oversized photos were all the same. There was no landscape, no context, no way of telling where the people were.

As Ru examined the photo more carefully, Sara's eyes strayed to the food table where a sturdy, broad-shouldered man was eating grapes and drinking wine. There was a tall, blonde woman sailing in his direction, and suddenly Sara wanted to get there first. Nudging Ru, she urged, "Wine now, photos later." He agreed and started pushing through the crowd.

When they got to the table, the woman was already talking.

"I'm Amy," she said, almost shouting. "I love your work, but couldn't you do something about the music?"

"I'm Jack," he put out his hand, "and I have tried."

"Well you should try harder," Ru interrupted. "Or you should complain to the bugger who runs this joint!"

"Under the circumstances," Jack said, "I think I'll avoid that."

"Good boy!" Ru patted him on the back. "Listen, there's a woman here who wants to meet you."

"Yes," the blonde said, "I was just telling him that I —"

"This is Sara," Ru interrupted again, pushing her forward from where she was hiding behind him. "I want you to meet her because she's also a —"

"Photographer. Yes, I know." Jack scanned the entirety of her long, black dress, pausing at the neckline and the shadow made by her chin. "I see you're not leaning tonight," he said. "I'm glad."

Sara shifted her weight involuntarily and tried to think of something to say.

Ru, handing them full glasses of wine, spoke for her. "To a great show, and to its brilliant creator!"

As they raised their glasses, Sara saw the blonde slink away.

"I didn't know if you'd come or not," Jack said after Ru had drifted off in search of other guests.

"I didn't know either," Sara yelled, "especially when I heard the noise. It's hard to talk. My throat's getting raw."

"That just means you need to lean in close," he said. "Why do you think I'm always going on about leaning?"

Sara smiled but didn't move.

"So, you like my photos, or what?" He was holding his wineglass with one hand while the other was jammed into the pocket of his jeans. "What do I need to do to get a compliment out of you?" He looked around. "I'd buy you a drink, if the wine wasn't free. Or maybe you'll join me for a coffee later."

"I'd like that."

"Great." Jack nodded. He was eyeing a middle-aged couple who were headed his way. "Remind me later, in case I forget. Excuse me." He turned towards the gushing words and the large wallets.

Just as the blonde woman had a few minutes earlier, Sara eased herself back into the crowd. Letting her hair fall forward to obscure the flush of her cheeks, she went looking for a glass of water.

After slipping into the bathroom and taking a long drink from the tap, she felt composed enough to embark on a self-guided tour of the photos. Starting with a naked baby, seen from above, and circled by six pairs of different-sized feet, she worked her way to the back wall, where Jack had hung the largest photo in the collection. It was a close-up of an old woman peeking through finger-spread hands — a coy gesture, uncommon yet comfortable on her wrinkled face.

Sara's eyes throbbed. Even though the photos were large and well lit, she struggled with the detail, trying to find clues about the photographer in the grainy backgrounds of his prints. When Jack brushed past her, she was leaning in and squinting.

"Forget your glasses?" he asked. "Or are you seeing something the rest of us have missed?"

Startled, she jumped back. "I have an eye condition," she said.

"I'm glad you don't look at me that way. I don't think I could take the scrutiny." He smiled before draining his glass of wine. "You don't like my work, do you?"

"I haven't decided yet."

"You're a photographer. I expect an honest answer."

She shifted from one sore foot to the other. "How do you know?"

"I saw the way you handled the camera — like it was an extension of your arm. And the way your body quivered when you pressed the shutter, like feeding on a shot of caffeine. You're hooked, I can tell. And I bet you're professional. Am I right?"

"I've taken a few pictures."

"A few million, more likely. That's why Ru introduced us — to make sure I'm aware of my competition!"

Sara was trying to unscrunch her eyes. She'd been holding them tighter than an angry fist.

"Your sight is bad, isn't it?" he asked.

"Yeah." She looked down at the black, tiled floor. "I'm on a leave of absence from work."

"So that's why you drooled over my camera."

"What?"

"Classic withdrawal. You have all the —" Someone was tapping him on the shoulder. "My camera's in the office if you need a fix." He was walking backwards, following a customer to the other side of the show.

In the silence of the space he left behind, Sara noticed that the loud music had been replaced by some frantic, but low-volume, jazz.

She wandered back to the wine table. Between handfuls of corn chips that she didn't really want, she watched a familiar woman walk through the door.

click
She bolts from a bed of needles, suffering immediate regret.

Ploughing her way through the remaining crowd, the acupuncturist headed directly for Jack.

After embracing quickly, the way distracted in-laws do, they started a brief exchange that Sara strained to overhear.

"Jack, the show looks great. I'd stick around, but I'm really not in the mood. I bet you'll sell lots." She turned to leave.

"Hey, wait a minute. Slow down!" He caught her by the shoulder and spun her around so that he could speak to her face. "You look tired. What's going on?"

"Lots of shit, but this is not the place to talk about it. I'll see you soon."

Taking his hand away, he let her go. Dazed, he walked to the food table and helped himself to another glass of wine.

Slinking into the shade of a potted fig tree, Sara hoped that he hadn't caught her staring.

Later, sitting at a small table across from Jack, Sara drank her coffee slowly. Still processing the intensity of his photos, and distracted by Sitara's brief visit, she was listening too much and talking too little.

Finally she asked, "How well do you know that Indian woman?"

"Sitara? Well enough."

"She's an acupuncturist?"

"Among other things, yeah."

"Have you been to see her?"

"Sure I have. She's great. You know, she could probably help you."

Sara took another sip of her coffee. "Perhaps."

"Come on," Jack said, "at my place there are three cameras that you still haven't met."

chapter 13

Abruptly, like the instant flash of a long forgotten face, Sitara thought of her plants. Worried about the possibility of them turning against her too, she hurried through the rest of her meal and then rode down to the clinic.

Opening the heavy red door for the first time in days, she felt a jolt of nostalgia. It had been part of her daily passage for more than five years. Once inside, she twisted the lock behind her.

Tending to her asparagus fern, she heard the telephone. After a few rings, the volume of her old tape-based answering machine startled her. She cringed when she heard her own voice explaining how the clinic was temporarily closed. Expecting a hang-up, she was surprised when someone left a message.

"Hi. This is Sara. I saw you a couple weeks ago about my eyes. Listen, I'm sorry for walking out on you. It was rude. I apologize and I'd like to try again. Will you make me another appointment?"

Sitara wasn't taking patients — especially ones who rattled her confidence — and yet, without knowing why, she picked up the phone and dialled.

"I could see you now," she said. "I have no plans for the afternoon."

When Sara arrived, Sitara was meditating — poorly — on the examination table. Hearing the bells that hung above the outer door, she took a last deep breath and climbed down.

"Come in," she said to the woman with the eye problems. She turned and walked into her office. With only a small hesitation, Sara followed. "Are your eyes still bad?"

"Yeah, as bad as ever."

"Have you been taking anything — bilberry, grapeseed, selenium, Vitamin A or E?"

"No."

"I think it would help. I'd also like you try a Chinese formula. Before you go, I'll see if I can find a couple of bottles." She motioned for Sara to climb onto the bed.

"Your eyes are blurry, right? Are they both the same?"

"No," Sara said. "The right is better than the left."

Sitara was checking her pulse. "How's your diet?"

"Not great," Sara confessed. "I'm often away from home."

Sitara hovered over her, performing precise and calculated movements. "Do you eat meat?"

"Yes, sometimes."

"Do you sleep well?"

"Not bad."

Sitara glanced up at the poster at the end of the bed. "I'd like to stimulate a few points, if that's okay." She paused before reaching for the bowl. "I don't have to use needles, but it is an essential part of what I do." She stepped back and took a long look at the woman's face. Her cheeks were still flushed from walking, and her skin was smooth and tanned. "Looks like the sun's been good to you," she said.

"I've just been in Portugal and Morocco taking photos."

"Ever been to China?" Sitara asked.

"Yeah."

"Try any acupuncture?"

"No. But I'll try it now. And I promise not to head for the door."

Sitara swabbed a spot on Sara's arm, opened a small paper package and pulled out a needle. "If I do my job right, you shouldn't feel this at all." Picking up Sara's right hand, Sitara rotated it so that she could have full access to the points on her wrist. Then, using her own right hand to insert the needle, she stroked Sara's fingers with her left. "Okay?" she asked.

Sara nodded.

"Are you still having headaches and dizziness?"

"Yeah. Mostly here." Sara used her free hand to illustrate.

"I'll see if I can fix that in a minute." She unwrapped another needle and inserted it into Sara's right ankle. "What did you see in China?"

"Beijing mostly. I was illustrating an urban story."

"Any herb markets?"

"None that I remember."

"Try to breathe deeply. It will help your circulation." She could see the build-up of tension in Sara's chest and shoulders. "You're doing so well," she teased, "I might not even have to lock the door."

"I always bolted at the dentist's office too," Sara said. "My father used to bribe me with his baking. I was promised a whole batch of gingerbread if I co-operated."

"I love ginger."

"Me too."

With one quick, controlled pull, Sitara removed the needle from Sara's ankle. Then, satisfied with the improvement in her energy flow, she removed the one from her wrist. "Alright, there's just one more thing I want to do." She walked around to the end of the bed and, after taking away the small rectangular pillow, she slid her hands under Sara's head.

"This was my father's idea," Sara said, staring at the sparseness of Sitara's ceiling. "I had something else in mind. Something fast and drastic. When he suggested acupuncture, I told him he was crazy."

"Sometimes I think my father's crazy too," Sitara said. She liked the feel of Sara's head in her hands. Working under the weight of it made her fingers feel strong. "I need to move one of your upper vertebrae. It's slightly unaligned." With slow, steady pressure, she started to turn Sara's spine. "Are you still okay?"

"Fine."

"Try to relax and let me move your head." Sara's hair had the kind of gentle curl that Sitara had always admired. Her mouth, too, even when she talked, was full and round like the petals of a lotus.

"And yet here I am," Sara said, "acting on my father's suggestion, as if I do everything I'm told."

As Sara spoke, Sitara could feel the reverberation of the vocal cords in her patient's neck. "Your father doesn't really control you, does he?"

"No," Sara said, "but it's an annoying part of the parent-child relationship. It feels like he's always trying to encourage or discourage me. Why, even at thirty, is it so hard to ignore the opinions of my family?"

"I don't know." Sitara was lost again in the topography of Sara's face. Upside down, her eyes looked like small, blue lakes, and her nose a gentle mountain.

"What if it's genetic?" Sara asked. "What if we're predisposed to believe the things our families tell us? Where does that leave us?"

Releasing Sara's head, Sitara sat down at her desk. Staring at her bookshelf, she said, "Some people think that's ideal. The Chinese would say that if each member of a family fulfills his or her role, then the family functions well."

"But what do you think?"

"I prefer to think our behaviour has less to do with genetics, and more to do with conditioning. That way, I have more power." Sitara turned and looked out the window. "I try to choose what I inherit from my mother." The sun was making green and yellow patterns as it fell through her collection of empty jars. She waved her hand through the stream of light and watched her skin change colour.

"Are you close to your mother?" Sara asked.

"Not exactly."

"Is it awkward when you see her?"

"I don't know. I haven't tried for years."

Sara stifled a cough. "And your father?"

"The same."

"Sometimes in my family, four or five months go by between visits. Any longer than that and someone freaks out. When I'm away they send hundreds of emails."

"Do you answer them?"

"Occasionally." Sara coughed again.

"You feel claustrophobic?"

"I don't know. Maybe I do, but I've never thought about it that way."

"It seems to me that you need a lot of space." Sitara was testing the strength of a wooden letter opener. "We all need space. Like a plant, there has to be room in the pot for growth."

"You mean, things that used to fit us as children eventually become too small," Sara said.

"Yes." She was thinking of her spice cupboard. "But some

things have always been too small. Plants need a huge amount of love and water."

"Actually," Sara interjected, "I'm always surprised at how well they survive."

"Surviving is one thing, thriving is another."

"I hadn't thought of that." Sara was swallowing hard, trying to keep from choking. There was water spilling out of her eyes.

Suddenly realizing that her patient felt trapped on the bed, Sitara jumped to her feet. "Sara, you can sit up now. I'm finished. I should have said something. I'll get you a drink."

Walking out of her office and reaching for the filtered water, Sitara blamed herself for losing track of time. In her clouded state, she'd forgotten that Sara was a patient.

"I'm sorry," she said, watching Sara drain the glass. "Are you okay now?"

"I'm fine." Sara had two wet paths spilling from each eye — a horizontal one that reached to her temple and a vertical one that ran down her cheek. She handed Sitara back the glass. After slowly climbing off the bed, she smoothed the creases of her shirt, ran her hands through her long, brown hair and fiddled with the stubborn straps of her leather sandals.

To give her privacy, Sitara was leaning into the doorframe, observing the grain of the wood floor through the thick bottom of the empty glass. "Can I buy you dinner?" she asked finally. She wanted to continue their conversation outside the formality of the clinic. "I was thinking of sushi."

"Sure," Sara said, "but I wish I had my camera."

"Why?"

"To prove that I've actually been here."

"You don't need a photograph for that," Sitara said. "I'll remember."

In the restaurant, Sitara ordered two bowls of miso soup, three batches of avocado maki and a pot of green tea. For the first time in days she was hungry.

Sara ordered a small selection of seafood maki, started to order a beer, and then asked for a glass of water instead.

Alternately sipping soup and tea, Sitara was silent. She liked how the steam moistened the air around her face as she drank, and how she could trace the intensity of the heat from her tongue to her throat and finally down to her stomach. Looking up, she could tell that Sara was framing a photograph in her mind.

"Do you want me to smile?" she asked.

"What?"

"For your picture," she said.

"I don't take photos all the time."

"Are you sure? I've seen you take three here already, and you took another six or seven on the walk over."

"I'm sorry."

"Why?"

Using both hands, Sara lifted her hair into a ponytail and took a deep breath. On the exhale she let her hair fall. "Because it's the only thing I know how to do."

"I bet you can ride a bike, or grow flowers, or cook great meals."

"I can cook," Sara said. "I learned it from my father, but —"

"But it's not your passion."

"No, photography is, and unless I'm taking photos, I don't feel whole."

"I can understand that."

"You can?"

Sitara nodded before draining the last bit of liquid from her bowl. She could feel the life returning to her blood. "It's important to know your passion," she said. "And even more important to act on it."

"What's yours?" Sara asked.

"Avocado maki." She laughed and then pulled a pair of bamboo chopsticks out of her bag. "Cheers," she said, before lifting the tamari- and wasabi-soaked morsel into her watering mouth. With her eyes closed, she pressed her tongue into the cold, creamy centre — caressing the avocado before biting into the rice and seaweed that surrounded it.

"I feel a little awkward being here." Sara smiled. "Maybe I should leave you two alone."

"No." Sitara put down her chopsticks. "It's great to have living, breathing dinner company for a change. I'll try to behave myself, I promise. It's just that it's so hard," she said, laughing, "to ignore my passions. Hey, you want to try one of these?" She gestured to her platter of sesame-seed-covered maki.

"I'll trade you," Sara offered.

"I don't eat fish. But please, have one of mine."

"Alright."

"Of course, I should warn you," Sitara said, as Sara took a rice bundle between her chopsticks, "that it could lead to a stormy new passion."

"I'll take that chance." Sara placed it gently on her tongue. Then, imitating Sitara, she chewed slowly, keeping her eyelids closed. "I could use a new passion," she said, when she was done. "I seem to have worn out my old one."

"Your eyes will get better, Sara. I don't think you have to worry about that." Sensing her resignation, and not wanting to let the energy of the moment slip, Sitara added, "I'll do everything I can to help. If you have a gift, you shouldn't give it up." Reaching across the table, she took Sara's hand in her own. "No matter how isolated and let down you feel, you're not alone."

"Thanks," Sara whispered. Absently, she added wasabi to a large, pink shrimp and then scraped it away again. "Were you a lonely child?"

"Why?" Sitara refilled her dish with tamari. "Were you?"

"No. I had a camera… and a sister."

"Younger or older?" Sitara asked, suspecting she already knew.

"Younger." Sara took a bite of her shrimp, dipped the remainder in tamari, and then used her teeth to yank the flesh away from the tail. Still chewing, she asked, "Are you lonely now?"

"I don't know," Sitara said. "My life is very full."

"But is it full of the right stuff? Recently, plain simple full doesn't seem good enough."

"I guess it's easy to fill time with distractions. We don't like having holes in our lives, so we plug them with whatever is close by."

"What do you plug yours with?"

"Work, mostly."

"Maybe it's none of my business," Sara said, "but what are you avoiding?"

Sitara smiled and pushed her empty platter away. "My parents," she answered, "and in some ways, my past."

"You're Indian?"

"Yes. And Canadian."

"Where do your parents live?"

"In Vancouver in the apartment where I grew up. For some reason, they've never felt the need to move."

"It's possible," Sara said, as if she'd never thought about it before, "that some people find it comforting to stay in one place."

"I suspect that's true," Sitara said. "But you like to travel."

"I like to have fresh perspective and changing scenery."

"Perspective is internal," Sitara said, becoming more sure of the words as she spoke them. "It's easily available if you know how to find it."

"Or if you're ready to find it," Sara offered, quietly.

"Hmm." Sitara nodded. *The problem,* she was thinking, *is that if I am truly open to all perspectives, I may no longer think*

I am right. She looked up at Sara, who was smiling. "What?" she asked.

"I just feel inspired," she said, "to try and improve."

"Must have been the good food. Maybe we should tell the chef." Sitara looked up and tried to catch his eye.

"Or maybe," Sara interjected quickly, "it was the conversation."

"Here's to perspective." Sitara raised her glass.

"And to confronting fears," Sara added.

Clunk. They banged glasses and drank.

chapter 14

Before meeting Jack for breakfast at eleven o'clock, Sara devoured a banana and a large cup of coffee. During the night, while still riding on the momentum of her evening with Sitara, she had done more thinking than sleeping. Now, as the sun followed its usual path in the sky, she was planning an adventure that she hoped would help her find a new path.

Standing in front of her bedroom closet, she was preparing to release her camera from its temporary prison. Pulling it out of the bag, she caressed it in her nervous hands. The moulded plastic body was the texture of leather, except where the constant presence of her thumb and fingers had nearly worn it smooth. Without thinking, she removed the lens cap, aimed the camera and pressed the shutter.

click
A closet full of boots and shoes.

After loading a film, she placed the camera back in its bag and checked the outer pockets for spare rolls. Wrapping herself in her long, black sweater, for security as much as warmth, she and her camera stepped out the door.

Walking to the coffee shop where she'd agreed to meet Jack, she kept pausing to take practice photos.

click
A tree spills over the sidewalk, its buds like tiny cabbages —
but twice as green.

click
A garbage can, overflowing with scrap lumber, waits to be
emptied.

As she burst through the door at the café and approached his table, Jack stood and reached for her lips. Soaking up the warmth of his wet mouth, she couldn't tell whose was watering more. Sitting down across from him, she placed her camera bag on the floor.

"How are you?" he asked.

"Hungry."

"For me or for food?"

"Maybe both," she said, "but I think I'll start with something sweet and drippy — and another cup of coffee."

"Up late? I thought you went to bed early when you weren't seeing me."

"I'm not a light bulb, if that's what you mean — on when you're here, off when you're not."

"Well, you certainly are *on* now. I take it your appointment with Sitara was good."

"It wasn't what I expected," Sara said. "It was better."

"I'll get us some food and then you can tell me all about it."

Jack got up to place their orders and kissed her on the forehead as he passed.

Following him with her eyes she thought, *He flirts well even on an empty stomach.* She reached down with her left arm and stroked the comforting surface of her camera bag, the way someone else might stroke a dog.

"Coffee and something sticky for you," Jack said, returning to the table. "And something wholesome and nourishing with a pot of herbal tea for me."

Sara smiled. "Do you always eat this way, or are you trying to impress me?"

"Is it working?"

"Not really."

"It was the cute girl behind the counter. She convinced me."

Sara laughed. The way he said the words "cute girl" made them seem foreign to his tongue.

"I see you brought your camera," he said, with a mouthful of bagel and egg. "Don't shoot until I'm finished." Using a napkin, he tried to cover the mess of tomato, sprouts and lettuce that was falling to his plate.

Sara raised her hands to her eye, making a square to frame him in.

click
Dirty lips that should be kept clean for kissing.

Slipping her hands around her coffee cup, she said, "I wouldn't dare."

"Wow. A polite photographer! Don't tell my mother."

"Actually, I want to talk about photography."

"I thought you wanted to talk about acupuncture."

"In a way," she said, "I want to talk about both."

Watching him use his fingers to pick up fallen pieces of

tomato and cheese, she thought he looked like a bird pecking at corn. He caught her watching and stopped.

"Alright," he said, pouring himself a strong cup of tea, "I'm ready."

"I guess," she was fidgeting with a bag of sugar, "I'm looking for some new perspective in my photos. I'm tired of taking the same old shots."

He nodded. "I hear ya."

"I fall so easily into comfortable ruts. I think I've lost sight of what I love about photography."

"Which is?"

"The unexpected. The surprise. The momentary convergence of things captured in time." She looked up. "Does this make any sense?"

"I don't know yet. Keep talking."

"I've been trying to evaluate what's really important in my life, and it keeps coming back to the same thing."

"Me," Jack said.

"No." Sara tilted her head and smiled. "I haven't known you long enough for that."

"Well at least I haven't become routine yet either." There was a hint of anxiety beneath his humour.

"Are you listening to me?"

"Yeah." He reached across the table for her hand, making her think of Sitara. "I'm sorry," he said. "Continue."

"I want to go with you on your next photo shoot."

"Why?"

"So I can see through your eyes."

"Alright," he said, "but only if you take me on one of yours."

"But Jack…" She stopped to search for words. "I'm not travelling anymore. What could I show you other than Halifax through blurry eyes?" With her arms crossed on the table in front of her, her chin was sinking closer to her hands.

"I bet you know a few fancy tricks." He leaned down to try to catch her eye. "Do we have a deal?" he whispered.

"Of course," she said, nervous that he would discover the narrowness of her depth of field. "I'm sure I can come up with something."

"Great. Let's get started."

"But I thought you had the day off!"

"No. I'm taking you on a photo shoot." He rubbed his hands together and looked around the room. "A small town post office. That's where we'll go."

"What?"

"Alright," he was grinning, "this is your assignment…"

Standing on the steps of the Hantsport post office, Sara was mortified. "We can't just stand here and take photos of people!" she said.

"Why not?"

"They'll think we're crazy!"

"Don't people usually think you're crazy?"

"I guess so, but —"

"Don't get squeamish just because it's too close to home. It's not like you're going to get arrested! And even so," he teased, "it's a familiar legal system. I'll get you out on bail!"

She whacked him hard across the face with her eyes, and then looked around for somewhere more protected to hide. Unable to find any big trees or railings covered in vines, she decided to cross the road.

"Hey, Sara!" Jack called to her from his position on the main steps. "How are you going to be able to see anybody from over there? I bet you've got half the post office in the frame."

Sara brought the Nikon to her eye. "Three-quarters of it," she said.

"This is not a landscape shoot." There was an old man crossing between them as Jack spoke. "You're not in Florence anymore. This is about faces and stories and people picking their noses."

"Jack!" His words made her feel even more exposed.

"Come on, Sara, we've got to get close if we're going to have any fun." He lifted his camera to his eye. "Here comes one."

A young woman, with three children trailing after her and another in a stroller, worked her way up the smooth, wooden ramp. Two of the kids were pushing and whining, while the third shuffled behind, lost in her own internal world. Sara followed them with her eye, but left her camera hanging around her neck. *Click.* She heard Jack's shutter. *Click. Click.*

Struggling with the door, the woman turned around to pull the stroller through backwards. Catching her boys as they pounded each other with small fists, she yelled, "Stop that! I promised Mama I wouldn't go mad 'til I was forty, and believe me, I got a few years left. Grab the door, will ya? I can't do this alone." *Click.* One of the boys held the door without taking his eye off his brother. *Click.* He managed an ankle kick below the height of the stroller. *Click.* Throwing a squinty-eyed glare at her boys, the mother yelled, "Remember, I've got eyes all over, so don't be stupid enough to try anything inside." *Click.* The little girl was spinning, watching her dress puff out.

Jack turned to Sara, but she was slinking away.

"Hey!" He followed after her. "How many frames did you take?"

"None." She was wishing she'd worn sidewalk grey for camouflage.

"I thought you wanted to come with me so you could see things my way."

"Is that how you always take photos?"

"No. Sometimes I'm in a formal setting — a park or a studio — somewhere posed and predictable. But those photos are usually crap."

Sara had her arms crossed to hide her camera. "Don't you ever ask?"

"When you're in Rio covering Carnaval, and people are dancing, screaming and parading by, do you ask?"

"No, but that's different."

He was still behind her, talking to the back of her head. "Sara," he stepped closer and put his arm around her, "what are you trying to capture when you take a picture?"

"That's a huge question. I can't answer that."

"You did this morning. 'The unexpected. The surprise. The momentary convergence…' Think about that young girl, orbiting in her own little world. If I'd gone up to her and asked, 'Excuse me kid, can I take your picture?' what do you think she would have done?"

"Posed," Sara said. "She would have smiled and showed off for you — and would probably have looked straight at the camera. You're right. There wouldn't have been any spontaneity."

"I'm a voyeur, Sara. I stare at people. And then, when they let their guards down, I snap."

She turned around and looked at him. "You're a creep," she said, but she was smiling.

"Thank you." He leaned in and kissed her. "Now come on, this is prime post office time!"

"Alright." She rolled her shoulders back and thought of the pact she'd made with Sitara — *To new perspectives, and confronting fears.* "You point, I'll shoot," she said.

After sharing dinner at a quiet restaurant, they walked down to the shore. Stumbling on the shaky wooden stairs, Sara felt drunk. Following Jack's lead, she had taken two rolls of film in the afternoon light. The candidness of the experience made her giddy. She'd used a telephoto lens to capture the surprise of a woman reading her phone bill, a portrait lens to frame the tears of a lover with a letter clutched to her chest, and a slow exposure for the awkward dance of two middle-aged men trying to hold the door for one another.

"Now!" Jack had coached. "Press the shutter. Don't think. You can work with it later. That's what cropping was invented for."

Although she had often worked fast before, it was hard for her to resist her obsession with alignment and centering and finding the perfect light. And it was hard to look into people's faces. For her, people had always been like extras on the movie set — they helped to fill in the background and frame the focal point. Once in awhile, by accident, she captured an expression or a gesture she liked, but mostly she avoided the unpredictable nature of the face.

Now, walking in the narrow path of sand between the rocks and water, she was trying to decide if the tide was coming in or going out. "What do you think?" she asked.

"About what?"

"The tide."

"It's on its way out. You can tell by the wet line it's leaving behind."

"Of course." She knew that. "I was watching the waves," she said. "Looking at the water, you'd think it was coming in."

"Sometimes the tide moves one way while the wind blows the waves another."

"I can sympathize."

"What does that mean?"

"Gravity pulling one way, the wind pushing the other. They either stand still or get ripped apart."

"I don't think you're going to get ripped apart."

"But I don't feel like standing still, either."

Looking down at the wet sand and the footprints she and Jack were leaving behind, she sighed. Although she had grown up near this same body of salt water, it was considerably tamer here as it rounded into a basin edged by tall, red cliffs. Walking into the wind next to the receding waves, she took Jack's hand.

"Where are you from?" she asked.

"A farm in Saskatchewan."

"So I asked a Prairie boy which way the tide was going?"

"Apparently, but I've been here almost fifteen years," he said.

"Fifteen years ago, I was fourteen."

"I was twenty and escaping from the States."

"But I thought you were from the Prairies!"

"When I was eighteen," Jack dropped the small, black stone he'd been carrying, "I started migrating towards the bowels of this land mass. I thought that to be an artist I needed to live in New York or L.A. The truth is, I was running from the flat land of my birth. I was terrified of all that emptiness — still am."

"So from the States you came here."

"Yeah. I moved up to the heart. It's always better to live above the digestive system, if you can!" He laughed. "What about you?"

"I grew up in Annapolis Royal," she said. "If we keep walking, we'll end up at my parents' door. We did that one summer when I was kid, my dad and I. We walked halfway to Cape Split — drawing and exploring at high tide, camping at night. I had a new camera then — my first good SLR. I took photos of everything."

"Do you still have them?"

"Yes."

"I'd like to see them sometime."

"Alright."

Using the hand that was joined to her, Jack guided her to a stop. Then, pressing her closer with his free arm, he placed his mouth on hers and tried to find her tongue.

Riding in the front of Jack's car with the windows rolled down and her hair flying everywhere, she was dizzy from the sound of his voice. For the last few kilometres, he had been recounting a series of recent conversations he'd had with a Toronto art dealer. Using an exaggerated imitation of the man's hard-sell tone, and an overly passive version of his own, he had Sara squirming with laughter.

"'I hope you're not one of those men with a ponytail,' Mr. Art Dealer said, 'because I don't trust men with ponytails.'" Jack laughed. "I guess I'll have to wear a scarf and a hat if we ever meet."

Sara leaned over and tried to remove the elastic band that was holding back his hair.

"Hey," he protested, "if you do that I won't be able to see."

"Then you'll be just as blind as —" There was a loud thunk, and she grabbed hold of the dash. "Jack?"

His hands were on the wheel, but the car was pulling towards the ditch.

"Hold on!" He hit the brakes and brought the car to an awkward stop. "Shit."

"What's happening?"

"A flat tire, I guess." Throwing open his door, he got out to look.

In the dark interior of the car, Sara drew herself into a ball. One by one, she made an inventory of her fingers and toes. Through the open car window, she asked, "You can fix it, right?"

"Yeah," Jack said, "as long as I have a spare."

"That's what I need," Sara muttered. "A spare."

click
A blown eyeball replaced with a shiny new one.

Climbing back into the car, Jack was itching his head. "The bugs are bad," he said. "Better roll up your window." Fishing for a flashlight in the glovebox, he reached in front of her. She could smell the blood on his scalp. "Shit," he said again. "I thought I had one." He turned around and checked under the seats. "There. Now let's hope it works." He flicked the long, red button and a weak trickle of light washed over the ceiling. "Well, it'll last a minute." He turned it off and opened the door.

Huddled in a pool of comfort, Sara was loath to get out. Instead, she twisted her spine around and watched Jack lift a tire out of the trunk. She could tell by the clanking that the tools were harder to find.

"Sara?" he asked, through her closed window, "can you hold this until I get the jack in place?"

Standing next to him, close enough to feel the heat of his body, Sara held the flashlight. Her skin crawled inward, and her toes, bare in their sandals, curled themselves in tightly. As Jack pulled off the hubcap, she jumped back. Then, sensing the ditch was not far behind her, she moved forward again.

As he stood and leaned his weight on the lugwrench, she tried to give him elbowroom, but she was distracted by what she could not see.

"Sara, I need some light."

"Where?"

"Here, where the bolts are."

The dim flashlight revealed little of the wheel, which was a black hole that took her light and ate it. Only Jack's skin glowed in the darkness — she could see his left temple pulsing from the strain.

"There's a lot of traffic tonight," she said. Even crouched down behind the shelter of the car, she could feel the dirty breeze of the large trucks as they passed. The fast lights made her want to vomit. Slapping her leg loudly, she killed another mosquito.

"Could you move that beam a little closer," Jack asked, as he grabbed hold of the new tire and lifted it onto the axle. "Thanks. Now you can turn it off."

click
The darkness begins to swallow her.

"Are you sure you can find them all?" she asked, quietly. "I'd help you, if I could see." She knelt close to him and searched the ground with a hand outstretched in front of her. "All I can find are rocks."

"It's alright, Sara. Relax. I know where they are."

She tried to reignite the flashlight, but its power had all been drawn. "They've got to be here somewhere," she said.

"I dropped them in a pattern, Sara, so I'd know how to find them. I'm putting the last one on now."

Bracing herself against the car, she tried to control her shaking. She could hear Jack's breathing and the sound of the lugwrench cupping and tightening the bolts. Then she heard the snap of the hubcap as he reattached it to the wheel. "Hop in," he said. "I can finish here."

Closing the door after her, she sank into the enclosed safety of the car. Numb to everything, including the bug bites festering on her arms and legs, she stared into the windshield.

After putting the tools back in the trunk, Jack followed her into the car. "I'm sorry," he said, wiping his hands on his jeans. "I bet you've never spent this much time on the side of the 101 before." He brushed against her thigh as he felt around on the seat for his keys. "Hey, what's wrong? You're trembling like a weed." Reaching behind the seat he found a blanket to wrap around her. As he tucked the fringe under her shoulders and legs, he placed large, warm kisses on her face. "It's not far now — if I can just find my keys."

"They're in the ignition," she said, almost laughing despite her fear.

Jack turned on the heater for her and, after reaching fifth gear, slid his hand under the blanket and rested it on her thigh. Finding comfort in the weight of his hand and the gentle glow of the dash lights, Sara melted into the interior of the car.

chapter 15

Sitara had already spent an hour and a half practising yoga when she moved her small bronze Buddha statue to check the clock. It was nine-thirty, which meant five-thirty in Vancouver. Replacing the statue, she turned Buddha face to face with the clock, hoping that he would take over the job of keeping an eye on the time. *Another few hours,* she thought, *I can't call until at least eight.*

Sitting at the restaurant with Sara the night before, she had decided — somewhere between the miso soup and the saki Sara had insisted on buying — to try communicating again with her father. In the days since Raj had left, she'd grown less and less sure of the accuracy of her memories. She was starting to wonder if they were more coloured by her own perspective than she'd been inclined to admit. Although she had no idea if he was still willing, she was hoping that another visit with her father would eliminate some of her uncertainty. He had been the one, after all, who had taken the first step.

Now, dusting her collection of books and belly-high mirrors, she was thinking of Sara. Making the shape of a square with her fingers, then closing one eye to look through it, she snapped an imaginary photo of her overflowing bookcase.

Smiling as she resumed her cleaning, she realized that she'd never had a camera. In the thirty years of her life, there had never been a time — with one important exception — when she'd wanted a way to remember. The past was something she had always preferred to let slide.

Slowly, after folding and refolding her damp cloth, Sitara worked her way into the kitchen. There were dust-covered grease puddles where she kept her jars of cooking oil — olive, sesame and flax — and little rose-coloured rings beneath the bottles of balsamic and red wine vinegar.

After wiping down the counter, and before attempting the stove or sink, Sitara went into her room to check the alarm clock. Ten-fifteen. Six-fifteen Pacific. Wandering back into the kitchen she opened the fridge, hoping to find a distraction. On the door, between the kalamata olives and a bottle of tamari, she found a box of henna. Pulling it out, she read the label carefully. *For all festive occasions,* it said. She smiled, remembering how Carrie had given it to her on her last birthday. Lounging all afternoon in her apartment, the women had covered each other's hands and feet in mehndi. Carrie had drawn Sanskrit words that she copied off book covers so convincingly that Sitara wondered if she understood them. She handled the tube's small-tipped cone as gracefully as she handled a brush. Watching her paint, Sitara was continually consumed by her skill.

Closing the fridge door, she took the henna to the telephone. Carrie was usually at her studio during the day, if she wasn't waiting tables at the new vegetarian restaurant, but Sitara tried anyway. As the phone rang, she rolled the end of the foil tube, like toothpaste, to push the liquid forward. Then, just as Carrie's voicemail answered, a crack opened and a spurt of henna covered her hand. Disappointed, and anxious to remove the dye before it made a blotch on her skin, she hung up without leaving a message.

After washing her hands, Sitara put on the kettle. Sometimes, a pot of tea could solve anything. Bringing her hand to her nose, she could still smell the henna. It was intoxicating — like her evening with Sara. Even after she took her hand away, there was a trace of mystery that lingered.

She walked over to the phone again. Summoning the courage to call Sara was easy — finding her number was not. In the phonebook, she fiddled with various spellings of her name before she gave up. The only place she could find it was at the clinic, and the kettle boiled before she had to admit that she wasn't ready to go back there yet.

Sitting in the sun she sipped her green tea, imagining that it tasted like sushi.

Sarasvati is beside me. I am wrapped in one of her sari's long, brown swirls. Holding it up to the light that spills into the cupboard, I pretend no one can see me through my protective veil. Walking through the playground this way, I will be invisible. I will watch the other girls and learn their secret games. I will listen to the things they say about me after they have turned and walked away. There are so many things I could do if I had a sari. "No, no, no," Parvati says whenever I ask her. "If you want new clothes, I'll buy you a sweater and some blue jeans." I bite my tongue but I want to tell her that there are no sweaters extraordinary enough to allow me to see without being seen.

Opening the cupboard above the fridge, Sitara pulled down a bag of powdered henna and put the kettle on again to make some more tea. Even without Carrie or Sara, she was hoping the distraction would last until it was breakfast time on the other coast.

Although it was easy to buy premixed tubes like the one Carrie had given her, she preferred the ritual of preparing it herself. She was mystified by the henna's metamorphosis as it transformed from dusty powder into a workable paste with the addition of strong black tea, a few drops of lemon juice and a small amount of sugar. Her feet, too, experienced a sort of metamorphosis — after being wrapped like a caterpillar in a protective cocoon, they emerged with the intricate detail of a butterfly's wing.

After achieving the consistency she wanted, Sitara used an old wooden spoon to funnel the liquid into a plastic cone. Then, crouching down on the kitchen floor, she drew a series of spirals on her big toe. The brown paste tingled for an instant as it began to sink into the pores of her skin. She had been decorating her toes with lines and circles and combinations of the two for more than twenty years — ever since her father first showed her how. When she was finished with the first foot, she stretched it out in front of her, being careful not to move her toes, and started slowly working on the second.

On the day her father brought home that initial bag of henna, he was shy. Having no first-hand experience with mehndi, he had relied on what he could gather from the package and what he remembered from the past. Growing up with six older sisters, he told Sitara, allowed him a privileged view of the inner world women usually keep to themselves. Once, as a small child, he had even pretended to be female in order to have the delicate patterns drawn on his own hands and feet. In such a large family, disguising himself wasn't hard — his aunts and cousins could never keep track of how many little hands and feet had already been painted and how many were yet to come — and his own mother, who was most likely to recognize him, was too distracted by the marriage of her first daughter to notice. Raj had revelled in his newly adorned hands, even though his brothers mocked him. Being so well decorated, he was sure the gods would see him.

"In India we use this for special occasions," he says. "Weddings, festivals and other auspicious ceremonies. Today is Holi, the festival of colour."

Awkwardly, he takes my hand. He knows this is something that should be shared between mother and daughter, but Parvati is embarrassed by the "old-fashioned" custom and will not be part of it.

"Try to be still," he says, although he is the one who is shaking. He paints my fingertips solid and then makes five curvy lines that culminate in a lotus flower in the centre of my palm. With some effort, he manages to make both hands match. Before he pulls off my shoes to start working on my feet, he walks over to the radio.

"I can draw better when there are voices," he says, "and laughter." To make me giggle he tickles my belly. I squeal until he stops because I can't tickle him back — he's already told me that the henna on my hands will take at least three hours to dry.

Now, Sitara craved voices and laughter too. Rolling up her pant legs before standing, she shuffled over to the stereo and chose a collection of Indian ghazals. Then, lighting a stick of incense, she watched the smoke billow and curl before it drifted out the window. Sitting down to continue work on her mehndi, she tried to imagine the voices of her ancestors, and of the extended family in India she'd never known. She wondered if they gossiped and laughed — the way women in groups often do — slipping easily between mischief and reassurance. She wanted to sit with them, to know what they knew, to paint someone else's hands while they painted hers.

Finally, with both feet and her belly covered, Sitara picked up the phone. Although she rarely used it, she knew her parents' number by heart — it had been her number too for almost eighteen years.

Listening to the high-pitched ring on the opposite coast, she was hoping her father would answer. For the last hour she'd been tracing and retracing the words she wanted to say to him, as if they were written in chalk. The dust from her eraser made a halo of doubt on the floor.

Gripping the phone with her right hand, her heart recoiled like the leaves of a mimosa plant. There was no one home to hear her practiced words, no one to accept her apology. She listened to two more rings, then hung up. She would try again in an hour.

Standing in the kitchen, waiting for her heart to unfurl, she heard the voice of Sarasvati.

"It is warm outside, Sitara, just the way you like it. There is enough wind to keep your thoughts moving through you, and enough sun to feed the blood beneath your skin. A long walk would make you feel good." She was leaning on the counter where a few hours earlier Sitara had wiped up the oil spills.

"Are you trying to tell me a walk will help me forget about my father?"

"No," Sarasvati said. "You cannot forget him. His seed runs too deep. He is in your heart, your liver, your eyes. But outside the air is warm and the sky is full of surprises."

Looking down at the henna drying on her feet, Sitara said, "But I won't be able to wear shoes."

Sarasvati laughed. "Are you concerned about your beauty?" she asked.

"No."

Barefoot, Sitara walked out the door.

Crossing the porch, she walked down the concrete sidewalk and around to the gravel driveway at the side of the house. Then, stepping carefully between the sharpest stones, she worked her way to the gate at the back of the house, across the soggy spring grass and onto the sunlit fire escape.

With her back against the railing, and her shirt still rolled up to reveal the eye she had drawn on her belly, she inspected the henna on her feet — worrying like she had when she was a ten-year-old that some pieces had already flaked off. Wishing her father had been there to answer the phone, Sitara criticized herself for having let him slip away. She knew that she had to start listening if she wanted things to improve.

Looking down into the yard, she could see that the lilacs were nearly ready to bloom. With their deep purple colour, they were screaming loud enough for her to hear. She noticed, too, that her downstairs neighbour had hung two lines of bleached white laundry that stretched from his back door, across the lawn, to the garage. As the wind shifted, the chemical smell became unbearable.

Inside, her apartment seemed dark and cool, and although her skin radiated light and heat, she paused until her eyes could make the adjustment. Then, walking to the telephone, she decided to try her father again.

"Hello? Who is this?"

"It's me, Bapa."

"Sitara?"

"Yes."

"Why are you calling me?"

She had to swallow before she could answer. "I want to apologize. I want you to come back to Halifax. I want to try again."

"It did not work before. Why do you think it will work now?"

"Because this time I'm ready, and it won't be a surprise."

"I suppose I should have called first."

"No," Sitara confessed. "If you'd called, I would have told you not to come."

"But now you are prepared to do battle. You are feeling strong and well armed."

"Bapa, I'm serious. I want to try again." She was picking at her henna, like a scab.

"No. I will not come."

"I could buy your ticket, find you a place to stay…"

"No, Sitara. I cannot leave."

"Why not?"

"Parvati is sick."

"So, wait until she gets better." Her chest was a tight cage that cut her breath short.

"She is not going to get better," he said, pausing before he spoke again. "Sitara, your mother has cancer."

C-A-N-C-E-R. The letters hung in the air like smoke from a deadly cigarette.

"Where?" she asked.

"Her breasts."

Subconsciously, Sitara ran her left hand over her own. "How long have you known?"

"More than a year now," he said. "I should have told you sooner."

Sitara was silent.

Parvati's fingers are cold as she measures me. I can feel them pressing into my skin at the centre of my back just below my shoulder blades. She pulls the tape measure tighter.

"We don't want it to ride up," she says.

I shift forward to compensate for the force of her grip. "What if I can't breathe?" I ask.

"Don't worry, it's just a bra." She laughs. "It won't kill you."
She coils the tape measure and stands back to have a look at me.
"You're smaller than I was at your age, but you may still grow."

"It is not going well," Raj said. "Even with her stubborn will, she has already lost one breast."

"I'm sorry."

"Right now, I am not sure which is worse — the cancer or the treatment. Sometimes I think the lump in her remaining breast is the least of her problems. Chemotherapy is very harsh, Sitara."

"You wanted to tell me this when you came to see me."

"Yes."

"But I wouldn't listen."

"Sometimes, Sitara, I do not speak very loud."

There was a long gap as she thought about the power of anger and resentment. "Bapa, what are you asking me? What can I do?"

"Come home, before it gets worse."

"What?"

"She is your mother, Sitara, and she is sick."

"Yes, but… Bapa, I need time to think."

"What is there to think about?"

"There is a big difference between seeing you here and returning to that apartment in Vancouver."

"You may have time in abundance, Sitara. But Parvati has very little."

Standing in the bathtub, Sitara scraped herself clean, leaving a crumbly riverbed of browny-green. Then, jamming on her sandals, she grabbed her keys and ran down to the car.

Her hands were sweaty on the steering wheel. Backing out of the driveway, she abused the clutch. At the traffic circle, she ploughed through the onslaught of cars and headed towards Herring Cove. Along the winding coastal road, past the yacht club and the large houses, she barely touched the brakes. Then, as the land dipped down at the mouth of the cove, she pulled into the parking lot and turned off the car. Leaving the keys in the ignition, she started to run. With the wind hitting her side-on, her cotton pants flapped towards the sea, and wisps of hair assaulted her eyes and nose. Beyond the barren rocks, she could hear the crashing waves.

"Your mother has cancer, Sitara. CANCER. As a healer, you've failed. Go home and clean up the mess you've made." The voice in her head was a trimurti — a trio of voices — hers, her father's and Sarasvati's. *At least,* she thought with a bitter laugh, *everyone agrees.* At the edge of the cliff, she kicked off her shoes, pushed her hands into prayer — and dove. As her face hit the water, the surface smacked her like a thousand unspoken words.

Blinded by the salt-sting and deaf from the roar of the blood inside her head, Sitara spit into the water and forced her way back towards the shore. Crawling over rocks that were slippery and wet with algae, she left a trail of emotion as black as tar. Then, with her feet out of the water and her knees pulled in close, she reached around and wrung out her hair. The cliff above her was jagged and steep. Clutching herself, as if her guts might spill out, she shuddered at the thought of how far she'd dropped.

Standing in front of the mirror, I compare one breast with the other. The right one is bigger. Horrified at my unevenness, I try to stuff it further into the bra Parvati has bought for me, but it doesn't stay. I decide I am cursed with uneven growth because my right ear is bigger too. Finally, resorting to the only solution I can think of, I fold two lengths of toilet paper and tuck them into the left cup of the stiff white bra. Lifting my left shoulder a little to enhance the effect, I determine that the illusion is acceptable — if somewhat uncomfortable. Although I am proud to wear my new bra, I am also afraid. I know it shows my age. Firm, round breasts are a sure sign of fertility and I am not ready for babies.

Shivering, she stood and started to claw her way up the cliff. After a few steps, she ripped her foot on a rock. Looking down she thought she was bleeding henna.

Finally, after fighting her way to the top, she headed inland and emerged in the middle of a family barbecue. As she walked past the silent picnic table soaking wet, with her clothes clinging ungracefully to her trembling body, everyone stared. Only the youngest boy continued squeezing mustard on his hotdog. Quickly, she crossed through their yard and made it to the road.

She was shaking and her breasts ached. With her arms crossed, she held them in her hands, massaging small circles into the flesh with her cold fingers. Walking barefoot along the shoulder of the road, she kept her head down. For the first time, the patterns in the gravel and dirt made sense to her. What had once seemed random now appeared to have purpose. She marvelled at the interconnectedness.

On the drive home, she started to see connections everywhere. The sky, the trees, and the shadows that crossed the road from telephone poles. The clutch, her hand, and the yellow line that kept opposing forces from crashing into one another. Only when she got home and saw the dried blood did she remember the connection between feet and shoes. Her sandals were still on the rocks at Herring Cove.

She crunched a handful of carrots and a two-day old samosa as she cleaned and bandaged the cut on her left arch. Remembering how, when she was young, her father had dispelled her sadness by using a brown marker to imitate the mehndi hidden beneath a similar bandage, she dug in the kitchen cupboards for a bottle of wine.

Then, with her feet still bare, she drove back to the ocean. After pulling a blanket from the back of her car, she started walking to the place where she had left her shoes. As she picked her way carefully over the rocks, she threw her voice into the wind and let her own thankful laughter wash over her. *Life,* she thought, *is better when I'm fully alive.*

Sitting on a flat rock, with the fiery sky blooming and dying behind her, she started to cry. For her, time had been a supple elastic with a limitless amount of give — at least until her father's words had caused it to snap. *"You may have time in abundance, Sitara. But Parvati has very little."*

Tilting her head back for another gulp of wine, she scolded herself for squandering so much time.

chapter 16

"I'm sorry about the tire," Jack said, in the morning. "I should have guessed your eyes would be worse in the dark. I didn't mean to scare you."

Waking up in the sunlight of his bed, Sara had almost forgotten about it. "It might be easier if I was fully blind," she said, "instead of this foggy in-between."

"How are you now?" he asked.

"I can see well enough to know you have a dangerous look on your face."

"Dangerous? Why?"

"Because you're about to —"

He dove under the blankets and started gnawing on her breasts, making loud chewing noises and letting his hand float up her thigh.

Laughing, she remembered his tenderness from the night before. After lighting candles in the bathroom, he had filled the tub. Moving through the dense steam, she had climbed in gradually, enjoying the spikes of heat-pain that travelled from her toes to her chest. "You're dirty too," she had said, sliding forward to make room for him.

Later, after drying her off with a soft towel, he had spread a clean white sheet over his bed and invited her to lie down. Then, carefully searching out every one, he had touched her mosquito bites with a drop of tea tree oil to take the itch away. Although they were mostly on her arms and legs, he lingered over her belly and thighs until she sighed. After a brief kiss on each nipple, he had rolled her over so that he could continue on her back.

"You run a beautiful spa," she had told him. "Maybe you should start a business treating battered old photographers who are scared of the dark."

"You realize," Jack had said, "darkness is half of light."

Now, in the middle of a bright May morning as he rubbed his bristled face against her skin, she thought of the Taoist symbol of balance — the black yang curving to fit the white yin, the white yin curving back, and each one supporting a dot of the other. Rolling over, she moulded herself into his curl.

An hour later, leaning against his kitchen counter with a coffee in her hand, Sara said, "I'm anxious to get my films developed."

"Why?" he asked. "I thought yesterday was about the process."

"But isn't the point of taking photos to get them developed?"

"Sometimes."

"Well, I want to see them." She lifted the mug to her lips.

"But why?"

"In case they look like shit."

Jack buttered a third piece of toast. "I was afraid you'd say that."

"I have to go downtown anyway. I have another appointment

with Sitara." Reaching for the coffeepot, Sara hesitated and then put it down.

Jack smiled. "She drinks coffee too, you know. You don't have to be totally pure. Still," he threw her a plum from the basket on the table, "you could eat one of these."

click
A spinning plum, the size and colour of a man's balls.

Walking along Gottingen Street with her camera bag in tow, Sara was beaming. She stopped at a variety store to buy a magazine and a roll of peppermints. All morning she'd been wishing for a toothbrush.

She flipped through the magazine as she walked, admiring the photos of a colleague before finding a double-page spread of her own. As she marvelled once again at her editor's choice of cropping, she felt a brief, but intense, pang of loss. Only four months had passed since her assignment in Central America, but suddenly it felt like a lifetime ago.

Stowing the magazine in an outer pocket of her camera bag and trying not to think about the holes in the next issue where her photos of Portugal, Spain and Morocco would have been, she kept walking. Driven by impatience, she decided that she would risk the unreliable rush of one-hour processing — waiting two days seemed like an impossible chore.

With the freshly printed photographs in hand, Sara looked for a quiet place where she could study them without the risk of coffee spills or interruption. In the end, she decided to go home.

As she walked up the steps to her third-floor apartment, she was dizzy with apprehension. Leaving her sweater and bag by the door, she pulled open the blind, cleaned off the low wooden coffee table in front of the sofa, and sat down. Then, opening the tall paper envelopes one by one, she revealed the truth of her post office shoot.

click
The orange and red torso of an out-of-focus girl.

click
A woman walking, mid-step, with her mouth open more than her eyes.

click
Grungy pavement, dotted with spit and dirt-encrusted bubble gum — a man's shoe swiftly exiting the frame.

Sara flopped back on the sofa and covered her eyes with her hands. Regretting her choice of one-hour processing, she wondered at the wisdom of having developed them at all. The film, while still sealed in its canister, had held at least the promise of hope.

Sitting up again, she winced at the barrage of botched photos sprawled out on the table. After stacking them carelessly, she stuffed them back into their envelopes and got up to use the bathroom.

Returning to her apartment's small living room, she was distracted by the flashing light on the telephone. Lifting the receiver, she learned that she had nine messages. As she listened to them, she rolled her eyes. There were two from her mother and seven from Kyle, all demanding that she call back immediately.

"You shouldn't be allowed," Kyle's recorded voice said, "to suffer alone in your apartment."

"Clearly," Sara said out loud between the beeps that separated messages, "if I'd been home alone, I would have answered the telephone!"

After hearing the last message, she paced through the kitchen debating how long she could put off returning their calls. In her bedroom, she decided to change out of yesterday's crumpled clothes. It would be easier, she reasoned, to face them in clean ones. Back in the living room, she decided to try her mother.

"Hello, River Bank B&B. How can I help you?"

"Hi, Mom."

"Sara! Where were you last night? You didn't return my call."

"I was in Hantsport with —" Sara started to say, but then she interrupted herself. "I just walked in and got your message now. Why did you need to talk to me?"

"It wasn't important, but when you didn't answer, and then you didn't call back I —"

"Mom! I was out late and then gone again early today. I'm sorry." She felt like a sixteen-year-old being interrogated for an unslept-in bed. Shaking her head, she changed the subject to the weather. "What's it like there today? I bet it's hot in the valley."

"It's warm enough. Your father has been in the garden all day. I thought he might come in for lunch, but he was apparently more intent on having a picnic."

"He'd do that on a cold day too!"

"True."

"Did you join him?"

Peggy snorted. "Contrary to your well-intended belief, picnics are not that romantic! I hate eating outside with the wind blowing dirt in my face and bugs landing all over my food. No, I stood at the sink and ate a five-day-old bagel. He's got pastry flour covering every other surface in the kitchen!"

Sara tried not to laugh. "What's he making?" she asked.

"Pasta."

For a moment, her mouth watered. Ron's fresh pasta with sun-dried tomatoes, mushrooms and pesto was almost worth flying home for. In her mind, she was lifting a bite to her mouth when she heard her father speak in the background. "What did he say?" she asked.

"Of course not," Peggy called back to him. "I wouldn't even know where to find it. Maybe you should ask the cat!"

"What's going on?" Sara said.

"He wants to know if I dug up his fennel."

"Did you?"

"No. I don't get involved out there. Like I was telling Karen yesterday, the backyard is his world. This time of the year, the two are inseparable. He doesn't think it's a problem, of course, because it's still a slow time for guests around here, but in a few weeks this town is going to explode and we'll have people in every bed in the house. And someone, I keep telling him, has to get the place ready for that."

Sara was fazing out, only listening to every other word her mother said. Sometimes, during these phone exchanges, she had the feeling she'd heard it all before.

"That reminds me, Sara, if you're coming up for a visit, you should do it soon, before all hell breaks loose. Sara? Sara, are you still there?"

"Yes, I heard every word. Unless I come and visit, all hell is going to break loose. I'll try to come soon, Mom. Listen, I've got a million things to do…"

"Are you alright, hon? You sound a little vacant."

"Fine, Mom. Everything's going really well. Say hi to Ron."

"Okay, hon. Thanks for calling back."

"No problem."

"One down, one to go," she muttered to herself as she hung up. Fiddling with the phone cord, she wondered if she had the courage to call Kyle. The sharp pain in her diaphragm made her doubtful. She'd broken up with him so many times already, she was afraid of repeating herself. He didn't take "no" easily, and she wasn't sure how well she could soften the blow. Her feelings for Kyle were a dead bloom, and more than anything she wanted to press them into the pages of a hardcover book that could be lost on the back of a shelf for the next twenty-five years while she was still vulnerable to the perfume.

Dialling quickly, she tried to resist the stomach-flipping urge to hang up. Holding her breath as his phone rang — its hollow voice booming in her left ear — she was feeling guilty for hoping that his machine would answer for him. With sweat collecting on her palms, she counted three rings, and then four.

On the fifth, a woman answered. "Hello?"

Surprised, Sara stuttered, "Is Ky-kyle there?"

"Can I get him to call ya? He's... ah... well..." She giggled. "He's right in the middle of something."

The woman's voice was familiar. Sara recognized the dismissive inflections in her tone. In the background she could hear laughter. "It's alright, thanks. I'll call again."

"Okay," the woman said. "But if you want, I can take your name and —"

"No." Sara panicked and let go of the phone.

"Hello? Hello? Is anyone there?"

Twirling and twisting, her sister's voice dangled a few inches above the floor.

Trying to recapture the freedom and alertness of the previous afternoon, Sara headed for the sea. Riding in a cab, she saw the familiar intersections, buildings and trees that made up the road to Herring Cove. She watched as though through a glazed window — only the fog was in her head, not in her eyes.

"The waves are high today, dear. Be careful," the cab driver said, as he pulled into the gravel parking lot.

I've heard the story before, Sara thought. *It's the same everywhere. The cab driver returns to learn the tourist has been drowned. "Walked too close to the waves," someone says. "Slipped on the rocks," another adds. "Was eaten by sea-monsters," an old woman claims.*

"I'll be fine," she said. "Just don't forget to come back in an hour."

The rocks were wet, stained black from the splashing water, but Sara moved easily in her running shoes — the soft rubber soles gripping as she flexed. Although she was in a rut of frustration, the wind blew wildly, stinging her face and sucking small insects out to sea. Holding her hair out of her eyes and mouth, she hoped the wind was strong enough to blow her somewhere she actually wanted to be.

After tripping on a loose rock, she stopped and kicked it into the water below. Looking down, she guessed it was a thirty-foot drop — about the height she had climbed and repelled with her parents when she was young. At the time she had enjoyed the backward descent more than the gruelling upward climb, but now she was wound too tightly to appreciate the freefall.

As she kicked another rock at the water, she berated herself for caring so much about Kyle and Lauren. She hadn't been in love with him for years. Even in the beginning, she hadn't taken their dating seriously. She had fallen for him in her first year of college because of his soft, absorbent shoulders and his big, sensitive ears — and because he loved being the subject of her photographs. For her, their love was always on the surface. Still, she had known him for a long time, and besides boxes and boxes of photos, there were other, less tangible memories that moved like alcohol — making her warm and giddy, but leaving her with an inevitable hangover.

And then there was Lauren.

In the years since Sara had left home, she'd seen her sister only at Christmas, in the summer, and otherwise by luck or coincidence. Distant not only geographically, they had, in Sara's opinion, hugely different priorities. *I shouldn't be surprised,* she thought, *that Lauren is attracted to Kyle. In some ways,* she bashed together two dull stones, *they're painfully similar.*

She imagined the two of them "cooking" in his kitchen — Lauren peeling the tinfoil off a frozen dinner, Kyle slipping it gingerly into the oven. He'd always loved the nostalgia of TV dinners, and Sara had suffered through many.

They both had an obsession with mirrors too — constantly pulling one out of a pocket or taking advantage of the shiny reflection of a building to fix their hair. All their self-analysis made Sara uncomfortable. She preferred the way the mirror in her camera allowed her to deflect the focus somewhere else.

Walking back to the parking lot to meet her cab, she thought of making love in the front seat of Kyle's mother's car. It had been winter and the condensation from their breath had covered the windows like a blanket. She remembered that, as Kyle cranked up the heater, she had been drawing faces in the disappearing steam.

Arriving at Jack's an hour later, she was calm. With a bottle of wine in one hand and a bunch of wildflowers in the other, she used her foot to knock on the door.

"Hey! I'm glad you're here," he said, as he accepted the bottle from her.

"I thought you might be."

"And not just because of this." He laughed.

"If I wasn't so broke, I would have brought two." She was stepping out of her shoes, trying to get close enough for a kiss.

Looking down at his clothes, he blew off a billow of white dust. "Sorry," he said. "I haven't had time to clean up yet."

"What were you working on?"

"I was hoping you'd ask. Follow me."

As she trailed after him down the hall, she tried to rub the dust off her lips, but it was stuck to her lip balm. Finally, using her finger to remove it, she wiped it on the seat of her pants.

"Alright," Jack said. "Sit here." He pulled a chair out from the kitchen table and waited for her to sit down. When she was comfortable, he reached for the black scarf that was lying on the counter. "Ready?"

"For what? Are you going to make the fruit bowl disappear?"

"No. I'm going to blindfold you to prolong the surprise."

"You could just ask me to close my eyes."

"Yes." Jack folded the scarf in half and then in half again. "But I think you're the peeking type." Gently, he stretched the black cloth over her face and tied it at the back of her head. "Can you see anything?" he asked.

"I wouldn't tell you, even if I could!"

"Can you see this?"

"See what?"

"Or this?"

"Jack!" She lifted the blindfold just in time to see the full length of his tongue.

"You weren't supposed to peek!"

"But you're making faces at me!"

As part of the game, she scrunched up her face and pointed her tongue back at him. Quickly, he leapt forward and tried to grab it. He missed and she bit his finger instead.

After they shared another dusty-lipped kiss, Sara slid the blindfold over her eyes and reached around to tighten the knot. "I'm ready," she said, sitting up straight and placing her hands in her lap.

Slowly drawing himself away from her, Jack went downstairs to retrieve what he'd been working on.

Breathing deeply as she waited for the sound of his return footsteps on the stairs, she hummed a song in her head. The floor was cold under her bare feet, and she lifted them to the rungs of the chair.

"Alright." Jack placed something large on the table in front of her and then stood back, breathing softly down her neck.

"What do I do?" she asked.

"Try and guess what it is."

"A box."

"No."

"A picture frame?"

"No."

"A cake?"

"Sara," he said, laughing, "why don't you touch it?"

She raised her hand a little, and then let it fall back into her lap. "I can't. What if you're a little boy pulling one of those try-to-gross-out the little-girl pranks? I don't want to put my hand into a pail full of worms."

"Cold spaghetti."

"Is that what they use?"

"I'm disappointed you don't trust me." His lips were at her ear. "This is something I made for you." Encircling her in his arms, he lifted her hands and placed them on the object in front of her. "What do you feel?"

"It's cold and smooth. Stone maybe, or plaster."

"What else?"

"It has deep grooves that feel like… waves."

"That's around the edges. What about in the middle?"

Moving both hands towards the centre of the object, she jumped when the feel of her own hand surprised her. Then, letting her left hand hover, she used her right to explore the bumps and rises more fully.

"So?" Jack asked, his voice still near her. "Any ideas now?"

"There are two holes here that feel like — wait!" She ran her fingers over the nose. "I know what it is, Jack. It's a face!" Using both hands, she outlined the eyes, the chin, and the mouth. She was laughing. "This is hair, not waves," she said, "and these are ears. It's a woman's face!"

"How can you tell?"

"I don't know. It's narrow, I guess. And soft. It has female curves."

"Do you want to kiss it?"

"No."

"Well, I do." Carefully, he removed the scarf from Sara's eyes and waited for her reaction.

Seeing the plaster carving on the table, she knew instantly that is was her.

After a dinner of rice, stir-fried vegetables and wine, Sara was still awed by her portrait. Staring at it again, she asked, "Did you carve it from memory, or from a photograph?"

"Both. My memory's good," he boasted, "but I wanted it to be accurate."

Jack's kitchen faced west, and as the early evening sun streamed though his uncurtained windows, it enhanced the effect of the wine by drenching them both in an enticing glow.

"So, how was Sitara?" he asked.

"I don't know. She wasn't there."

"What do you mean?"

"I waited for a long time, and then I knocked and knocked, but she didn't answer. I'm worried about her."

"She's resilient. I've seen her bounce back from worse." Jack picked up the wine bottle and refilled Sara's glass.

"What about you?" she asked.

"I was getting to that." Lifting the bottle, he tilted his head back and savoured the last drop.

"I mean about being resilient. Do you heal fast?"

"Why? Are your eyes bad tonight?"

"Don't evade," Sara said. "Just answer the question. Do you heal fast?"

"It depends. Skin, pride, heart… Each has its own speed."

"Have you ever been seriously wounded?"

"Yeah."

"Where?"

"For that I need more wine." He got up and searched the back of a cupboard, finally producing an unlabelled bottle. "From one of my customers," he said. "I have no idea if it's any good."

Watching him with the corkscrew, Sara twirled her glass and said, "There are some things I wish I could just wash off."

Jack put the bottle on the counter. "You know, we shouldn't waste this beautiful light," he said. "Come on, before I lose you to the throes of sorrow."

"But I don't have a camera."

"I'm devising a plan," he said, "where it won't matter." After filling his glass, he took her by the hand and led her through the tall streaks of sunlight into the living room. "Hmm," he said. "The light level's low. Let me get a tripod."

Surveying the room while he was gone, Sara calculated the necessary settings for shutter speed and aperture. Then, without thinking about it, she turned to the corner and took a mental photo.

click
A wooden rocker accompanied by its multi-runged shadow.

Returning, Jack set up his camera and tripod.

"No Hasselblad?" Her tongue still tingled with the sound of it.

"Nah, if I use it all the time the others get jealous." He covered the sides of the camera with his hands as if to block its ears. "This one's not as good, but I have a bunch of film for it."

Sara was squinting, taking a close look at the features of the camera. "What year did they start making this model?"

"Shit, I don't know. It's been around for awhile." He snapped an 80-millimetre lens into place. "I need something to focus on. Can you hold up that pillow?"

"Sure." She crossed into the light. "Like this?"

"Raise your arm a little."

"Why?" She was standing with her back against the window.

"Your arm is blocking the light. Just raise it a little."

Click. She heard his camera automatically advance.

"Hey!" she said, throwing the small square pillow at him. "How much of me was in that shot?"

"Not a lot, but this one will be better." He dropped the pillow on the floor and pressed the shutter. *Click.*

She winced at the painful finality of the sound. "Jack!"

"What?" he said. "I've got to take pictures of something!"

Her face flushed through a whole spectrum of reds, including one called merlot. "But…"

"I suppose I could take pictures of the couch, or the end table, or that pile of crap in the corner. But I prefer people! And you're so much more beautiful than the couch!" When she didn't say anything, he added, "What do you want me to do — take pictures of myself?"

She laughed. "Wouldn't that be difficult?"

"Not with the timer."

"True." She hadn't thought of that.

"Here." He picked up a stool and brought it over to her. "Have a seat — and let me find you something to read."

"Is this how you distract all your customers?"

"You're not a customer. You're a subject. And so far, the most difficult one I've had." He handed her a gardening magazine.

"You have photos in here?" she asked.

"No. I bought it for an article."

Flipping to the table of contents she tried to scan the titles, but the text was too small for her to read. "Do you have a garden?"

"Every year I plant some seeds. You might try page seventeen."

"Why?"

Click. He caught her face looking up at him.

Quickly, she hid behind the shiny magazine.

"Hey!" He moved towards her, brushed her forehead with his lips, and ran his hand along her spine. "What's wrong?"

Letting the magazine drift to her lap, she admitted, "I'm feeling really shy."

Smiling widely, Jack tried to suppress a chuckle. "You spend all day with cameras!"

"Yes, but," Sara looked down at her hands, "I'm usually on the other side."

"Well, go ahead then. I'll sit on the stool."

"Really?"

"Sure."

Sara stood up and positioned herself behind Jack's camera. Looking through the viewfinder, she saw him sitting with his legs crossed and both hands resting on his knee. "Can you move your right — no wait — your left hand somewhere?" she said.

He reached up and held his breast. "Is this good?"

"No." She laughed. "Try holding the edge of the stool."

"Like this?"

"Now you look posed!"

"I am posed. You put me here."

"Okay, then look natural. Pretend you have an itchy leg. Or stand up… Try resting your foot on the stool… Okay. That's good. Hold still." After a pause, Sara screwed up her face. "Jack, does your shutter usually stick?"

"No."

"Well, I can't get it to work."

"Do you want me to have a look?"

"Yes, please."

click
A puzzled man takes a large step.

"Got ya!" Sara clapped her hands and grinned. "Thanks, you were great!"

Catching her in his arms, he spun her around until his own laughter made him stop. "You're really bad, you know! Actually, let me rephrase that. If you keep going like this, you could be really good!"

"Thank you," Sara tried to say, but he smothered her in a kiss.

Then, after leading her back to the stool, Jack said, "Let's use the rest of the light."

Breathing more easily now, Sara carefully copied a defiant pose she'd learned from Katherine Hepburn.

"You make a good hot-headed leading lady," he said.

As she watched, Jack fussed behind the camera — shifting the tripod and adjusting the height. Then, suddenly, he was moving towards her. "I have an idea," he said.

He ran his hands down the front of her shirt and gently undid the buttons. To remove it from her shoulders, he slid his thumbs along her collarbone.

"What are you doing?" she asked.

"Improving the photograph."

With his mouth on hers, he sank his hands into her pants and drew them to the floor. After she stepped out of them, he angled her slightly to the left, letting the light drip from her breast, to her hip, to her thigh.

The sun was warm where it embraced her, and she eased herself into its care. Jack was tender and gentle, and she was beginning to enjoy the slow, agonizing seduction he had started. Posing easily, she let him take a whole roll.

Between films, she asked, "Have you ever done this before?"

"I've photographed other nude women," he said, "but you're the first photographer."

Fuelled by her body's desire, Sara whispered, "Let me take some of you."

"Alright."

Before she could reach him, he'd pulled down his hair and dropped his shirt to the floor. Pressing her breasts into his chest, she lowered his zipper, reached into his faded jeans, and pulled out the subject of her next photo.

click

chapter 17

In the passenger's lounge at the airport, Sitara didn't even pretend to read a magazine. Instead she sat cross-legged on one of the grey vinyl chairs facing the women's bathroom, unconsciously sorting people as they came out — breast cancer patient, both breasts intact, breast cancer patient, both breasts intact. She knew the current statistics were one in eight — every eighth woman was at risk. She was sorting the beads on her left wrist too — staying with one for a long time, and then leaving seven behind. Ever since childhood she'd been drawn to the singled-out ones, the different ones, the sick ones.

She had been dropped off at the airport by her friend Carrie, who was the only one brave enough to tackle the impish personality of her car.

"Be peaceful and decent," Carrie had told her as they stood on the pavement ready to say goodbye, "but don't take any shit you don't deserve. Call me if you need a kick in the ass."

Sitara had felt Carrie's boot bounce off her jeans. "Thanks," she said.

The two women embraced and Sitara felt her friend's lips on her ear. "Call me for anything, really. I'm always here."

And then Sitara was alone, watching her car zigzag and sputter down the airport road. *Shit,* she thought, *if I can't even fix a simple car, how am I going to help my mother?* Although she knew the anatomy of cars almost as well as she knew the anatomy of people, lately she'd been having trouble keeping the Honda on the road. On a good day she could coax it as far as White Point Beach. On a bad day, it was stubborn and sullen and refused to get out of bed.

Uncrossing her legs, Sitara shifted her gaze to the men's washroom. She watched two short balding men come out before a thin man with a baby went in.

After fishing for her shoes on the floor, she grabbed her bag and stood up. She didn't want to be there when the man with the baby came out.

We are at the train station, waiting for Bapa's brother to arrive. I'm squirming under the ruffles of my itchy pink dress, wishing Parvati had let me wear my pants instead.

"Your daughter has to pee," she announces without asking me.

"I will wait for my brother while you take her."

"Public bathrooms disgust me — very unclean. You go."

"Parvati!" Bapa's eyes blaze like sequins caught in the sun. "She is five now, and not a baby. She can no longer come with me to the men's."

"I can't bear to do it. There might be a stink," Parvati says, pouting.

"Will you go on like this in front of my brother too? Here we have luxury compared with India. What will he think of you?"

Standing still, I try to use the long pink dress to hide the puddle I've made on the station floor.

As she resettled herself, Sitara's wool sweater exhaled the essence of her apartment. All day as she packed, it had smelled of jasmine mixed with dahl — a scent so perfect she had let her suitcase hang open as long as she could, hoping to capture and preserve it, the way film captures a moment. Recently, she wasn't happy relying on memory alone.

The meal she'd made the night before, and the leftovers she'd heated for lunch, comprised some of her favourite ingredients — onion, garlic, ginger, ghee and, of course, moong dahl. She'd rolled chapatis too, to round out her own farewell dinner. In Sitara's life, all important events were marked with food.

"In India," Bapa says, *after devouring a good curry, "we ate like this every day — not just on weekends, like we do here. Weekend Indians,"* he complains. *"That is what we are."*

"And the rest of the week?" Parvati asks.

"Fast-food Canadians."

Pizza. Fish and chips. Single-serving bean pies. Anything that came in a box. Parvati loved being a "modern female." On the phone to relatives, she bragged about it. *"Ten minutes in the oven, and the meal is done!"* Only on the weekends did she soak dahl or boil rice. Then, paying homage to a family tradition, she hummed scales while rolling out chapatis.

"This is why I married her," Raj would claim. *"A beautiful woman from a long line of exceptional cooks."*

Sometimes on Saturday nights, Sitara even saw her mother smile.

As her plane touched down at the Vancouver airport, Sitara's nerves hit the tarmac with a thud.

Waiting to collect her luggage, she realized that she'd never entered the province before, only exited. Growing up, her family had never travelled further than the Queen Charlotte Islands. She had loved their holidays of canoeing, hiking and sleeping in the tents her father had borrowed from a friend at work. But Parvati preferred Victoria with its smooth sidewalks, cafés and four-star hotels. Raj, as usual, was caught in between, trying to keep them both happy.

After pushing her way through the crowds of families gathering around the new arrivals, Sitara took the bus to her parents' apartment building. Riding on streets that had once been familiar to her was like walking into an old house that had been fitted with new furnishings — the layout was the same, but the details had changed. Scanning carefully, she tried to find the drycleaners where Parvati had sent her every Friday night to pick up or deliver skirts and jackets for work, the store where her father had bought her unauthorized candy and milk to wash the food colouring away, and the street where Fatima lived with her gracious and loving stay-at-home mother.

The block leading up to her parents' building had changed so much that she missed her stop and had to walk back from the next one. Standing by trees that had once been shrubs, Sitara questioned her decision to return. Looking up, she noticed that the metal-panelled balconies were painted brown instead of green — snot green, her friends had called it — but already the brown had started to peel.

Drawing on the strength she'd found drinking wine by the ocean, she dragged her suitcase over the crumbling pavement to the lobby door. With an unsteady hand, she ran her finger over the directory of names next to the buzzers. Her parents were not listed. She panicked, wondering if her father had forgotten to tell her that they'd moved. Then, closing her eyes, she let her hand drift over the panel. When she looked again, she saw a yellowed tag with faded ink. Third row, fourth from the top. The square button was stiff when she pressed it, and she held her breath.

"Hello? Hello?"

The scratchy echo of the voice paralyzed her before she remembered what to do. Leaning towards the microphone, she said, "Bapa, it's me."

"Okay, good."

He unlocked the door and let her in.

The lobby, with its fake leather furniture, half-dead potted plants and film of stale smoke, was barely lit. *"Hides the dirt,"* Parvati had always said, and for years Sitara had wondered if that was good or not.

In the elevator, she held the waist-high metal railing and counted as it chugged its way up. When the door opened on the fifth floor, she was scared to get out. On the airplane, while she dozed somewhere over Ontario, she had dreamed about stepping into the past — an altered past, where she was the mother and Parvati was her child.

After a deep breath, she stepped over what seemed like a dangerously wide gap, then turned to watch the elevator door jerk closed behind her.

Following a worn and soiled path, she pulled her suitcase through the carpeted hallway in the same way she had pulled her doll buggy when she was five. Although today the distance to her parents' door didn't seem as far, she still felt small.

In front of her, at the end of the hall, there was light spilling over the carpet. Blinded by the brightness, she slowed her pace. As she walked, she saw a figure the size and shape of her father hovering in the door.

"Welcome home, Sitara."

The apartment smelled like garlic and grease. She trembled and had to stabilize herself by grabbing the doorframe.

"You haven't moved anything," she said.

Her eyes panned from the curry-coloured curtains to the glass and steel tables that held her father's plants to the box-style sofa and easy chairs her parents had bought the year before she was born. Their wedding portrait still hung in a gold frame on the wall, next to Parvati's business school graduation certificates and her papers of Canadian citizenship.

"It is a small room — like a puzzle. There is only one way to make everything fit." He was still standing by the door, waiting for his daughter to finish stepping through it. Her suitcase was parked across the metal sill that marked the boundary between apartment and hall.

Sitara smiled weakly. She felt like cream being churned into butter — all of the emotion was slowly making her solid.

"The lamp is new," Raj offered. "So at night I can read."

She followed his guiding arm. The lamp had a hinged brass stand and a pleated plastic-covered shade. The sofa sagged where its light shone, and there was a stack of books on the table nearby.

"And this too." Raj walked over and rubbed a slipper on the soft pile of a black area rug that made a puddle at the foot of his favourite seat. "Sitara, come in and close the door."

"I'm sorry." She lifted her suitcase through and pulled the door shut, immediately remembering how flimsy it was.

"What is the point of closing the door," I scream, "when the neighbours already know every time I take a pee!"

"Only the rich can buy privacy," Parvati says. "If you get a good job, then you can have a big house where no one will hear."

"I want that house now," I say, "so I don't have to listen to you!"

"Here, Bapa." She extended the potted fern she'd bought for him at the airport, hoping it hadn't been crushed by the turbulent tension in her hand. "This is for you."

With a bow of his head, Raj accepted the plant and put it down on the coffee table without unwrapping it. "Like the ones in your clinic," he said.

"Yes."

"Very thoughtful. Come, sit down."

Sitara hesitated before choosing one of the armchairs. She worried sitting down would mean staying indefinitely.

"I can make tea," Raj said.

"I'm not thirsty."

After a silence as disastrous as dead air on the radio, Raj shifted his kurta. "Today is a very auspicious day," he said slowly, as if calculating his daughter's reaction. "My violets have started blooming."

Sitara let her eyes fall on the cluster of purple and pink blossoms by the window.

"I'd like to see Parvati," she said.

"Of course."

She rose and started walking down the hall. On her left, there was a linen closet with its door firmly sealed to keep out bugs and light. Further down was the windowless bathroom. She could hear the toilet running and a slight drip from the tap. She put off her desire to wash her face and kept walking.

Her parents' room was next on the right. It had been eleven years since she'd laid eyes on Parvati. The cancer, she knew, would now be visible on her face.

The door was partly closed and she knocked on the wall before entering. The smell that emanated from the room was deep-fried oil mixed with muscle rub. She squinted into the darkness, but could find no one in the bed.

She was shaking as she backed into the hallway and took the seven steps from one bedroom to the other. Outside the door that she thought had been forever closed on her childhood, she pressed her sweaty hands into prayer. Then, lifting them above her head, she placed herself in a makeshift temple and forced herself to breathe.

No one answered when she knocked, but she turned the knob and went in.

Even in the heavily filtered light, she recognized her old dresser, still pushed up under the window, and her desk with its built-in cabinet full of shelves. The square light fixture was the same, although the saris that hung over it had all been taken down.

Lying on the bed, Parvati looked pale. *Like almonds with their skins peeled off,* she thought, *although a little more green.* Her cheeks, which were from a much rounder woman, sagged like balloons at the end of a long party. Her ravaged hair, which was too short for its usual stylish cut, now stuck up in tufts like a newborn's. And even though her eyes in their sunken sockets were closed, Sitara couldn't tell if her mother was sleeping or not.

Watching from the doorway, it was Parvati's stillness that disturbed her the most. In her memory, her mother had always been in motion. Even when she was sitting still, some part of her was twitching, twirling or tapping. *"You have the giggles and your mother has the jiggles,"* Raj used to tease. *"Perhaps a good walk would cure you both."* But Sitara couldn't remember ever walking with Parvati, and now it seemed impossible.

"I'm not hungry," she said, as Sitara got closer. "Stop trying to feed me."

"I haven't brought food."

"How did you get in? Does Raj know you're here?"

"Everything's fine, Mother. He invited me."

At the word "mother" Parvati opened her eyes.

"Sitara? How can that be you?"

"I came as soon as he told me."

"I wish he hadn't told you at all."

"He pretty nearly didn't."

"So," Parvati's voice was a rough whisper, "I ask you again, how can that be you?"

"Mother, I might be able to help you."

Parvati closed her eyes and turned her head painfully to one side. "You lost the right to call me that a long time ago."

"Did I?"

"The day you walked out of here without saying goodbye."

"So, if I'm not your daughter, who am I?"

"I don't know. Perhaps you can answer that. Who are you?"

Sitara thought for a moment before she said anything. "A breathing bag of blood, bones and bile."

"What?"

"A healer who has come to try and help you."

"If I'd wanted your help, I would have asked for it."

"Bapa asked."

"Great. Then go heal him."

"He's not sick."

"Are you sure? He invited you here."

"Parvati, please. Stop being stupid."

"The only stupid thing, Sitara, is that you were ever conceived in the first place."

Sitara flew into the kitchen.

"I can't talk to that woman!" she hissed.

"Sitara, your mother is dying."

"Possibly. But that hasn't changed her. She's just as close-minded and arrogant as ever." Without thinking, she put water in her father's kettle.

"I am not saying you are wrong." Raj was leaning forward, staring deeply into his interlaced hands as they rested in front of him on the table. "I just wish you would sit with her. That is all I am asking. You do not have to talk."

"I will try." Sitara turned to her father and let an exhale turn into a small smile. "I'm sorry, Bapa. I know things are bad for you too."

"I will survive. Especially," he said quietly, "now that you are here."

Sitara pulled a chair out from the table and sat down. "You should have warned me," she said.

"About what, beti?"

"That she was in my room."

"It has not been your room for a long time."

"Still, I was surprised."

"This way I can sleep. She mutters in the night. And moans."

"*You* could have made the move, slept in my old bed."

"Yes," Raj said, slowly changing the interlacing of his hands. "But that would have been harder."

In the bloated silence that followed, Sitara thought, *After all these years, my cage is now hers.*

Sitara slept — badly — on the sofa and left the apartment without eating breakfast. Instead, she had a bowl of miso soup at a diner on the corner. She could tell it had been reheated from the night before — the rubbery tofu gave it away. She had a brief and cynical thought about microwaves cancelling out the benefits of miso, but it was lost somewhere in a spoonful of seaweed. Sushi, chicken teriyaki and vegetable tempura on one side of the menu, and hamburgers, fries and grilled cheese on the other. *Japanese and Canadian Food*, the sign out front advertised. For years, it had read, *Chinese and Canadian Food*. Although the cook was new, the waiter was the same. "*Oh, very good. Best item on menu,*" he always said, nodding to assure her, no matter what she ordered, or when.

Now, as she stared into the chrome-edged tabletop, she thought about the irony of change, about how life was filled with an ever-advancing string of pebbles that could, from certain angles, look unmistakably the same.

I am wrapped in blankets and propped up in an armchair where Bapa can see me while he reads. I have been cold for three days. Nothing seems to warm me. Parvati is buying groceries — something she loathes and saves for the first Monday of every month. Bapa and I have another hour together, maybe less. Then she will hold the buzzer until I'm deaf in one ear and he will go down to the car to carry the bags while she recalculates the receipts to make sure no one has cheated her.

"Bapa?" I ask. "When she gets home, can I have burfi and tea?"

"Perhaps," he answers. "We can try."

He knows as well as I do that we're not allowed to eat anything on the first night — that the full cupboards need to stay full, at least until tomorrow after Parvati goes to work. I'm hoping that this time she will make an exception because I am sick.

After the soup and a soothing pot of green tea, Sitara took a bus to Chinatown, where she was hoping the comforting smells and numbing chaos would help her think.

Wandering though the crowded sidewalk stalls of meat and vegetables, she found a small, dark spice shop. Walking in, she recognized it instantly. There was an old woman behind the counter who looked less ancient than before. Perched on a stool, she was filling small plastic bags with turmeric using a carved wooden scoop. She had a different scoop for each spice in the store — and each one hung from a bit of twine on a row of pegs behind the cash. None of them were labelled but the woman never mixed them up.

In the dimness of the fragrant shop, as Sitara scanned the bottles and jars for herbs that would help Parvati, she filled her lungs with calmness. Light fell from a single bare bulb in the ceiling, and from a crack around the window where the blind didn't quite meet the frame. Spices, she knew, preferred to live in the dark.

As the old woman behind the counter switched from turmeric to blood-red paprika, a rain of dust clouded Sitara's vision.

"Namaste," the woman said. "I see you have answered your bapa's call. Your order is ready." With a long, spice-stained hand, the woman pointed to a neat paper bundle on the counter. "This time, it is more — forty-eight dollars, seventy-five cents." She kept shovelling paprika.

"He didn't mention an order," Sitara said. "He didn't even know I was coming here."

"Your bapa always knows," Sarasvati said. "Take it. He can pay later. And here," she added a small plastic bag, "this is for you." Then, bumping down off her stool, she slipped through a beaded curtain into the storeroom.

Alone, Sitara inspected the paper bundle. There was an itemized list marked in pencil. She could read it even though it was written in Sanskrit.

The bag Sarasvati had added was cardamom.

Returning to her parents' apartment building, Sitara hurried through the lobby and the elevator and the long, carpeted hallway, thinking deeply about how she might help Parvati. Immune system deficiency, she knew, could be attributed to many factors, but she kept reflecting on the Seven Emotions.

Anger, overexpressed or held within, damages liver function, which, in turn, causes toxins to stagnate in the blood.

Parvati's anger filled the air like spilled vinegar, permeating everything and lasting just as long.

Grief, too, could weaken immunity.

Long periods of extreme grief injure the lungs, causing the body's stores of vital energy to coagulate.

Sitara could see the textbook in her mind — the strong red cover, the small cramped type, the black and white illustrations of the cycles of energy flow. Following the paths with her inner eye, she could see that the meridians of liver and lung crossed at the breast.

As she formed a fist to knock on the familiar door, her father opened it.

"Hello, Bapa," she said.

"You were gone before I woke up this morning. I no longer hear so well in the night. Do you remember, I always used to hear you?"

"Yes. You woke up when I was sick."

"And when you were scared."

"And when I was trying to sneak in late at night."

Raj laughed. "I remember that too. Lucky for you, Parvati sleeps like a rock."

"How is she?"

Raj shook his head. "Not good. But what about you? Did you sleep well?"

"Fine."

"Do not lie to me. I know the sofa is no longer comfortable."

Sitara squirmed before she admitted, "You're right."

"And there are many ghosts for you here too. Perhaps you should get a hotel."

"I booked one this morning, Bapa. It's only a few bus stops away."

"Good. That will be better." Wiping the perspiration from his forehead, Raj shuffled to his place on the sofa and eased himself down.

"I brought gulab jamun," she said, putting a sticky bag on the kitchen table. "Three pieces each."

"You are still good at spoiling me," he said with a smile that opened like a lotus, the full blossom too big for his tired face. "Later, we will have them with tea."

"Raj... Raj?" Parvati's slow whisper floated towards them from the back room.

Pushing himself up, he said, "I must go."

"No." Sitara picked up her bag of acupuncture supplies. "You rest. I'll go."

"After yesterday, I am surprised you are willing."

"This is what I came here for, isn't it?"

"Yes, but I did not think that —"

"I can be her healer, Bapa, without being her daughter — if she won't accept me as that."

Raj nodded his head. "Good luck, beti." Proudly, he waved to her as she started down the hall.

As she drew nearer to Parvati's room, the hollow stench of vomit reached out to greet her. Opening the door, she could see her mother propped up on the bed with a collection of dull-coloured pillows. Her face changed from blue to green and back again as the soundless television flickered in the dark room.

"So it was you at the door, not Leslie."

"Who's Leslie?"

"My nurse."

"Do loud noises bother you?"

"No."

"Would you like me to turn on the sound?"

"No." Then, after a moment, Parvati added, "I am watching the pictures."

Sitara knelt down beside the bed and pulled a package of needles out of her bag.

"What are you doing?"

"I want to try to calm your stomach."

"Seeing you in this room," Parvati said, "is enough to upset any stomach."

"If I could do this from the hallway, I would. But I need your arm."

Putting her needles aside, Sitara slid her left hand slowly over the blankets and reached out for her mother's thin, wrinkled wrist. Parvati flinched, but did not pull away. As their skin met, a spark travelled up Sitara's arm and spiralled around her breasts, putting pressure on her already tense lungs. Their fingers blended perfectly, as if their hands were a pair, separated only by the passage of time.

Disarmed by the warmth and smoothness of her mother's hand, Sitara coughed and returned to her needles. "Your qi is blocked," she said. "This should help."

After working on her mother every day for five days, Sitara asked, "Do you feel any better?"

"No. Am I supposed to?"

"I hope so."

"A few pokes of your precious needles won't help me now," Parvati grumbled.

With grated teeth, Sitara forced a pleasant smile. "But they won't hurt you, either," she said. Then, putting her needles, cotton swabs and alcohol back into her bag, she asked, "Would you like some tea or juice?"

"No." Parvati screwed up her face and, unable to hold back any longer, opened her mouth to vomit.

Sitara grabbed the dishpan from under the bed and slid it onto Parvati's lap after the liquid had already started to fall.

I have been puking for three days and I am not allowed out of my room because Parvati is afraid I'll soil the carpet. "We can't afford to have them cleaned again," she says. I puked once on the carpet before — when I was four — and she still hasn't forgotten. That time it was small, just one ricey blotch. I had been spinning, first with my arms out and then with them tucked behind my head. I cried because I didn't know what had happened, or why Parvati was so mad. This time she's not taking any chances. She brings me a pot if I need to use the toilet, and wipes me down with damp towels if she thinks I need a bath. I keep hoping that if I puke just a little more I'll be thin enough to slip under the door.

Sitara took away the rubber tub and handed her mother a bath towel. Then, after peeling the top blanket off the bed, she rolled it into a ball and piled it in the corner with the other dirty laundry. When she turned back, Parvati was pulling at the remaining blankets.

"Hang on, I'll go to the cupboard and get you another one," Sitara said.

"No. I am already too hot."

"Then I'll get you a damp cloth and some tea."

Parvati said nothing as Sitara stepped out of the room and made her way down the hall.

Roused by her presence in the kitchen, Raj asked, "Teatime already?"

"First, I'm making some for Parvati."

"I thought maybe she threw you out!"

"No. But she didn't invite me back, either."

"Sometimes..." Raj paused until his daughter turned to look at him, "you do not have to wait for invitations."

"But before I go to the trouble," Sitara said, "I like to know that I'm welcome."

"In my home, you are always welcome."

"Thanks, Bapa." On her way out of the kitchen, she leaned down and placed a small kiss on his forehead. "I'll come back when it boils," she said.

Leaving Raj with a sleepy-eyed grin, she stopped in the bathroom to get a facecloth, then climbed back into the darkness of Parvati's cave. Waving the white cloth like a flag, she handed it to her mother. She was tired of being at war.

"Too hot," Parvati said, although the water Sitara had used was cold. "I told you already, I'm too hot."

"You're having heat flashes," Sitara said. "When they pass, you'll be cold again."

"I am not cold until I say I'm cold." She fumbled, dropped the facecloth on the bed, then tried to make it look intentional. "Take this horrible thing away. When I want to wash, I will go to the bathroom."

"I can take you now, if you want."

"I am not a child going for a car ride. I will pee when I have to pee." Parvati folded her hands across her stomach and winced at her own pain.

Feeling helpless, Sitara crouched down at the side of the bed and watched as sweat accumulated on her mother's tired face. On the bedside table, in a tarnished frame, there was a photo of Parvati and her two younger sisters. Shanti and Meena were dressed in saris, each with a single long braid and a nath from nose to ear. Parvati too, wore her hair in a long braid, but her sari had been replaced by a pale business suit. The picture, Sitara knew, was taken on the day her parents left for Canada. It was the last time Parvati had wrapped her protective arms around her sisters who, despite years of cajoling, had decided to remain in India.

Suddenly, her mother forced a series of painful swallows, and Sitara reached again for the rubber dishpan.

My mother's life is ending, she thought, *in the same bed mine started in.* The one that had, over the years, absorbed so many of her precious liquids — blood, tears and baby pee. No matter how many times the sheets were changed, the mattress still held the secrets of her childhood dreams and nightmares. For years, it had felt unbearably small. But now, as she stood there watching, it seemed to dwarf her shrunken mother.

Wandering the anonymous streets of Vancouver, Sitara decided it was time to go home. *The mind is a porous organ,* she thought, *except when it's filled with lies.* And denial, she had finally decided, was also a lie.

After a week of insults and resistance, she admitted that she had been unable to reach her mother. It was also hard to tell if the acupuncture was helping, especially when Parvati was so closed to it.

"Your daughter is here to see you," she'd overheard her father say as she arrived one day.

"Raj, she is not my daughter," Parvati had answered. "I didn't want her then, and I don't want her now. Stop trying to convince me."

Sitara had surprised them both by letting herself in with the key Raj had given her. *Bapa's short-term memory,* she'd thought, *is not as good as it used to be.*

Now she turned down a side street, seeking shelter and shade. The heat bouncing off the concrete was giving her a headache, and the accusing stares from strangers as she tried to say hi were shrinking her already shrivelled resolve.

Leaving was the easy part. It was informing her father that was hard.

chapter 18

"Jack?"

   "Yes?"

   "Where are you?"

   "Having a soak in the tub."

"Seriously!"

"Why, do you need me?"

"No. I just want to know where you are."

They were working in the blackness of Jack's bathroom, which, with the lights off and the windows and door sealed, doubled as a darkroom.

   "I'm still at the counter," he said. "I have one more reel to wind."

   "I thought you had four to do!"

   "Yeah."

   "How can you go so fast?" Sara asked. "This is the most delicate process."

   "Practice, I guess. How many have you done?"

   "Two."

   "So hurry up, before I turn into a mole!"

The day before, when Jack had suggested they develop some black and white negatives together, she had hesitated. It had been a long time since she'd been in the darkroom and she didn't know how much she'd be able to remember. However, as soon as she saw the equipment, her professor's droning voice came back to her. *"Line up your materials first. Spread them out and memorize their location. When I turn the light off, it's going to be dark."*

Dark didn't begin to describe it — for in every shade of dark, Sara had believed, there was still a little light. But in the lab, when her professor pulled the switch, it was black. Tar black. Panic black. Blind black.

"Where are you now?" she asked.

"Leaning on the bathtub, waiting for the perfectionist to finish her rolls."

"When you see them, you'll be dazzled by their quality."

"If we don't die of asphyxiation first!"

"Oh come on, Jack. It's not that bad."

"Well, stop talking so much. You're using up all my air."

"Fine," Sara said. "What's on all these rolls anyway?"

"You."

"On all of them?"

"No. Some of them are old. From the winter, probably. I already developed the important ones. On these, I was just screwing around."

"Experimenting is the technical term."

"Yes, I've heard of that — it makes it sound so tidy. How are you doing there?"

"I'm done," she said.

When Jack turned on the amber safe light, she was sitting casually on the toilet with her shirt off and both hands tucked comfortably behind her head. "Nice spot," she said.

He smiled. "Yes, I come here often."

"Does it always stink this bad?"

"No, sometimes it's… more organic."

As Jack made a lunge for her, she picked up her shirt and laughed. "We have photos to develop!"

"But I prefer this development." He was bending over, running his lips along her shoulder.

"Jack! We can't stop mid-process."

"You're right. We can't." Spreading his legs, he straddled her and combed his hands through her hair.

After a long kiss she whispered, "It's chemical time."

"If you're talking about pheromones, I agree."

"I'm talking about photographs!"

"Alright." As he eased himself away from her, she slipped on her shirt.

"I hate to disturb your mood lighting, but do you mind if I turn on the big light?"

"Actually, the bulb's burned out." Grabbing a timer from a small, wooden cabinet, he added, "I wish there was a more natural way of doing this."

"I guess it's called digital," she said.

"Between you and me, I can't bear the thought of turning a face into pixels."

"It is pretty bizarre, isn't it?"

On assignment in certain countries, Sara had been tempted by the simplicity of working with a digital camera, especially when it came to submitting images to her editor. In Hong Kong, she had seriously considered buying one. But, in the end, she couldn't imagine a camera being ready until she had tucked a film leader into the spool, closed the camera back and heard the satisfying creak of the initial wind.

After they had carefully processed the first batch of films, Jack said, "Alright. Let's fix them."

"What about a stop-bath?"

"I wasn't going to bother."

"It won't take long."

"Okay." Jack grabbed another bottle of chemicals.

"May I?" Sara took one of the tanks in her hands and tapped it on the edge of the counter.

"What's that for?"

"To remove any bubbles. Otherwise you might have dark spots on your negatives."

"I've never noticed any."

Sara smiled. "Then I guess you've been lucky."

Impressed, Jack asked, "You want to do this part?"

"Sure." She accepted the bottle from him. "You know, you can use water too."

"Too, or instead?"

"Instead, if it's at the right temperature."

Even in the dimness of the safe light, she could see that Jack was smiling.

After she had finished with the stop-bath solution, they poured fixer into the tanks and began gently shaking them.

"This part always makes me feel like a bartender," she said.

"Personally, I go for less potent drinks."

"Ah, but you haven't tried one of mine!"

At the end of the fixing process, while they waited for the films to rinse under running water, Sara pressed herself against Jack's chest and nibbled gently at his neck. "This is fun," she said. "I'd forgotten."

Then, as they hung the negatives over the tub to dry, Jack asked, "What do you think?"

"I like the subject matter," she said, pinning up a strip of his naked torso.

"Seriously!"

"I think they look pretty good."

"Yeah, and they'll look even better when they're big!"

"Unless they're all blurry."

"Nah, they won't be blurry. We used autofocus." Snapping the excess water from a length of film, Jack added, "Sara, that's something you should consider."

"No thanks." For a long time, she had been convinced that it was a cheap shortcut, like substituting a microwave for an open grill. There was no subtlety. No room for the cook's skilled hand.

"It's not a crime, you know. Lots of professionals use it."

"You don't."

"Sure, I do. We did the other night."

"Well I don't. I'm allergic to point-and-shoot."

"I just thought that —" Jack looked up and tried to catch her eye. "Never mind." Then, after pegging the last strip to the line, he said, "I have another box of undeveloped rolls. Want to do this again tomorrow?"

"I can't." She was rinsing the remaining traces of chemicals from her hands. "I'm going to see my parents for a few days. They run a bed and breakfast, and pretty soon, as my mother keeps reminding me, they won't have any spare beds."

"But what about me?"

"You can live without me for a few days! And besides, I'm going to be on assignment."

"Oh yeah?"

"Yep." She smiled and pulled him into her arms. "When we go downstairs, I'll show you my new business cards."

Feeling elated, Sara waited for the bus. Wrapped in the energy and clarity that working in the darkroom had given her, she was planning the promotional shots her father had hired her for.

click
The historic exterior of the River Bank B&B with its proud lines reaching towards the sky.

To her, the house was overly large and grand, but shot from below — with her camera flush to the ground — she was hoping the effect would be more impressive than imposing.

Inside, her father would want photos of the kitchen, since his remodelling was apparently the talk of the town. "A *very small town,*" her mother had said, laughing.

And, of course, she would take photos of each of the bedrooms because, she figured, the guests would want to see the details of where they were going to stay.

click
An ornate ceiling fan made of cast iron and tin.

click
A small lamp shade, like an overturned flower, on a base of imported wood.

click
A collection of other small items long coveted by the photographer.

As the bus pulled up, she was dissecting the anatomy of her parents' house — there were so many rooms that she didn't know how to label them all.

Riding out of Halifax, she thought of Jack. She tried to imagine him as a young man seeing his first tree-surrounded lake, or his first hunk of blasted rock. She wondered what he took photos of year after year on the flat, monochromatic prairie. Although she'd never been to Alberta or Saskatchewan, she compared it in her mind to the desert, which she'd experienced twice. For three days she'd trekked through Iran on camelback and, a few years later, she'd taken a series of day trips to the Sahara in a Jeep. Both times she'd felt lost in a landscape of repetition. Without streets or rivers or forests, she had nothing to anchor herself to. Like a pencil nestled in the end of a compass, she liked to circle around a fixed centre point, expanding or contracting the radius as needed.

Jack, she suspected, was different. He made his own anchors and, she realized, could find subjects for photos anywhere. She wondered if his parents still operated the family farm, and if there was a barn with a loft where, with a young woman, he'd taken his first nude portraits.

As the bus neared the last hill before Wolfville, she started to fidget in her seat. Even though the windows were heavily tinted, she could see the blaze of sunlight gathering in the sky. Without thinking, she reached down for her camera, held it to the window and waited for Blomidon to come into view.

click
Clear sharp spikes of red bathe the mountain in light.

Recognizing the temporary clarity that autofocus afforded her, she'd reluctantly taken Jack's suggestion and pulled her old camera out of storage.

click
Clear sharp blades of marsh grass in a river of mud at low tide.

As she put her camera away, she was singing under her breath.

"Good morning," Ron said, as his daughter stumbled into the kitchen. "Sleep well?"

"Uh-huh." Sitting down at the table, Sara chose a chair in the curve of the bay window and tried to keep a smile from turning into a yawn. She didn't want to tell him how much she missed Jack.

"I see you didn't place your order," he teased, holding up one of the square slips of paper that guests used to indicate their breakfast preferences. "Would you like pancakes with blueberry-mango sauce, or eight-grain granola with dried cranberries and your choice of soy milk, rice milk, goat's milk, or cow's milk? I'm afraid it's still too early in the season for my famous fruit plate!"

"How about some toast?"

"What? You don't like the chef's specialties? There's a greasy diner down the road!"

Wiping remnants of sleep from her eyes, she laughed. "Actually the granola sounds good, since I'm trying to eat well."

"With rice or soy milk?"

"I can get it myself."

"I'll put them all on the table and you can choose." Ron put his hand on the refrigerator door. "Or, if you're feeling brave, you can mix them."

"Just regular milk will be fine, Dad. I can't stand that other stuff — although I know it's probably good for me."

"Changing your lifestyle takes a while, Sara."

"Yeah."

"And you need to have a good reason to do it in the first place."

"Which I have." She covered her mouth with her hand. "I'm sorry. I can't stop yawning."

Placing a bowl of cereal on the table in front of her, Ron said, "I heard you and Peggy up late — laughing. I hope you weren't talking about me."

"Of course not. We were talking about Grandma's foot, actually."

"Peggy loves telling stories about my mother, doesn't she?"

"I have to admit, it was pretty funny."

"For you, maybe." Ron sat down at the table. "You didn't have to carry her out of the office and into the car, with her screaming the whole time about how the good-for-nothing doctor had made her foot ten times worse!"

"I thought she liked her doctor."

"He was away. This was a young guy. 'Too young to even know what a goddamn sore foot is,' my mother said."

"But Peggy said she doesn't have any broken bones or anything…"

"True, although it has been bugging her for years. It swells up so bad she can't get her shoes on."

"And that's when she calls you!"

"Ron to the rescue!" He laughed. "I keep telling her there's a good naturopath in the valley. It's possible diet and herbs will help. But you know her, she won't touch anything she hadn't heard of before 1940!" The kettle interrupted with a thin, sputtering whistle. "You want some tea, Sara?"

"Sure."

As her father rinsed out the teapot, she slipped into the hallway where she'd left some of her bags the night before. It had been a long time since she'd seen her grandmother, and she was contemplating the ramifications of asking Ron to make the drive to Digby. On a good day, her grandmother was likeable enough, except that she continuously called her Lauren no matter how many times they had tried to set her straight. It irritated Sara that the woman who complained resentfully about having only two grandchildren insisted on using the same name for them both.

When she returned to the kitchen, she put her rattling bag down on an empty chair.

"What's all that?" Ron asked.

"My dispensary," she said. Reaching into the bag, she pulled out nine plastic bottles, naming them as she went. "Vitamin A. Vitamin E. Vitamin C. Selenium. Bilberry. Zinc. Grapeseed.

Beta Carotene. And an unpronounceable Chinese blend my acupuncturist gave me."

"Very impressive. Are they helping?"

"I don't know yet."

"Looks like you bought half the store! You want a glass of juice for those?"

"I'll wait until the tea cools down."

"You like the acupuncturist?" he asked, scanning the label of one of the bottles.

"Yeah, she's great. But I still don't like the needles."

"Painful?"

"No. At least not physically! It's the psychological damage I'm worried about!" She waited until her father looked up to add, "I'm kidding. The woman's really great, and I think the treatment is helping. At least at the end of it I feel calm and centred."

Ron reached over and topped up her tea.

"Dad, thanks for looking after me."

Winking at her, he said, "I do this for all my guests."

"No, I mean thanks for saving me from surgery."

He put the teapot down. "Well, I'm glad you're less stubborn than I am — I never listen to my own advice!"

Sara smiled. "How about listening to some of mine?"

"That depends."

"On what?"

"On the topic."

She winced as she swallowed three vitamins in a single gulp. "Try two tea bags next time instead of four. Besides being bitter, your tea is way too thick."

Ron pouted and then took another sip. "Thankless daughter," he said. And then he choked on the sludge at the bottom of his cup.

"Are you alright?"

"Physically, yes," he said, grinning. "It's the psychological damage I'm worried about."

"Very funny." She leaned down and unzipped her camera bag. "Can you pick up your mug again? I feel like catching you in the act."

click
A wicked grin on an otherwise gentle face.

"Is that the same camera you always use?" he asked.

"No. This is an old one I bought in school." Leaning towards her father, she cupped her hands around the camera, pretending to plug its ears. "It thinks it's smarter than I am, with all its *auto* features, but I know where the override is!"

"It looks pretty swanky," Ron whispered.

"Don't be fooled by good looks, Dad."

"So, do you want to get started on those pictures?"

"No, it's such a grey day they wouldn't look like much. And Peggy's still fussing anyway, trying to make everything perfect. If the sky clears, I'll take them later. I was thinking I might go for a walk."

"There's an umbrella by the door you can take."

"Thanks."

Wandering the streets in her thick shades, Sara wore an unintentional disguise. Even on a dim day, the light bothered her eyes.

Although the house was new to her parents, she'd grown up in this town, with its tall trees, old houses, rose gardens and tourist shops. And she'd taken her first photos here — the leafy pumpkin shot that had won first prize, the series of old windows she'd sold to a magazine, a gull landing on the water at

dusk against a fiery sky. The houses, the fences, the fancy painted signs — these things dotted her first photo palette. She'd
found pleasure in the cracks of pavement, the brightly coloured
walls, the blooming flowers or budding vines, and the tempt-
ingly grassy embankments of the fort.

As a child, she had often sought refuge behind the constrain-
ing walls of Fort Anne. In fall and winter she could hide away
undetected for hours, while in spring and summer some helpful
tourist would inevitably try to drag her to the lost and found.

In the early evenings, when the air had cooled off and the
noise of the town had quieted down, Sara would venture to more
visible places. She would sit with her magnifying glass or binoc-
ulars, framing photos, cropping details, always watching. She was
absorbed by the visual world around her — the way water met
sky, the way stone met earth, the way windows reflected images.
She thrived on the exotic details of her ordinary world.

And then, after college, she saw Paris. And Berlin. And
Vienna. And the great stone forts of Scotland and Wales. And
suddenly Annapolis Royal seemed small.

As she walked along the main street, the wind picked up
and, as she predicted by the mass of cloud in the sky, it started
to rain. Quickly, she opened her father's umbrella and headed
for the edge of the water. The wharf had been recently repaved,
and a large mural had been painted at the far end. Removing
her shades, she stood above it, gazing at the colours, keeping
one small section of it dry at a time. She'd never made an image
like this — with a brush and a can of paint. Her images already
existed — the art was in knowing when to press the shutter.

The rain poured hard against the pavement and against the
plastic shelter above her head. Slowly, tilting the umbrella with
her, she lifted her face to the sky. She was tempted to open her
eyes, as if it would somehow cleanse them of their malfunction.
But instead she opened her mouth and let it fill slowly with

water. As the rain collected on her tongue, it seemed sterile and unforgiving. She spat it into the harbour and ducked under her umbrella again.

Drawing her skin tightly around her, she turned away from the water and walked towards the mossy green house across the road. Seeing lights on, she placed her knuckles on the wet glass and knocked. A woman, with hands covered in clay and hair the colour of silver, motioned for Sara to let herself in.

"The door's open!" she said.

Sara brought a gentle river with her and then stood creating a small pool. "Ingrid, do you remember me?"

The potter wiped red clay on her apron and then lifted her glasses to her face. "Sara! It's been a long time."

"I know. I've been away."

"Have you brought me pictures from someplace romantic and warm?"

"No. Just a lot of rain."

"That would have come anyway." The woman smiled, trying to find the young face she had known. "Hang your things there, and I'll make you tea."

Sara followed her past shelves of bowls and mugs and hand-built plates. In the years since Sara had visited the studio, Ingrid's glazes hadn't changed. They were still vibrant and strong with splashes of colour where Sara least expected them. Ingrid had tried earth tones, she claimed, and lost a husband because of it.

The air that had felt cool and damp at the front of the studio grew warm and dry as they reached the back. The kiln was quiet, but the kettle steamed on the woodstove. Ingrid lifted down a teapot that was cracked and broken and, Sara estimated, at least fifteen years old.

"So, what's brought you home?" Ingrid asked in her fading German accent. "I trust your parents aren't ill or anything."

"No, they're fine."

"Just fine?"

"Well, you know," Sara said, "the same as always. I mean, did they ever get along?"

"Oh god, I don't know. You see them more than I do."

"Not really."

"Milk with your tea?"

"Please." In the past, Sara had tried it without, but hadn't been able to hide her wincing faces. Grabbing a dry cloth from the rack above the stove, she wiped a chair clean for herself. In Ingrid's studio nothing escaped the dust. Then, stretching her feet towards the fire, she tried to dry her jeans and sandals.

Chatting easily with Ingrid again reminded her of the past. She had spent many long evenings watching and asking — but never helping or imitating. Getting her hands dirty didn't appeal to her, and she had no desire to colour or construct things. It was Ingrid herself that fascinated her.

"You still haven't told me why you're home," Ingrid said, "although I do have a suspicion." The twinkle in her eye suggested something whimsical or foolish like marriage — a topic that appeared to be a favourite of hers although she had no interest in it for herself.

"I just want some time off — away from work, away from travelling." Sara tried to make it sound casual, as if it was nothing at all. But she could tell Ingrid knew better.

"You've been fired."

"No!"

"You've been bad-mouthed in some popular magazine."

"No."

"Then what?"

"I'm just having troubles with my eyes."

Ingrid sat down and faced Sara. There was steam rising from her mug. It acted like a veil and she swept it aside. "Sara, you are always welcome here." The way she said it made her sound like a grandmother or an aunt — someone who always expected Sara to need her.

"How's business?" Sara asked, quietly.

"Fine. Or at least I hope it will be. It's always slow over the winter. I work hard until Christmas, and then, like a bear, I practically hibernate until spring." She opened her mouth wide when she laughed, showing off her teeth and gums. "I feel like I'm just waking up now," she continued, "all groggy and hungry for food."

"Do you really sell enough to make a living?"

"Well, I'm alive." Ingrid laughed again. "But according to statistics, of course, I live way below the poverty line."

"That's all relative," Sara said.

"Yeah, by the look of me, I'm not suffering too badly." She grabbed the flesh of her belly and threw her head back in another rattling laugh. "Well," she said, "not everyone would like it, but I can't imagine living any other way. What about you? You're not going back to that fancy magazine, are you?"

"I don't know."

"The only way to be happy is to be in control of your own life. That's the best advice I can give you on a rainy day."

Walking home, Sara wondered if it was advice that she'd been seeking, or just some warmth and comfort. Either way, she kept hearing Ingrid's words like a mechanized mantra, over and over again in her head. *Take control of your life. Take control of your life. Take control of your life.*

"Shut up," she moaned to herself out loud. For in many ways, she felt like she already had.

"Ron? Ron?"

Sara was in the front study. It was the one room that she recognized, since it was set up almost exactly the same way it had been in every house her family had lived in. The busy shelves had fascinated her since childhood. They were full of books and magazines and small handmade decorations. There were a few pieces of Ingrid's pottery, and there was her father's collection of wooden boxes. He liked places where he could tuck away small pieces of himself, where memories resided alongside smells and bits of coloured paper.

"Ron, can you hear me? I don't have all day!"

Sara didn't know where her father was, but she didn't blame him for ignoring her mother. Too often, Peggy's impatience spewed out of her mouth, spraying everyone within earshot and leaving a film of irritation. As she was fond of reminding them, she came from a family where quietness meant laziness, and artistry was a luxury unless it paid the rent.

"Ron!"

Although rich in character, her parents' new house was large and cavernous, and it exaggerated her mother's voice. Following the sound of it, Sara went out into the hall.

"Can I help you with something?" she offered.

"Thank goodness someone listens around here. Well I guess this means you're not going deaf too. You know, your father has selective hearing."

Sara cringed invisibly. "Mom, what are you doing?"

Peggy was bashing at the wall with the back end of a stapler. Her target was almost at ceiling height and she was standing on a rolling chair. "The clock must not be visible enough, because our clients never seem to see it."

"What, are they always late for breakfast or something?"

"Something like that."

"Maybe you should put clocks in their rooms."

"People should travel with watches or alarm clocks of their own," Peggy said.

"I guess." Sara thought of all the times her watch had

been broken or stolen. She'd tried all kinds — wrist, pocket and pendant. Her own internal clock seemed to fight with outside time.

"You still have that clever little one I bought for you, don't you?"

"Yep." She'd traded it in Peru for a guided tour and a car ride, although the photographs she'd taken had never been used. "Here, Mom. Let me do it."

"Nah. I got it now. Just hold the chair."

Sara grabbed the rounded plastic arms of the padded, tilt-back office chair and tried to hold it steady. There was something inherently unstable about her mother, even when she wasn't standing on a chair.

With an overstated thump, Peggy stepped down. "So, what do you think?"

"About what?"

"About the clock. Unless," she joked with her daughter, "you're so blind you can't see it."

"It looks great, Mom. You should have done it ages ago."

Satisfied, Peggy turned back to her desk. "Well, it's done now."

Dismissed, Sara walked into the kitchen, where her father was quietly working at the counter.

"Dad?" She approached slowly, seeing Ron's mind adrift — separated entirely from his vegetable-chopping body. "Where are you?"

"In the garden," he said, "picking herbs." He blinked and then smiled at the reality of having his grown daughter right in front of him.

"Really? You were rocking."

"The wind was strong."

She pulled up a stool, lifted a cookbook from his rarely used shelf and started choosing recipes based on the mood of the photos.

"Well, the beast has been tackled," she said, licking her finger and flipping quickly from page to page. "There will be no more late dinner guests."

"We haven't had any guests for weeks. But, of course," he rolled his eyes, "we're preparing for the upcoming stampede."

"Don't you think it will be busy?"

"Perhaps, but I didn't just hire you so that I could see you again. I really think we need to advertise."

"But if there are no guests, then what's the classy platter for?"

"Sometimes I do catering on the side. Marsha's having a grand reopening sale."

"Tonight?"

"Tomorrow. I'm going to wrap it tight."

"I didn't know you guys still hung out with her."

"It's a small town, Sara." Ron rinsed off his cutting board and opened a package of cheese. "I'm leaving early in the morning. I could use your help — that is, if you want to come."

"Alright." She was concentrating on a photo of sautéed mushrooms. *The composition is good,* she thought, *but the lighting is all wrong.* She would have used a different angle and a more concentrated light. She pushed the book aside. "Dad, do you have a flashlight? I want to try something."

"A flask of what, Sara?"

"A flashlight," she repeated, surprised by the degree of his distraction. "I want to illuminate the underside of a mushroom."

"Sara," he said, skillfully wielding a paring knife, "I'm really glad you're here."

Looking up, she saw that he was cutting hearts out of a block of pale-coloured cheese.

chapter 19

Patrick was jittering more than usual as he stared at the ceiling of Sitara's office. She was feeling badly about cancelling his last appointment, but she was also wondering if he was starting to rely too heavily on their time together.

"Breathe slowly, Patrick. Remember, fifteen in and twenty-five out."

She usually advised her patients to breathe in for three counts and out for five, but with Patrick everything was accelerated.

Removing needles from his ankle and calf, she was reminded of Parvati. Laying her fingers over his wrist, she checked his pulse again. It was still slightly wiry and rapid, but it had improved.

"Ever been to Vancouver?" she asked.

"No, but I lived in Seattle. Just never made it up the coast."

"Where else have you lived?"

"Do you want it chronological or alphabetical?"

"As it comes to you," she said.

"Toronto, Montreal, Quebec City. Back to Toronto. Then Seattle, New York, Winnipeg, Sudbury and here."

"Well, you certainly have the continent covered." Sitara checked his pulse again, then removed the last two needles. "Alright," she said, "you can go."

"That's it?"

"Were you expecting more?"

"No. No. Of course not." Without hesitating he sat up and jumped off the bed. "Same time next week?" He reached into his back pocket and pulled out a little red calendar.

"I'll be here," Sitara said.

"Oh good. Then I'll write it down in ink."

Watching him go, she thought, *Most of his anxiety is contained in that book.*

After smoothing the bed and changing the pillowcase, she took a long drink of water from a glass bottle on her desk. Then she went into the waiting room to find her next patient.

Sara was sitting by the door flipping through a magazine.

"That's heavy reading for a woman with bad eyes," Sitara said.

Quickly, Sara snapped it shut. "Actually, it's pretty pictures mostly."

Sitara walked over to have a look at the cover. "Are they any good?"

"Honestly?" Sara smiled. "They're pretty terrible." She dropped the magazine back into the wooden crate where she found it. "I'm glad you're back. Did it go well?"

"A bit turbulent, but as the Chinese say, 'No wind, no waves.' Come on." She motioned towards her office. "Let's talk about you." When Sara was positioned comfortably on the bed, Sitara asked, "In the middle of the day, do you ever rest your eyes?"

"No."

"Never?"

"Not unless I'm sleeping."

"Hmm."

Blinking rapidly, Sara asked, "If I did, how could I see?"

"It's not about seeing. It relaxes your eye muscles — lets you look inside. Have I showed you any exercises?"

"No. I don't think so."

Sitara let her hands rest on the bed as she spoke. "There are four, but I like the one involving the sun."

Standing in front of the window, she spread her feet shoulder-width apart and rotated her upper body slowly. Even with her eyes closed, she could feel the sun's energy as it passed across her face, warming her skin and seeping deep into her consciousness.

"It's called sunning," she said, reluctant to end her demonstration. "Take as much time as you need with it — maybe ten minutes at a time."

"Okay." Sara had barely moved from her position on the bed.

Sitara smiled. "You can sit up, if you want, to see better."

Sara's face flushed and she rolled over onto her side.

"Another good one for you might be this." Sitara rubbed the palms of her hands together and then cupped them firmly over her open eyes. "There shouldn't be any pressure on the eye, but make sure you have a good seal. And try not to let any light in."

Sara nodded. "I'll try to remember."

"Sit like that as often as you like," Sitara continued, "holding it for maybe five minutes at a time. I did it a lot on the plane last week."

"You don't like flying?"

"I don't mind. For me, the exercise is more about finding perspective." She let her hands fall away from her eyes. "The world always seems different when I come back to it." She looked over at Sara, who was lying with her head propped provocatively on one arm. With the speed of summer lightning, Sara's face went pale. "What's wrong?" Sitara asked.

"Nothing."

"Something happened."

"I guess…" Sara's cheeks were starting to burn. "I guess I just felt the weight of my health fall from your hands into mine."

"Because of the exercises?"

She nodded.

Sitara sat down in her wooden armchair and took a deep, belly-expanding breath. "All of this is new," she said. "I'm not surprised it's overwhelming. But you're not alone, Sara, and you're not the only one working on a solution."

"I know, but —"

"You feel like a frog in a well shaft looking at the sky."

Sara giggled and returned to a more stable position on her back. "Is that another proverb?"

"Yes." Sitara smiled as she stood up. "You can tell what I was reading as I fell asleep last night!"

"Did it help?"

"I don't know. I found a lot of answers. But I guess I haven't formulated the right questions yet."

"Are there any *wrong* questions?"

Sitara tapped a needle into Sara's wrist. Watching her face, she wondered if Sara had even noticed. If so, it was the first time she hadn't flinched. "I can lend you the book, if you like."

"No," Sara said. "Sounds like it might confuse me, and I feel like I'm just starting to get things sorted out."

Inserting a needle into her ankle, Sitara said, "I envy you." Then, rubbing Sara's shoulder, she added, "I'm going to leave you here for a minute to cook. Keep breathing. I'll be back."

Grabbing the bottle of water from her desk, Sitara stepped into the waiting room. Since returning from Vancouver, she'd been single-minded about getting caught up with her patients and had worked through lunch every day. As her stomach rumbled, she tried to pacify it with another drink of water.

Going back into her office, she slipped into the cupboard where she kept her herbs. As she scanned the shelves for the formula she had chosen for Sara, the door swung closed behind her. In the dark, even with the tall stacks of herbs surrounding her, she panicked.

I hear the apartment door open and realize Parvati is home early from work. I try to bolt for the dining room, but she comes into the kitchen and drops her bags on the linoleum floor, blocking my only way out. It must be something special, like Bapa's birthday, for her to have gone shopping instead of being at work. I worry that if it is, I haven't made him a present. I want to ask her, or check the calendar that is pinned up by the phone, but I will get sent to bed if she finds out where I am. Sucking on a cardamom pod, I hear her humming as she stacks her groceries on the counter one by one. I have to plug my ears because the clunk of bottles and cans is like thunder above my head. I retract into the smallest ball possible, hoping that when Bapa comes home, she will go to meet him at the door.

Flicking on the light, Sitara tried to breathe. Then, with her hand on the container she'd been looking for, she opened the door and walked back into her office.

Sara turned her head and smiled. "Get lost?" she asked.

"Just a little." Placing the herbs on her desk, she said, "I know they're a bit expensive, but I think they're really helping."

After checking the progress of the needles, she removed them. Sara's energy flow had greatly improved. "You can sit up now," she said. "How do you feel?"

"Good — a little spacey."

"Do you have to drive?"

"No. I walked." As Sara slid off the bed, she admitted, "I took a cab, actually."

Nodding, Sitara asked, "What would you like to do now? Do you want to make another appointment? Or do you want to call me?"

"I'll call."

Sara picked up her belongings and walked into the waiting room. As Sitara followed, she felt a heaviness in her head and a chaos in her body that she remembered from childhood. Sara, on the other hand, appeared so light and buoyant that Sitara wondered if she might float away.

"You look a little dreamy."

"Yeah," Sara said. "I think I'm still drifting — drinking in the gift of your hands."

Sitara smiled as she motioned for the next patient to wait in her office. The man was old and he crossed the waiting room slowly.

Watching Sara glide out the door, Sitara saw a flash of gold and burgundy. When she turned, Sarasvati was sitting by the Zen garden, arranging the folds of her sari and using her fingers to draw question marks in the sand.

"Here you are again," Sarasvati said, "isolating yourself. Is there something wrong with having friends? Is that why you prefer to hide in cupboards?"

"What do you expect me to do?"

"Well," Sarasvati said, "you could run after her."

Without blinking, Sitara opened the clinic door and looked for Sara. She was halfway down the stairs. "Are you busy later?" Sitara called. "I'd really like to get together and talk."

Turning around, Sara said, "I'd be happy to change my plans."

"I'm done at four. Can you come back then?"

"I'll be here." She smiled, then continued down the stairs.

As Sitara turned back to the waiting room, she looked for Sarasvati but, of course, she was gone.

Three hours later, Sitara was standing on a chair, cranking the skylights closed, when Sara opened the door.

"Hey!"

"I'm so glad you're done," Sara panted. "I ran pretty fast, but this is still starting to melt."

Sitara climbed down off the chair. "What is it?"

"Raspberry sorbetto. It seemed like you could use some." Sara put the paper cups on the coffee table and opened her sweater. "I think I've spent too much time in warm climates. I was cold when I left the house." She sat down and fanned herself. "I hope you like sorbetto. I thought the sugar might perk you up. Sometimes it's good to have a cheap thrill."

Sitara smiled. "I've never turned down a raspberry before."

Leaning forward, Sara picked up one of the paper cups and handed it to Sitara. "This one's for you," she said, "since I've already started on the other one."

"Thanks." With a cool spoonful of frozen fruit on her tongue, Sitara closed her eyes. After she swallowed, she said, "This is so huge, maybe we should go outside. If I scream in here, my neighbours will think I'm crazy."

Giggling, Sara followed her out the door.

On the sidewalk, away from the clinic, Sitara felt like a bird released from its cage. Spinning as she walked, she threw her arms open and embraced the air.

"Long day?" Sara asked.

"Yeah. Sometimes I wish I wasn't so popular. I would have enjoyed being outside."

"Was it warm in Vancouver?"

"Warm and rainy — you know what it's like in the spring."

"Actually, I've never been there."

"It has certain charms — probably more than I give it credit for. But for me it's so linked with the past, I have trouble seeing it objectively."

"Was it really that bad?" Sara asked, reaching out for Sitara's empty cup and dropping it, along with her own, into a green garbage and recycling bin.

"Some parts were."

"I like the town where I grew up, except that no one recognizes me anymore."

"Were you an infamous kid?"

"I was certainly noticeable. I was the one sticking a camera up everyone's nose!"

Laughing, Sitara said, "I can see how that would make you memorable."

"But that's the thing. No one remembers me, because I'm not in any of the photos. Years later, no one remembers the photographer, just the faces in the photograph."

"Hmm." Sitara smiled as she digested the irony of the profession. "Maybe the invisible photographer needs to switch to the visible side of the camera."

"I tried that recently."

"And?"

"And…" Sara turned away. "I felt a little exposed."

"You mean, like falling in love?"

"No." Turning back to Sitara, her face was fully flushed. "I was making an occupational joke — you know, exposed on film."

Feeling badly, Sitara said, "I was just teasing."

"I know." Stopping in the middle of the sidewalk, Sara looked around, then whispered, "Actually, there is someone."

"You don't need to tell me this. I didn't mean to —"

"No, it's okay. I think he's someone you know. He says you saved him from back pain a few years ago."

Sitara nodded her head. "I've fixed a lot of bad backs."

"He's a photographer."
Sitara dropped her gaze to the ground.

"Jack!" I scream. He is hanging out my third-storey window, with one hand clutching the wooden frame and the other holding up his camera.

"Man, this is a great view," he tells me. "I've got to come here more often."

Horrified, I turn away.

"Check it out," he says. "Come on, I'll hold you."

Ignoring him, I smooth the sheets on my new examination bed and decide to buy a white paper lantern to replace the ugly fixture that is currently installed above my desk.

"You're not afraid of heights, are you?"

"Not usually," I say. "But unlike you, I haven't had ten glasses of wine!"

"Come on, Sitara. It's a party. You're going to be working here now — you should check it out!"

"Maybe after a few more glasses, I will."

Raising her head, Sitara said, "You must be talking about Jack! You didn't stand in front of *his* camera, did you?"

"I'm afraid so."

Sitara smiled. "Then I'll look for you at his next show."

"I hope not." Sara blushed again and bit her bottom lip.

"I wouldn't worry," Sitara added. "I'm sure the photos he took of you are lovely, and just think," she dug her hands into the pockets of her black cords, "now you won't be so invisible."

Walking silently, absorbed in her own world, Sitara's thoughts turned from Jack to her mother. She tried to imagine what Parvati had been like as a thirty-year-old woman in love. Had she blushed at the mention of her sweetheart's name? Had she laughed at his stories of growing up surrounded by so many other kids? Had she been foolish and blind and drunk with the thought of kissing him? Or was there no room in her business plan for that kind of abandon?

Her parents, she knew, had chosen each other instead of being chosen for each other. And it had been a long courtship, with Raj trying to make enough money to buy their tickets to Canada before they held the ceremony. In the end it was Parvati, as she reminded her daughter whenever she could, who had actually raised the needed funds. *"I worked two accounting jobs,"* she was fond of bragging, *"one in the daytime and one at night." Very noble,* Sitara thought, *but not very romantic.*

"Damn!" Sara tripped on an uneven slab of sidewalk and threw her arms out to catch herself. "I'm always doing that!"

Sitara looked down, expecting to see Sara in clunky high heels, but she saw flat leather sandals instead. Straightening her own spine, she was surprised that Sara was so tall. "Are you alright?"

"Yeah. I'm just so clumsy!"

"Who are you angry at?" Sitara asked, the context of her thoughts still spinning in her head.

"What?"

"Do you often lose your balance?"

"Well," Sara said, "I feel fuzzy a lot — and dizzy."

"Do you have any idea why?"

"I blame it on not being able to see."

"But you're not blind."

"No, but because of my eyes I can't anchor myself with defining objects like walls and floors, and the other straight lines that let me know I'm upright."

Instead of waiting for the traffic light, they turned and headed towards the water. The wind was calm and the harbour was filled with boats.

Sitara smiled. "Physical balance is affected more by the ears than by sight. Even if you closed your eyes, you'd be able to walk along that curb without falling off."

Looking skeptical, Sara asked, "Why did you ask me about being angry?"

"Because…" Sitara stopped herself. "Because I was thinking of my mother. Anger depletes yin energy and allows yang energy to ascend to the head, which causes headaches, dizziness, blurred vision and mental…" Sitara stopped again. "I'm sorry."

"She's dying, isn't she?"

"Yes." Sitara nudged a small stone into the water and watched the ripples expand outward.

"Were you able to help her?"

"I don't know. I feel like all I can do is combat the side effects of the drugs they keep pumping into her. But I'm not even sure that it was working. Acupuncture takes time."

"I don't know much about chemotherapy."

"You don't want to. It's designed to kill all fast-growing cells — that's why a person's hair is always affected. The drugs are indiscriminate. They kill everything, good and bad."

"Can't she decide to opt out of it?"

"I think she's scared and doesn't know what else to do."

"I know that feeling." Sara shivered. Although they were walking briskly, the sun was momentarily blocked by a building. Buttoning her sweater, she asked, "Are you going to go back to her?"

"I don't know." She was struggling to keep up with Sara, who seemed to be in a hurry to get somewhere. She wondered if it was because of flying that Sara seemed so preoccupied with destinations.

"But if it really is that bad, then…" Sara prompted.

"I don't think she wants me there."

"What about your father?"

"He's the one who called me."

With her hands buried deep in her sweater pockets, Sara said, "It's scary to be sick, but I think it's also scary to be left behind."

"I know."

"If it was me, I'd go back to her — to be there with her at the end."

"I just wish I could reach her," Sitara said. "She has such thick skin."

"'No wind, no waves,' you said. Maybe you need to blow her over."

Sitara turned and watched the length of Sara's stride. She didn't walk like someone who tripped on sidewalks — her steps were long and confident. "Thanks for reminding me," she said.

As they approached the entrance of Point Pleasant Park, the cranes, the cargo ships and the stacks of colourful containers made Sitara feel vulnerable. She didn't like being near so much steel and concrete, and the noise and smell from the heavy machinery made her cringe.

As if sensing her discomfort, Sara said, "This is a strange place to put a park!"

Sitara smiled. "You can look at it that way, but the trees and rocks have been here much longer."

"You're right. We've screwed up a lot of things, haven't we?"

"Yeah."

After a long silence, Sara said, "I've just learned that my great aunt has the same condition I have — only she's eighty-three."

"How is she doing?"

"Not great, I guess. The doctor suggested the family buy books with large type and a magnifying glass. Of course, my father mentioned acupuncture since it's already helping me, but they just laughed."

"Not everyone's open to it."

"Doesn't that bother you?"

"No. I don't expect everyone to like raspberry sorbetto either." Sitara winked. "You're not still worried about it, are you? You said yourself that your vision is getting better."

"That's because you're good at what you do."

"You've done a lot of the work too."

Sara stopped walking. "I can't believe I was going to have surgery!"

Scalpels. Sutures. Seeping scars.

Sitara could see the words, like a swarm of bees, targeting Sara's head. To protect her, she grabbed her friend's hand and started to run. "Come on," she said. "We've got to be fast!"

Laughing, they ran through the parking lot, past the junk-food shack, and along the crowded gravel path. When they were far enough away from the shipyard, Sitara led them to a sheltered slope where they threw themselves on the grass.

"Did you see that woman with the snarly dog?" she asked.

"No." Sara was still out of breath. "All I could see was a blur of scenery and your hair streaming like a horse's mane behind you. Was she scary?"

"She had a face full of indignation, as if the path was reserved for one kind of traffic only. It's amazing how some people start to look like their dogs!"

Sara thumped the ground in time with her waves of giggles, as Sitara tried to imitate the woman's, and then the spotted dog's expression.

Sitara couldn't remember the last time she'd watched someone laugh so hard. It was one of the acts of abandon she loved. Sara kept trying to say something, but the words wouldn't come out. Finally, she sat up and squeezed her cheeks flat with her hands to keep from smiling. As she caught her breath, she massaged her aching facial muscles.

"If I was a photographer," Sitara said, "this is what I'd take pictures of."

Reaching into her canvas shoulder bag, Sara pulled out a book of photographs and handed it to Sitara. "None of them are recent," she said, "but they'll give you an idea of what I do — or at least, what I used to do."

"What do you mean, *used* to do?"

"My ideas are changing."

Sitara sat up and flipped open the cover. There was an impressive photo of an ornate mosque.

"Turkey," Sara said, "a few years ago."

Sitara traced the outline of the minarets with her finger before she turned the page. On the next spread, there were two shots of stone ruins, both taken at sunset, with long shadows and vibrant skies. "Turkey too?" she asked.

"The first one, yes. The other is Greece."

"Any of India?"

"Not in this collection, no."

"Where is this?" She was looking at a crisp blue sky, clear water and a white sand beach. "It almost doesn't look real."

"It's Fiji," Sara said, "and sometimes I wonder why I didn't stay there!"

"Does the whole island look like that, or is there a sign for foreign photographers that reads, 'this way to the picturesque beach'?"

Sara smiled. "I don't know. I didn't have much time to explore."

"Let me guess, you met someone on the beach!" Sara kept her lips sealed while Sitara flipped the page. "I'd like to go there!" She was looking at a photo of rugged green hills with mist in the foreground and a crumbling castle in the upper left.

"Scotland," Sara said.

"I might have guessed."

"The beer was good too. Dark and thick."

Sitara sighed. The accompanying photo was of an urban square at night. "I bet you tried this pub," she teased, pointing at a fluorescent sign in one of the windows.

"In Glasgow, they're on every street corner, and unfortunately rather hard to avoid."

"Sounds unfortunate to me!"

Sara laughed. "It's one the hardships of the job."

"You miss it, don't you?"

"Yeah, in some ways I do."

"Do you think you'll go back?"

"I don't know. I've been working around here a little — taking advertising shots mostly. Not really exciting stuff. And I'm doing a wedding for Jack in a few weeks because he's double-booked."

"You'd miss him if you were on the road."

"Yeah."

Sitara looked down again at the photo album open on her lap. "These are beautiful photos, Sara. Flawless, in fact, except for one thing."

"They lack soul," Sara said. "I know."

"What I think they lack is *you*."

Hesitantly, Sara reached into her bag and pulled out a large, brown envelope. She played with the flap for a few seconds before she slid out a stack of photos. "Here are some of the ones I've taken since I met Jack."

"Wow," Sitara said. "These don't look like Jack's."

"No, we have different styles. But he did remind me to stick my camera in people's noses again. For so long, I've been too removed from my subjects. I'm relearning how to look deeply."

"What are you working on now?"

"Nothing specific yet. I'm just experimenting."

"Well, call me when it's time for the gallery opening," Sitara said. "I love cheap wine, and if the photographs are anything like these, I might have to buy a few!"

chapter 20

Standing with her feet planted firmly on the wooden floor, just as Sitara had shown her, Sara rotated in and out of the sun. Although she tried to focus her mind, her thoughts changed quickly, like an overexcited slide show.

click
She wants to experiment more with black and white.

click
If Kyle calls again she will scream.

click
Her bananas are going bad fast.

click
She will make pasta with red peppers and olive oil for dinner.

click
In Sitara's office, it is much easier to feel calm.

Opening her eyes, she could see a knot of fruit flies swarming above the kitchen counter. Sighing, she turned her back. She had no idea how to get rid of them.

Eager to escape her apartment, she grabbed her camera bag and a handful of cash. With a combination of words and images echoing in her head, she bought three rolls of black and white film and a bottle of grapefruit juice. Then, after taking a few steps along a shady side street, she knelt down and loaded her camera.

click
The curved petals of a flower against the sharp crosses of painted lattice at the foot of a wooden porch.

click
A camera bag and a bottle of juice.

click
A street of tall trees, their trunks like telephone poles, betraying human involvement.

Standing, Sara decided to move on. With her camera hanging around her neck, her extra films safely stowed, and her grapefruit juice at her lips, she felt like she was on assignment again. Only this time, she could enjoy the blissful, clear-headed sense of purpose that she gained from an organized shoot, without any of the editorial constraints.

Although Sara's relationship with her editor had always been amicable, it was, by nature, a power struggle. With her youthful sophistication, Sara had a fresh eye for the old cities of the world, and with her vehemently denied rural upbringing, she had an intuitive flair for the otherwise tired scenes of life in the country. Often, especially in the beginning, Joyce had argued that she was too inventive for the magazine's middle-aged readership. So, as the years went by, Sara learned to photograph creative variations of the expected — original, but not too wild.

Now, without commercially imposed barriers, she wanted to rediscover what, for so long, had been suppressed. After dropping her empty bottle into a recycling bin, she held her camera to her right eye and surveyed the street frame by frame as she walked. Smiling, she remembered how as a child her father had teased her about being a spy.

click
A boy on a skateboard uses both hands to hold up his pants.

Growing up, she had enjoyed being a voyeur but, unlike Jack, her awareness of modesty and discretion had sprouted with her hormones and blossomed with her magazine job.

click
Abandoned on the sidewalk, a rusted tricycle rests on its seat and handlebars.

Changing lenses, Sara got closer.

click
The spokes of a small tire, chipped by flying stones.

click
The name "Alex" written with a thick black marker on the seat.

As she took the photos, she was thinking about freedom. Her first bicycle had been a two-wheeler with a banana seat, a plastic basket and brightly coloured streamers dangling from the handlebars. For one whole summer she rode up and down the sidewalk in front of her house, laboriously turning the bike around at the imposed boundaries of her route. But by the end of the second summer, she had grown tired of her fifty-foot cage and was eager to break free. One afternoon, with the sun pounding down on her skin, she rode past her usual turning point into a stretch of deep shade. Then, with one simple turn of a corner, she escaped her family's hold and developed her taste for travel. Even now, she remembered the heavy thumping in her chest, the tremble in her legs as she pedalled, and the weightless, dizzy feeling that filled her head.

As she waited to cross the street, she could hear children laughing and screaming. Although her instinct was to keep walking, she followed the voices instead. Partially hidden by the chain link fence, she lifted her camera to her eye.

click
A dozen kids in motion.

Without thinking, she switched lenses again and stood on her toes to get a clearer view. Using the top of the fence to steady her hand, she focused on a small group of kids.

click
Two boys trying to climb up the bottom of a playground slide.

As one of the boys turned and starting running towards her, she sank to the ground, keeping her camera trained on him.

click
A small boy with a metal fence obscuring his face.

Frustrated, Sara stood up and looked for a gate.

On the inside, as she scanned the faces of the supervising adults, she almost backed away. Even after years of photographing sacred monuments, large cathedrals and closely guarded government buildings, she was intimidated by the grave expressions of authority. Only after catching the eye of a young girl did she relax.

click
A girl with braids shows a missing tooth.

Moving from the shady grass of the entrance to the hot sand of the playground, Sara knelt at the bottom of the slide. One of the boys was still climbing. Positioning herself as low as she could, she pointed her camera towards the sky.

click
A boy scaling a mountain of steel.

Curious about the view from the top, she walked around and climbed the ladder.

click
Two gripping hands followed by a very determined mouth.

Turning to her right, she noticed the swings. As she tried to decide what to focus on, the little boy made it to the top of the slide.

"Watch this!" he said, as he flipped onto his stomach and let go of the sides.

click
Feet, legs, torso.

click
The sole of a white running shoe.

click
Arms raised in victory.

Smiling, Sara climbed down from the slide.

"Now, watch this!" the boy called, but she was already on her way to the swings.

Positioning herself at the mid-point of the triangular cross-braces, she dug herself into the sand and waited for a young girl to look her way, but with hands tight-fisted on the chains, the girl was in her own zone of power and speed. Sara remembered the duality of feelings — the thrill of going forward and the stomach-flopping ache of going back. Raising her camera to her eye, she snapped a trio of images, one in each position: forward, centre, back.

Wanting to experience the sensations first-hand, she squeezed her hips into the next available swing. Walking backwards with the chains in her hands, she gave herself a strong push-off and then extended her legs as she swished forward. Careful not to drag her feet on the ground, she worked hard to gain height. Then, fascinated by the accentuated blur, she wrapped her arms around the chains and used her hands to control her camera.

click
The sky.

click
Her legs.

click
The sandy ground.

In the middle of her back and forthness, she caught glimpses of a small girl bent over her camera bag. Allowing herself to slow down, she eyed the girl carefully.

"Is this yours?" the girl asked.

"Yes."

Squatting beside it, she was poking her fingers into each of the compartments. "What's it for?"

"To protect my cameras."

"Oh." The girl took her fingers away. "What's your name?" she asked.

"Sara."

The girl giggled. "My name is Terra, and I have a cousin named Clara."

Sara smiled, wishing she could think of something else that rhymed, but she couldn't. "Do you want me to push you on a swing?" she asked.

"No. I like the monkey bars."

"Where are they?"

"Over there!" Terra pointed. "You could come and take a picture of me!"

"Alright."

Sara got off the swing and lifted her camera bag out of the sand, just as Terra grabbed her hand and started running.

"Come on," she said. "Come on!"

When they got to the nearest ladder, Terra hoisted herself onto the second rung and then turned back to make sure that Sara was still watching.

click
The anxious eyes of a seven-year-old.

"Not yet," she said. "I haven't done anything!"

"You tell me when you're ready, and I'll take another one."

As the girl climbed quickly upwards, Sara moved to the centre of the structure, hoping to capture her face. Leaning against the metal bars, she waited for Terra's signal.

"I'm ready!" She swivelled her head around until she located Sara's camera. "Watch this."

With her legs folded over one of the rungs, she flipped upside down and dangled above the ground.

click

Inverted, a girl lets one arm hang free while the other keeps a pair of red sunglasses plastered to her head.

"Did you get it?" she asked, after she pulled herself up and slid her sunglasses back over her eyes. "I can do it again."

"Yep, I got it. Why don't you show me what else you can do."

"Okay," she said, "but you should move over there."

Looking up as she walked, Sara was fascinated by the geometry of the coloured bars against the smooth lake of the sky. Like a skeletal umbrella, the structure offered comfort without providing any real protection. Setting her camera for a long exposure, she followed one of the lines as it curved down to the ground.

"Look what I can do!" Terra called from where she was perched on top of the bars, her arms outstretched wide.

Glancing up, Sara wondered how the girl was able to balance. *Maybe gravity doesn't apply to kids,* she thought, as she manoeuvred into a better position.

click

With a cheeky grin, a young girl poses for the camera.

"Excellent," Sara called up to her. "That was a good one."

Already on the move, Terra said, "Wait, I have one more!"

Lying down in the sand, Sara watched the girl from below. Inspired by the intensity of the sun, she ignored her light meter and opened the aperture wide. Then she waited until Terra was right above her.

click
Washed out, an angel hangs upside down.

Drenched with sweat and sun, Sara returned to her apartment. The fruit flies were still clinging to the overripe bananas and, keeping the bowl at arm's length, she placed it outside and closed the door. Smacking a few stragglers between the palms of her hands, she decided to call Jack. She felt like cooking him dinner.

After three rings, she left a message on his answering machine. "I just bought groceries. Come over if you're hungry and feel like eating my cooking. Or come over anyway, if you want. I'm just stepping into the shower."

She locked the front door and brought the phone with her into the bathroom. Feeling decadent, she started to run water for a bath. With her shirt unbuttoned and her cargo pants on the floor, she leaned over the sink to look at her eyes in the mirror. There were lines in the irises she'd never observed before, like tiny roadways mapping the intricacies of everything she'd seen. As she pulled at her skin to get a better view, she was startled by the shiny reflection of her own finger. Looking carefully, she noticed for the first time that she could see her whole face reflected in her eye.

Shutting off the tap just before the tub overflowed, she pulled a clean towel from the stack behind the door and stepped into the water. Swishing the melon-scented bubbles from side to side, she let the hot water penetrate her skin.

When the phone rang, she dried her hands before answering it.

"Hello," she said. "Are you coming?"

"What do you mean? Coming where?"

Quickly, she sat up, creating a backlash in the tub. "Oh, Kyle. I didn't know it was you. I… I was expecting someone else."

"I hope you're not disappointed."

"No." She waited while he breathed into the phone.

"So, ah, what are you doing tonight? I hear there are some good bands in town."

"I have other plans."

"Well, if not tonight, then what about —"

"Kyle, please stop calling me! I haven't changed my mind."

"I know, but I thought maybe —"

"Why don't you call Lauren?"

"Why?"

"Well, you seem to be hanging out with her!"

"No, I'm not. She's in my riding group, and I guess she's been over a few times with the guys… Come on, Sara, we can all go out together."

"No! It's over, Kyle. Good night."

Dropping the phone to the floor, she sank back into the tub. The water that had felt luxurious before, now seemed pointless and vulgar. After dumping some shampoo on her hair, she slid down to rinse it off. With her eyes closed and her ears underwater, the image of Kyle pounded through her head.

click
His eager face cloned onto the bodies of a hundred uniformed men — each armed with an automatic camera.

click
A hundred deafening clicks bombard her.

click
*Her clothes, flimsy and one-dimensional as a paper doll's, fall
to the ground when she tries to cover her ears.*

click
Naked, she lies there with her mouth contorted into a scream.

Sitting up, she pulled the plug and let the water drain.

After getting dressed with loud music on and her bedroom
door pushed closed, she called Jack again and left another message on his machine. "I'm coming over. I have a bunch of food
and some films I want to develop. See you soon."

Covering herself in a hooded black sweater, even though
the evening was warm, she waited by the door for her cab to
arrive. Then, with her bags of groceries piled beside her, she
stroked the smooth skin of a red pepper and watched the tick-
ing meter as they got caught at every traffic light along the way.

When Jack didn't answer his door, she tried the handle.

"Hello? Hello? Jack, are you here?"

"Sara?" His muffled voice floated down the stairs. "I'm in
the darkroom. Make yourself at home."

Leaving her bags in the hallway, she ran up the stairs and
pressed her face against the door. "I tried to call," she said. "I
brought food for dinner. Can I use your kitchen?"

"I'm doing some enlargements, and I might be about an
hour, but go ahead. I hope you can hold your pee that long!"

"It's my nose I'm worried about!"

He laughed. "Your cooking should fix that. I'll be there
when I can."

"Okay."

When she was halfway down the stairs, he yelled, "Help yourself to the wine on the counter."

Taking her groceries to the kitchen, she smiled at the piles of photos spread out on his square table. Unable to restrain her curiosity, she poured herself a glass of red wine and sat down in the chair with the best light.

On top, there were two envelopes with their prints spilling out. She recognized them from their day of developing. Some were of her, posing with a pillow in the glow of his living room, and the others were of dairy cows and the farmer who tended them. She studied the way he had cropped the prints, impressed by the expressiveness of his eye.

Lifting the lid off a brown and white shoebox, she pulled out some negatives that were obviously from Christmas — a family around the tree, sitting at the dining room table, lounging by the fire. There were no close-ups and Sara couldn't tell who any of the people were. She put the family aside and kept looking. Next, she found some strips of a naked man. There were shots of legs, chest, arms and feet, but no head — no face to identify the dissembled limbs. The man was attractive and well built but, after careful examination, she decided it wasn't Jack. Hearing a noise from upstairs, she buried the unknown man back in the box, but Jack did not emerge.

Confident that he was still in the darkroom, she dug further into his archives. The next batch she pulled out was, like most of his others, unmarked — no date, no location, no coded initials. She wondered how he remembered it all. She had tried at first, but after confusing Pakistan with Afghanistan, and a beach in the Caribbean with one in Australia, she had learned to keep methodical notes.

Squinting, she discovered rows and rows of women — some in fields in the afternoon light, some in bathing suits fresh from the water, some with children on their laps or grabbing at their ankles. She stared at their tiny inverted faces trying to guess who they were and how well they had known Jack.

Picking up a magnifying viewer to lessen the strain on her eyes, she fed one of the strips into the light. The woman she saw was stunning. With her head bent forward and her hands gripping a trowel and spade, she was on her knees in a flower garden. By the angle, she could tell that Jack had been standing — possibly on a stool. In another shot, the woman was laughing as she held her tools out to the camera. With her mouth open, and her eyes visible, Sara could see that she was flirting with the camera, the way Jack flirted with distance and light. *With or without their clothes on,* she thought, *his camera exposes people, makes them beautiful. Makes them equal.* The woman, Sara guessed, was in her late sixties, although Jack had photographed her as if she was a young girl. Even now, the playful tension between subject and photographer made Sara feel giddy.

"I don't smell anything yet!" Jack called to her as he came down the stairs.

Standing up quickly, Sara grabbed another glass and filled it with wine. "I got a little distracted," she said.

Jack smiled and accepted the wine. "See anyone you know?"

"Other than me, no."

"Oh good." He raised his glass to prepare a toast. "To dinner — whatever it might be!"

After they drank she said, "Pasta with fiery red pepper sauce."

"Sounds good to me. Can I help?"

"Do you want to chop?"

"I'd rather kiss," he said, sliding in behind her as she pulled an onion and a few cloves of garlic from her bag. Burying his face in the melon scent of her hair, he added, "But I'm willing to chop."

"Do you have olive oil?" she asked.

"Above the stove. There's a bottle of extra-virgin, and the tall one is infused with basil."

Sara laughed. "Basil would be good. Actually, I should go get my book." From the back of her camera bag, she retrieved a small Italian cookbook. "I stole this from my dad," she said, "because of the photographs."

Looking over her shoulder, Jack nodded. "Not bad. A little contrived, maybe, but the colour's good."

"There are others in the book that are better." She put a pot of water on the stove to boil. "What were you developing?"

"A roll from a few months ago — ice formations, mostly."

"Today, I shot three rolls of black and white."

"Where?"

"In a playground. I was going to cross the street, but a boy on a slide caught my eye."

"I didn't realize you liked them so young," Jack teased.

"Hey!" She flicked water at him as she washed the peppers in the sink. "I got totally absorbed following a little girl around, trying to see the world from her point of view."

"You had fun, didn't you?"

"Yeah. It's been a long time since I've played in the sand, and for the first time in years, I think I was actually improvising!"

"And that felt good?"

"Yeah," she said, slapping her hand with a wooden spoon. "In fact," she walked over and snapped the cookbook closed, "I'm not going to use that."

When Sara woke up, it was already eleven o'clock. She rolled over and looked at Jack. His long brown hair was splayed out around him and his left arm lay strategically over his eyes. He quivered a little when she kissed his bare shoulder, but showed no other signs of movement.

Feeling thirsty, she looked around the room for a robe or something cozy of Jack's to wear. Settling for her own skirt and tank top, she shuffled down the stairs.

In the kitchen, she poured herself a glass of filtered water and stood by the back door watching two birds hop around on the long, unmowed lawn. Turning back to the room, she saw Jack's photo boxes stacked in a pyramid against the wall. There was an image of a woman hanging laundry, with a white sheet billowing as much as her hair, that Sara wanted to see again.

Bringing several brown envelopes to the table with her, she sat down, untucked the flap of the first one, and let the contents spill out. Flipping through the collection, she realized they were all wedding proofs — formal, functional and taken by a tired eye. She had seen other wedding portraits of Jack's that were more inspired, but looking closely at the anxious, worn-out couple, she thought, *We can only work with what we're given.*

In another envelope there were colour prints of three girls, obviously sisters, playing with buckets and shovels on a beach. Sara smiled. In one shot, she could see the photographer's shadow.

After taking a long drink of water she picked up a third envelope, still hoping to find the woman with a clothesline that had burned itself into her memory. Untucking the flap, she reached in and pulled out a stack of black and white photos. What she saw took her a moment to calculate.

Sitara with a swollen belly.

Sitara with a smaller swollen belly.

Sitara with barely a hint of a swollen belly.

Fanning the photos out on the table, she saw the entire progression of Sitara's pregnancy, photographed side-on under a revealing but moody light. Shifting her eyes from belly to face, Sara guessed that the photos were at least ten years old.

Turning away from the uncertainty raised by the images, Sara drained the rest of her water. As she heard Jack's footsteps on the stairs, she made no attempt to return the photos to their envelope. Instead, she tried to pluck a question from the chaotic orchard ripening in her brain.

"Good morning," Jack said, as he entered the kitchen. "You left an empty hole in my bed." Walking over to kiss her, he looked down and saw what she was staring at.

"Do you want to explain this?" she said.

"Why should I?"

"Because I'm asking you to."

"Well, they're my photos. I didn't invite you to look at them, and to be honest, I'm pissed off that you're invading my privacy." He took the photos, slid them back into their envelope, and returned them to the stack by the wall.

"How come you've never mentioned this before?"

"There's nothing to say."

"Those photos would suggest otherwise."

"Sara, photos don't tell the whole story. You of all people should know that!"

"Then perhaps you could enlighten me about the parts that are missing."

"I can't do that."

"Can't or won't?"

"What difference does it make? They're my photos and I shouldn't have to explain them to you."

Standing up, Sara said, "I have to go."

"I thought you had films you wanted to develop."

Picking up her camera bag, she swept past him and made her way to the front door. "Change of plans," she said. "Goodbye."

chapter 21

As Sitara moved down the long hallway of her parents' apartment building, she reminded herself that patience was the invisible mortar that would hold everything together, if she could just remember to use it. Knowing that Parvati was as run-down as the plastered walls and patterned carpet around her, she was arriving with a well-stocked repair kit including herbs, needles and an open mind. In a park a few blocks away, she had meditated for an hour before beginning the last leg of her journey. Breathing deeply, she could still feel the calmness floating through her veins.

When she knocked on the door, Raj answered it quickly.

"Welcome home, Sitara." He opened his arms and embraced her. "Now that you are here, I must go."

As he fumbled with his wallet, she asked, "Where are you going?"

"To buy flour and tea."

"Bapa, I can go."

"No. You stay with Parvati. I need some air. I do not get out as often as I used to." He smiled. "Do you need something else?"

"I'm fine, thanks."

"Okay." With his wallet in one hand and a cotton grocery bag in the other, he started down the hall.

As she turned around, Sitara realized the apartment was awkwardly quiet without him. Wheeling her suitcase into a corner, she paused before she pushed open Parvati's door. There was a bell hanging from the handle that she had never seen before. Assuming that it was designed to signal her mother's departure rather than a visitor's arrival, she smiled, thinking that both warnings were fair.

"Hello Parvati," she said, as she entered the dark, rank room.

Parvati moaned. "I don't want whatever it is you have."

"I have brought nothing," she said, "and I ask for nothing in return. I just want to sit with you." Cleaning off a chrome and vinyl chair, Sitara sat down near the foot of the bed, deciding not to speak until she was spoken to.

Parvati closed her eyes but did not turn away.

There were bottles and cups on a table by the bedside, and a stack of magazines with their pages all ripped apart. On the wall above her mother's head, there was a map of the world with a pencil line from India to Canada that Sitara had drawn when she was ten. Standing on her pillow with her knees pressed against the ridges of the headboard, she had spent hours tracing the shape of the oceans that separated the stories of her parents' childhoods from her own. *"You are a lucky girl to grow up here,"* her mother had often told her. But during those long days of map tracing, she didn't feel lucky.

"Some water," Parvati said, raising her arm a little to point at the table.

Sitara poured half a glass and handed it to her mother. "Would you like to sit up?" she asked.

"No." Parvati patted the blankets until she found a straw.

Sitting down again, Sitara watched her mother sip water in slow, short pulls. When she had drained the glass, she let it roll onto the bed. Then, flicking the straw dry with her fingernail, she let it fall in the same direction as the glass.

With her hands folded in her lap, Sitara made no attempt to interfere. Looking down, she noticed an ink stain on the carpet that hadn't faded with cursing or time. She remembered the day the pen had burst in her hands and the explosive night that followed, with Parvati yelling, *"Scrub!"* and Raj trying to rearrange the furniture. There were many such blots on her mind — more, she guessed, than were ever on the carpet.

"Who is running your clinic while you are away?" Parvati asked, after carefully coating her lips with moisture from her tongue.

"No one. My clinic is closed."

"How can you make money if it is closed?"

"I can't."

"Have you finished your taxes? It's important that you submit them on time."

"It's June now. Tax time is over."

"June? Raj said it was April."

Watching her mother lick her lips again, she asked, "Would you like something for those?"

"No. I am too old for that kind of nonsense. I have no boy's cheeks to smudge."

"I don't mean lipstick. What I have is just beeswax mixed with peppermint oil."

"Maybe. But just a little."

Reaching into her bag, Sitara pulled out a small tinted glass jar. Then, after unscrewing the lid, she handed it to Parvati. As she watched her mother dip her middle finger into the cream-coloured wax, she felt like a four-year-old discovering the mysteries of being a woman.

Standing on a stool at the bathroom sink, I hold a lipstick in my right hand. Staring at my open mouth in the mirror, I try to coat my lips like Parvati does. It's hard to keep my hand steady and I keep drawing outside the lines.

"Sitara, are you okay?" Bapa asks through the closed door.

"Yes," I say. But I am mad because what takes Parvati only a few seconds might take me all day.

After Parvati finished smearing her lower lip, she handed the jar back to Sitara. "Aren't you going to poke me today?" she asked. "Since your business is closed, maybe you need a patient."

Surprised, Sitara looked into her mother's eyes. "I will if you want me to, but I wasn't sure if you liked it."

"Does that matter?" Parvati said. "You need to keep working so your muscles don't go soft."

"Alright, I'll get my needles after lunch."

"I'm not hungry. I don't want to eat."

"Perhaps not, but I do. I've been up for a long time, and the food on the plane wasn't great."

Returning to the chair, Sitara crossed her legs and re-experienced the nondescript mush the airline claimed was vegan cuisine. In her rush to get to the airport, she had forgotten the bag of snacks she had packed for herself.

"Where is Raj?" Parvati asked.

"He went for a walk."

"You let him go?"

"Yes. The exercise will be good for him."

Parvati moaned. "I hope he doesn't get lost."

"Why would he? The streets haven't changed in thirty years."

"But he has changed. He forgets things. I'm always having to remind him."

"He was going to the corner for tea and flour," she said, trying to reassure her mother. "He'll be back soon."

"Yes," Parvati said, wincing at a sharp pain. "All of the family is coming back — only yours was a very long trip to the store."

When Raj returned from his walk, Parvati was asleep and Sitara was in the living room skimming through a stack of magazines.

"Those are ready to be torn up," Raj said, as he closed the door. "For Parvati. A whole magazine is too heavy for her to hold."

"Did you enjoy your walk?"

"Yes, very much." He placed his grocery bag on the telephone table and, without bending down, exchanged his shoes for his black and red checkered slippers. "How is Parvati?" he asked.

"Sleeping," Sitara said. "Can I help you put those things away?"

"No, no." Raj took the bag into the kitchen and set it on the counter.

Following after him, Sitara remembered that he never put food on the floor. "Is it warm out?" she asked. "It was lovely this morning."

"Warm for you maybe, but still cold for me. Look what I have," he said, holding a plastic sandwich bag in each hand. "Half a sub for you and half a sub for me."

"Thanks, Bapa. What's on it?"

"Vegetables and a lot of hot peppers." His whole face curved into a grin. "No matter how many he puts on, I always ask for more."

Sitara smiled. It was the only time Raj liked to start fires. In their family, he was usually the one who put them out.

"Do you have garlic?" she asked. "I feel like I could use a dose."

"Up there." He pointed. "And fresh ginger too."

Opening the cupboard, Sitara saw two shelves full of bottles and jars. "Bapa," she asked, "have you always kept the spices here?"

"For a long time, yes. There is ginger and garlic in the basket."

Before lifting the basket down, Sitara said, "But I thought the spice cupboard used to be down there."

"When you were a girl, yes. But it was too damp. I always told Parvati spices belong where it is dry. Sitara, there is a cutting board behind the toaster," he said. "You chop. I must go wash."

As soon as she was alone, Sitara hoisted herself onto the counter. Quickly, sorting through the spices, she looked for cardamom. When she found the short, round jar, she shook it, throwing the tiny pods into orbit. After they settled, she removed the lid and poured a few into the palm of her hand. Then, climbing down from the counter, she opened the lower cupboard door.

It was filled with stacks of cooking pots and plastic containers. Leaning forward, she could smell mildew and cleaning supplies, but not even a trace of spice.

After closing the door, she sat with her back against the greasy fibreboard and squished a pod of cardamom between the fingers of her right hand. The fragrance sang a lullaby around her.

"Bapa, are you here? Bapa?" Using Parvati's key, Sitara unlocked the apartment door. It was noon and she had spent the morning meditating and walking, looking for a way of combining the past and present into a paste she could digest. Dropping her patchwork shoulder bag, she toured the apartment, calling to her father softly. "Good morning, Bapa. I'm here. Bapa?" She hadn't intended to arrive so late.

When she had looked everywhere else, she peeked through the half-open door to Parvati's room and saw Raj doubled over, trying to help her sit up. As he lifted her a few inches at a time, he whispered to her, telling her the pain would only last a minute and that she'd be more comfortable when he was done. As Sitara watched silently from the doorway, Parvati kept her eyes trained on her husband, smiling at him between the stabs of pain.

"Okay," she said. "I can finish now." As he backed away, she planted her arms on the bed and pulled her hips towards the pillows he had stacked against the headboard.

"There," he said, smoothing the blankets around her. "Now you are ready for tea. I will come right back."

Ducking into the hallway, Sitara walked quickly back to the living room. When Raj came out, she was opening the door to the balcony. "Good morning, Bapa," she said.

"Sitara. I did not hear you come in."

"I thought you might be sleeping, so I tried not to make a sound."

"I am making tea. Would you like to have some?"

"Sure," she said. "Bapa, are you alright?" He was shaking and the moons around his eyes were dark.

"Yes. Fine. But Parvati…" His gaze dropped to the floor as his voice trailed off. "She can no longer get out of bed. How will I bathe her, or help her when she needs to pee? She has no will, Sitara, and I have no strength in my back." Raj covered his mouth with his hand as if he'd already said enough. Then he used it to rub his eyes and wipe his brow. "I must make tea," he said.

"Sit down, Bapa. I'll make it."

Without a word, Raj sank into his well-worn place on the sofa, let his head drop back and closed his eyes. Sitara went into the kitchen and put tap water in the kettle, shrinking away from the smell of chlorine. She kept forgetting to buy a filter.

In the living room, she sat down next to her father and took his left hand in hers. Starting at the base of his fingers, she massaged fresh blood into each of his tired muscles.

"She puts on a brave face," he said, "especially when you are here. But I have seen her when she thinks no one is watching. There is no life left in her eyes."

Sitara squeezed her father's hand, and then reached across his lap for the other one. "I think you're doing a good job of making her comfortable," she said.

"It is hard, Sitara. She is in too much pain."

"I will try to help her, Bapa, after we have tea."

"Forgive her," he said, pulling his hand away, "so that when she dies she will be free."

The kettle was boiling, and Sitara went into the kitchen. Filling the teapot, she watched as the hot water turned into steam.

Raj was stepping out of the bathroom, with a mist of woody cologne following him, when Sitara said, "Bapa, I'm going to check out of my hotel and stay here instead." She could feel the warmth emanating from his bath-soaked skin. "I want to be closer — in case Parvati needs me."

"Thank you, beti." He opened the door to the balcony to hang up his damp towel.

"I'm just going to get my things — I'll be half an hour at the most."

"Very good."

On the street, she let her facial muscles fall. She'd been pretending for hours — they both had — knowing that Parvati was getting worse. She walked a little faster, imagining Raj with a bedpan trying to help his wife.

Stopping at a phone booth, she decided to make a call — collect.

"Hello?"

"I'm sorry to call you like this. I'm on a payphone. Can you hear me?"

"Yeah, the volume's fine, but you sound strange."

"Sara, if I buy you a ticket, will you come and take photographs of my mother?"

"Now?"

"Soon. Tomorrow or the next day. She's slipping away."

"I don't know. I'm… I'm feeling awkward."

Sitara rubbed her stomach, wishing she hadn't asked. "I know it's a long way for you to come and not a lot of notice, but —"

"It's not that."

"Then what?"

"I'm feeling awkward about you and Jack."

Sitara pressed the receiver closer to her ear and used her finger to block the street noise from entering the other one. "I don't understand."

"I was looking at some old photos at his place the other night, and I found a whole collection… of you."

"And?"

"I've asked him about them, but he won't tell me anything."

"What do you want me to say?"

"Well, a little explanation might be helpful."

"It seems to me they're pretty self-explanatory." Sitara let her head fall back against the glass of the phone booth. "The swollen belly should give it away."

Pulling on the emergency brake, he leaves the car running for warmth. In the dark shadows of the tree-lined street, he leans over to kiss me. I let his lips touch mine, but I don't open my mouth. I dread parked cars, having spent far too many hours in them waiting, forgotten, as a child. He tries to part my lips with his tongue. I sink as far as I can into the cushioned seat, but cannot get away. He doesn't understand my discomfort, as I have never rejected him before. I reach for the door and fumble with the handle. Somehow I have locked myself in. Pulling away, he stares at me blankly. I can see his eyes shining in the mottled light. He searches my face for answers I do not have. I don't know why he suddenly repulses me, I just know he does.

"Tara, please," he says. But I shake my head and he takes me home.

"Don't you think it's reasonable of me to want to know?" Sara asked.

"It was a long time ago."

"Still…"

Sitara shuffled her feet on the concrete floor of the phone booth, and waited while a woman and her child walked by. "Jack and I were never lovers, Sara. Over the years, I've fixed his back a few times, and I always try to make it to his shows. But there's nothing to be jealous of."

"So, it wasn't his baby?"

"No," Sitara said.

He is pale – the colour of ghee, the colour of my enamel bath-tub. His moustache moves when he talks, making me want to laugh. His beard scratches me, and my skin suffers from the bris-tle of his attention. And yet when he kisses me, I kiss him back. He has unbuttoned the top of his shirt and I see a few greying hairs, not unlike my father's. He runs his hands down my spine and lets them fan out over my hips. I am eighteen, although he thinks I am twenty. I find comfort in the two-year lie.

"Tara," he says — for I have dropped the Si from my name, "let me buy you dinner. I'll take you to the Palace."

I stare at him blankly before I nod. I have spent all day in the kitchen making fettuccini and cream sauce — badly. But as usual he prefers rice and curry and takes me to a restaurant where, no matter what we order, the waiter brings two dishes — mild for the bearded professor and hot for me because of my skin colour. When the young waiter turns his back, we use a spoon to combine the two. I eat with my hands to please my lover, although I prefer to use a fork.

After dinner, he takes me to a small back-alley café. He proudly orders something the menu calls chai, which appears to be nothing more than weak tea with too much milk and sugar and a small dash of cloves. Although I consider it, I don't tell him about cardamom. I bury the memory in my nose and order a strong black Colombian instead. Recently, coffee and I have become good friends.

When I talk, he listens to every fifth or sixth word, but expects me to hear every one of his. He researches and teaches languages, and says that now he wants to study mine. I give him a puzzled look, because mine is a language of spices, silences, and mirrors that deflect the truth.

"Where is the baby now?" Sara asked.

"I don't know. I think the adoptive parents lived in Ontario." Sitara could remember ten vacant birthdays. "It's not something I like to think about."

As he reaches under my blouse, I can no longer contain the thought that has been exploding inside me all day. I push his hand away.

"What's wrong, Tara? You're tense."

"I'm nervous," I tell him, "because my period is late."

"Oh, is that all. I'm sure you've just miscounted," he says. "It will come soon enough."

Undeterred, he pulls my zipper down and tries to slide his hand inside. I make my decision without lifting my eyes to him. I will flee — although it may not be tonight.

"But," Sara said, "I still don't see how Jack fits into all of this."

Sitara sighed. She was worried about being away from her mother. "I decided that I wanted photographs. Or rather, Ruth, my employer, did. She thought that I might someday want a record. So she arranged a food-for-photos barter deal with a young photographer who was always advertising on our board." Sitara poked the phone's coin return flap. "That's how I met Jack… For a few boxes of granola, he agreed to take my picture every four weeks."

"Oh."

"I was pregnant when I arrived in Halifax on the bus, thanks to a university professor I met when I first left home. But I never told him. I left the province without telling anyone." She flicked the coin return flap again and listened to its hollow, metallic sound. "My parents still don't know."

In the sterile hospital room, I have only a moment to hold you. In my arms, you are red and vibrant and your eyes shine. Even though the cord has been cut, there are invisible lines that connect us. You look at me as if you've heard everything, as if you know that we have only these few minutes together. "I'm sorry," I whisper, "that I have to give up so much to start over."

"Are you still there?" Sara asked.

"Yes."

"I'm sorry I asked about all this. I was being stupid — thinking about myself and not about you."

Sitara let out another long sigh. "Don't worry about it. Maybe after this, I'll finally be able to let it go. It's been weighing on me for a long time." She kicked the swinging door with her foot. "So, will you come and take pictures for me or not?"

"Yes," Sara said. "Of course, I will. I'll try to book a flight for the morning."

When Sitara opened the door to her parents' apartment, she saw that Raj's slippers had fallen to the floor at the end of the sofa. Removing the open book that was lying across his chest, she covered him with an old blanket and tucked a small pillow under his head.

"Sitara," he said slowly, "I will move now."

"No, Bapa. Stay where you are. I'm going to read for awhile."

"Is she coming, your friend the photographer?"

"Yes, if she can get a ticket. I will know soon."

"You could have stayed at the hotel, beti. You would have been more comfortable."

"I'm okay here, Bapa. You get some sleep."

By the time she had leaned down to kiss him on the forehead and had switched off the light, he was breathing deeply again, with the gentle hint of a snore.

Slipping into Parvati's room, Sitara curled up on the small, hard chair and watched the motion of her mother's restless dreams.

In the quiet stillness of the apartment, she could hear three distinct sets of lungs.

When Sitara woke up, the room was still a moist fog of darkness. Although she was hungry and her neck was sore from being jammed against the wall, she had no idea what time it was or how long she'd been asleep. As she rolled her head slowly from side to side, she caught Parvati's eye.

"Raj," her mother said. "I want Raj."

Shaking her legs to encourage the blood flow, Sitara

stumbled to her feet and reached for the door. The hallway was bright and full of morning although it had no windows of its own. Stopping in the bathroom, she splashed cold water on her face and then used the roughness of the line-dried towel to stimulate her skin.

"Your friend called this morning," Raj said, as she stretched and yawned her way into the kitchen. "She is on her way now. I told her where we live and which bus to take. I hope she can find her way."

"She's travelled a lot, Bapa. I'm sure she'll be fine."

"She was very nice on the telephone. Very polite."

Sitara smiled. Politeness was important to him. *"Parvati, that is rude,"* she could hear him saying. *"Do not speak in front of your daughter that way, or she will grow up badly."*

"I'm glad you like her," Sitara said. "When will she be here?"

"By two o'clock, I believe. If you are hungry, there is tea and… cinnamon toast." To make her laugh, he wiggled his head in time with the spice's syllables, as he had done when she was a child.

"Thank you, Bapa. I'll have some."

"Did you sleep well?"

"Alright. Parvati is asking for you."

Raj finished the fruit he was eating and hurried down the hallway. "She does not like to wait!" he said.

After pulling two pieces of raisin bread out of the bag, Sitara dropped them into the old four-slice toaster. It took three tries before she convinced the large plastic button to latch. Inhaling the smell of burned crumbs, she took a mug of tea to the window and stared at the busy traffic light below. *If Parvati is stop,* she thought, *and the baby is go, I'm the one lost somewhere in between.* When the toast popped, she burned her fingers spreading it with her father's special mixture of cinnamon and ghee.

"Sitara?"

She jumped. "Yes, Bapa?"

"Parvati needs to use the toilet, but she is too weak to make the trip down the hall."

With a mouthful of bread, Sitara said, "She could use a bedpan."

Raj shifted his weight from foot to foot, but did not move.

"Don't worry, Bapa. I'll go. You can finish my toast."

"Okay." Without looking at her, he sat down.

It was the first time she'd seen her father recoil from any natural function of the body. *"Coming from such a big family,"* he used to boast, *"there is nothing that I have not seen!"*

In her mother's room, she pulled the green bedpan from under the dresser and unwrapped it. "Did the nurse leave this?" she asked.

Parvati turned her head away.

"It might be easier than walking to the bathroom."

Without agreeing or disagreeing, Parvati stayed still while Sitara lifted the blankets and rolled the pink and white nightgown around her waist. Then, with as little movement as possible, Parvati accommodated the bedpan that her daughter slid into place. Turning her back, Sitara ran her hands though the twenty-year-old curtains, dislodging memories and bits of dust. With a series of sneezes, she cleared some of both away.

"I'm done," Parvati said.

Gently, Sitara removed the bedpan and set it by the door. She straightened her mother's nightgown and replaced the blankets over her one by one.

"Do you feel better now?" she asked.

"What is better? There is only worse and worse."

"I could get you some tea or water."

"No," Parvati winced. "If it goes in, it comes out."

"Would you like the TV or a magazine?"

"No, Sitara. Just sit."

Knowing her mother's invitations often sounded like commands, Sitara sat down on the chrome chair and waited. "I'm sorry for fussing," she said.

"You are like my mother, with her medicines and questions and poking, poking, poking." Parvati looked away while a wave of pain hammered her chest.

Sitara gripped the underside of the chair and resisted the urge to stand up.

"She was a healer too, Sitara, with a cure for everything. She was not a professional like you, but still she embarrassed my father with her success — although he should have been proud."

Sitara had never heard Parvati speak fondly of her mother before. Usually, she denounced her for being too traditional and for teaching her daughters old ways. "Did she practise Ayurvedic medicine?" Sitara asked.

"I don't know. She used herbs and spices and was always checking our pulse."

"Did she ever heal you?"

Parvati closed her eyes, and thought before she said, "No. I would never let her. But she saved Raj from malaria when we were first married. We couldn't leave for Canada until he was well."

"How did she feel when you left?"

"We fought about it. She claimed I was throwing away my heritage." Parvati shuddered from another swell of pain. After it passed, she added, "Now, I realize that healing him was her blessing."

Looking at her mother, Sitara saw a mirror of her own watery eyes. "Parvati, I wish that —"

"Call me Ama, Sitara. We have argued long enough."

When Sitara heard the buzzer that signalled Sara's arrival, she was fixing the front of Parvati's veil. For an hour, the two had been struggling with the sari.

Sitara, who had only seen photos of it, was amazed when Parvati asked her to retrieve it from the top of the linen closet where it lay bandaged like a wound in long strips of cotton and plastic. Inside, the delicate silk was folded between sheets of yellowing tissue paper with dried flowers to keep it fresh. Opening it at the foot of her mother's bed, Sitara was silent. The only saris she'd been aware of as a child were the ones sent from India by aunts and sisters, the ones Parvati dismissed as old fashioned and gave to her as toys.

"What will my husband say when he sees how foolish we have been?" Parvati sang out in a voice her daughter almost didn't recognize. The secret of the bridal sari seemed to give her strength.

"He'll want to marry you all over again," Sitara said quietly. "Are you alright?" Wrapping her mother in the vast length of silk had been fatiguing for them both. "I can get you another pillow."

"I'm fine. Now, go. Your friend is here." They could hear Raj greeting Sara at the door.

"You look lovely, Ama."

"Thank you," Parvati said. As her daughter turned and headed for the door, she added, "If there was time, I'd ask for mehndi too."

chapter 22

At the apartment door, Sara paused and prepared her formal greeting. She had met the parents of friends before, but she had never photographed them. On the phone Sitara's voice had been calm and strong, and Sara hoped she could be as graceful.

As she knocked on the flimsy wooden door, she drew comfort from the camera gear that accompanied her. Visualizing the contents of her bags and cases, she let a stream of silent words cross her lips.

"Hello, Sara," Raj said, when he opened the door. "Welcome to my home. I see that my directions were not so bad."

"No," Sara replied, surprised by the depth of his smile. "I had no trouble finding you."

"Come in, please. Are you tired? I can make tea."

"I'm okay, thank you." She set down her small suitcase and lowered the handle.

"Sara. You're here!" Sitara's voice lit up the hallway. "Bapa said you got an early flight. Did they feed you? Do you want some tea?"

"I have already offered," Raj said.

"And I have declined."

"Because you were being polite," Sitara asked, "or because you really don't want any?"

"I'm fine."

"Well then, come and meet my mother." Sitara gestured towards the hallway. As they walked, she pressed her hand into the centre of Sara's back. "I'm so glad you're here," she said.

Following Sitara through a door that was already open, Sara wiped her sweaty hand on the seat of her pants.

"Ama, this is my friend Sara, the photographer," Sitara said.

"Hello," Parvati whispered.

"Hello." Sara hung onto the doorframe while her eyes readjusted to the lack of light. The smell reminded her of motion sickness on an overcrowded bus.

"It's nice to meet you," Parvati said. "Sitara has told me that you are very good."

"She exaggerates because she likes me." Sara smiled.

"Do not underestimate yourself. Think big and you will go far."

"That's what Sitara says too."

"She learned that from me," Parvati said.

Sara looked over at Sitara, who was now standing between the window and the bed with her hands in her pockets and a pleased expression on her face. "It's lucky that wisdom runs in your family," she said. "I won't tell you what runs in mine."

Both Parvati and Sitara smiled.

With a camera bag over each shoulder and a tripod in her arms, Sara was still standing in the doorway. It was a small room, and she was speculating on how to get the distance she required.

"Where do you want to set up?" Sitara asked. "I can move anything you like."

"I think this area will work." She leaned her tripod against the closet door, and watched Sitara move a basket of laundry. As she unzipped one of her bags, Raj came into the room with the flowers she had brought for him.

"Oh Parvati, who is getting married?" he said, when he saw his wife. "I have never seen such a glittering jewel."

"You do not have to lie, Raj. I am not a fool."

"It is not a lie." He turned to Sara. "That is the sari," he explained, "that she wore for our wedding ceremony."

"It's beautiful."

"Yes." Raj smiled. "But it is the woman inside who makes it beautiful." He stood admiring Parvati before he placed the vase of flowers next to her bed. "Now I see what you two were doing in here," he said to his wife and daughter. Facing Sara again, he added, "I have not been allowed in for over an hour."

"Thank you for the flowers," Parvati whispered.

"They are lilies," Raj said.

"They are very nice."

Looking through the lens of her Nikon, Sara saw the glow of an elderly woman draped in turmeric-coloured silk with a border of red and gold embroidery. "Is it possible to open the curtains?" she asked. No matter which aperture setting she tried, the sari's radiance had no effect on her light meter.

"It bothers Parvati's eyes," Raj said. "I could try the over-head bulb."

"Nonsense, open the curtain — or do both. I'll be fine."

Raj switched on the light and Sitara drew the curtains. As sunlight flooded the room, Sara closed her aperture. "That's better. Thanks." Squeezed behind her tripod, with her back pressed into the wall, she smiled at the family breathing around her. "I'd like to try a few, if you're ready," she said.

Parvati nodded.

click
Beneath shrunken cheeks, a proud woman smiles.

click
Lying above layers of blankets, her shrivelled arms lead to wrists filled with bangles.

"Hang on." Sitara stepped in, pulled the blankets to the foot of the bed and smoothed the folds of Parvati's sari.

click
With a patient smile, a mother lets her daughter enhance her beauty.

"Okay," Sitara said, repositioning herself by the window. "I'm finished."

Releasing her camera from the tripod, Sara moved away from the wall. Kneeling carefully on the end of Parvati's bed, she took a series of hand-held portraits.

click
Nose, mouth, eyes.

Waiting while Parvati blinked, Sara noticed that she and Sitara shared the same cinnamon eyes. Returning to her camera bags, she decided to try the Hasselblad.

"I didn't know you had one of those," Sitara said. "It looks like Jack's."

"It is Jack's." She removed the lens cap. "He let me borrow it."

"I have never seen one so big," Raj said.

"It's a medium format camera," Sara explained, "which is good for making enlargements. I was thinking we could try a few frames with all three of you."

Instantly, Raj licked his finger and smoothed his hair. "Tell me where to stand," he said, "or maybe you want me to sit."

"Can you both fit in, one on either side of Parvati?"

As she focused the Hasselblad, Raj and Sitara each perched themselves on the edge of the bed.

click

Two strangers holding court at the bedside of a woman they have never met.

"Could you move a little closer?" Sara asked. "And relax. Parvati is the only one who is smiling."

Together, Raj and Sitara sighed. As Sara suspected, they had both been holding their breath. Inching closer, Sitara held one of Parvati's hands. Following her cue, Raj held the other.

click

A dying matriarch, with a deep yellow veil, brings together the forgiving hands of her family.

"Perhaps one with just mother and daughter," Sara suggested, enjoying the feel of Jack's camera in her hands.

As Raj left the bed, Sitara stretched out her legs to match Parvati's and then looked to Sara for direction. "Any ideas?" she asked.

"I don't know," Sara said. "Maybe —"

Letting her bracelets clank, Parvati raised her right arm, and Sara pressed the shutter.

click

A wrinkled hand reaches for a daughter's strong chin.

Sara shivered, and thought of her mother. "Now just the two of you," she said, gesturing to Sitara's parents.

Raj smiled at his wife. "This is just like on our wedding day," he said, "where I was the envy of all the men."

"On that day you had a flute," Parvati whispered.

"Yes, but I played very badly."

"I remember it another way."

"Parvati, now it is you who lies."

click
A face drenched in empathy smiles at one drenched in pain.

"Parvati is growing tired," Raj said. "That is enough for today." He lifted her hand to his lips and planted a kiss.

Then, while Raj closed the curtains, Sitara unwound the veil from her mother's head and helped her to lie down.

"Thank you," Parvati said, as the blankets were pulled up to her chin.

"Sleep well, Ama."

"Good night."

As Sara finished putting her cameras away, she heard Parvati whisper, "Sitara was right. You are very good."

Letting Parvati's face fill her eyes entirely, Sara mouthed the words, "Goodbye."

In the hallway, Raj wrapped his arm around Sitara's shoulders. "It was good of you to think of the sari," he said.

"It was her idea, Bapa. I didn't know she still had it."

"Yes. 'A bride keeps her sari as long as she is married.' That is what Parvati always told me. Seeing her wear it made me happy. I thought she looked very good for the pictures."

"She did, Bapa, and so did you."

"Flattery will not get you mango kulfi today," he said, grinning. "You are too old for ice cream."

"No, she's not," Sara said from behind them. "I've seen her clean out a bowl of raspberry sorbetto in no time."

"Well," Raj said, "then I will not tell you what is in the freezer!"

Exchanging glances, the two women smiled.

"All this talk of food is making me hungry," Sitara said.

"I will make dinner."

"No Bapa, I can take care of it."

"I am concerned that, besides ice cream, there is not very much in the fridge."

Standing in the living room with her camera gear at her feet, Sara said, "Point me in the direction of a grocery store and I'll take care of that."

"Thanks Sara," Sitara said.

As Sara stood up to clear the plates from the table, Raj asked, "Do you have a place to stay tonight?"

"I don't know, actually, I guess I'll —"

"Don't worry, Bapa, it's all taken care of," Sitara interrupted. "I've booked a room at the place where I stayed before."

"Very good." Raj turned to Sara. "Do you know how to get there?"

"No, but I'm sure Sitara will tell me." With a damp rag, she wiped the table clean.

From the kitchen, Sitara called, "I'll take you. Maybe we can walk there."

"She is always trying to escape to the sidewalk," Raj teased, in a hushed voice. "Just like a puppy."

Smiling, Sara dried the table with a tea towel and then, after pushing the empty chairs in, joined Sitara in the kitchen.

"Let's just leave the dishes," Sitara said. "I'll do them when I get back." She eyed Raj to make sure he understood.

"I will not touch them," he said.

"Alright, we'll go as soon as I check on Parvati."

After she disappeared down the hall, Raj motioned for Sara to follow him to the window. "It started blooming the day she arrived," he said, fingering the pot of a dark purple violet. "And now there is no end of blossoms in sight."

"My father likes plants too," she told him.

"Does he have south or west?" Raj asked.

"Both," Sara said. "And an outside garden as well."

Raj raised his eyebrows. "I am sure it makes him very happy. It is rewarding for old men like us to watch things grow."

Sara wanted to say, *When you come to Nova Scotia next time, I'll bring you to meet my father,* but she bit her tongue. Instead, she said, "He likes his herbs the best, and his cherry tree."

"I'm ready," Sitara said, as she came down the hall. "Parvati seems okay. At least she's sleeping."

"I'm ready too." Stepping into the hallway, Sara waited for Sitara and her father to say goodbye.

"I'll be back soon, Bapa."

"Life is a combination of things, Sitara. Some like oil and water, others like garam masala. I think you and Sara mix well together. You should go out tonight and have fun."

"Perhaps we will, Bapa. Thank you."

"Good night."

Sara smiled and pretended she hadn't overheard.

"Thanks for buying food," Sitara said, when they were tucked safely into the elevator. "How much do I owe you?"

"Don't worry about it."

"But you will let me buy your ticket?"

"I will."

"You impressed my father, you know, with your cooking.

Did you notice how he ate a lot of your mixed vegetable, and hardly any of my chickpea and potato?"

"I'm a novelty, Sitara. Don't take it personally."

"Yeah, but I liked yours better too! Where did you learn to make curry like that?"

"On my father's knee," Sara said, as she pulled her suitcase and camera bags through the lobby.

"Here, let me take that," Sitara offered, as they manoeuvred through the awkward set of front doors.

"Thanks." Sara transferred the handle of her carry-on to Sitara's hands.

"Is this all you brought?"

"Yeah, I don't trust airports," Sara said. "I prefer to keep all of my baggage close at hand."

"You should talk to someone about that," Sitara teased. "Hanging onto your baggage could seriously jeopardize your health."

Sara threw her head back and laughed.

In the lobby of the hotel, Sara said, "There's a bottle of wine in my bag."

"I think I could use some of that."

There was a large crowd in front of the elevator and, turning to Sitara, Sara suggested, "Let's take the stairs." She disliked having loud strangers in her space.

From the stairwell, she led Sitara down the plush, muted hallway until they got to the room that matched the number on her key. After opening the door, she walked to the window and peeked through the curtains.

"There should be glasses in here," Sitara said, vanishing into the bathroom.

Sara lifted her suitcase onto the bed and pulled out the bottle of wine. "Compliments of Jack," she said, removing the paper bag as Sitara returned.

"So my photos didn't screw things up?"

"Not at all."

"Are you sure? I still feel badly about it."

"Don't worry about it, Sitara, please."

"You did a great job today."

"Your mother has a formidable presence. She made it easy."

"Will you try some more tomorrow? She may protest if she's not in her sari, but I'd like to remember her both ways."

"Of course," Sara said. Struggling with the corkscrew on her pocketknife, she asked, "Are you any good at this?"

"I can try." Putting the bottle between her legs, Sitara pulled a few times before she popped the cork. "To friends who travel long distances," she said, after Sara had generously filled their glasses.

"And to those brave enough to return home."

With glasses raised, they locked eyes before drinking.

"I'm really glad you came," Sitara said, as soon as she'd taken a sip. "And I'm glad Jack sent wine! To absent friends," she added, and they raised their glasses again.

Sitting down on the edge of the bed, Sara said, "I think your father is very charming."

"He was playing it up for you."

"I felt bad laughing, with your mother so sick down the hall."

Fingering the unbroken string of beads at her neck, Sitara said, "But what else can we do?"

"I suppose."

"The irony is, I feel better about Parvati than I have in years. She told me some amazing things yesterday about my family. She offered me a connection with my past — with her mother, especially." Sitara sat down on the wooden table next to the TV. "My grandmother was a healer too."

"You didn't know that before?"

"No. My mother never talked much about those days. She was an accountant, and she liked to keep her life in orderly columns, with subtotals at the bottom of every page. There was a column for husband and one, reluctantly, for daughter, but there were none for her family in India."

"What was your grandmother's name?"

"Lakshmi, after the goddess of prosperity. I wish I'd been able to meet her."

"Did she die a long time ago?"

"Yeah, when I was nine. She was already an old woman then — close to ninety, I think."

"I don't know much about my grandparents, either," Sara said, "although they live here in Canada."

Tracing patterns on the top of the TV, Sitara asked, "Do you still have all four of them?"

"No, just three. My mother's parents live in Truro and my father's mom lives alone in Digby. I see them each a couple of times a year."

"I never met any of mine. I just saw photos." Sitara drew her knees into her chest and rested her chin on them. "That's why I wanted you to come. Soon, photos are the only things I'll have left."

click

Shaded by the mechanical box at her side, she slumps — her face in disquieting shadow.

"Are you comfortable up there?" Sara asked. "In the absence of a sofa, we could share the bed."

Smiling, Sitara slid off the table and curled up next to the headboard. "This room is identical to the one I had," she said.

"Hotel rooms all look the same."

"If that's true, why didn't someone choose a more interesting model? I would hang saris from the ceiling, make the lampshades all purple and red, and have CD players instead of TVs."

"That would be quite an improvement, but don't you think we could also lose the ugly carpet, the bedspread, and the putrid green drapes?"

Sitara laughed and unfurled her tightened limbs a little. "How are you feeling?" she asked. "How are your eyes?"

"I can see well enough to know your glass is empty." Sara climbed off the bed and reached for the wine bottle. "When all else fails, drink Italian wine," she said. "It has never disappointed me."

"Thanks," Sitara said, as her glass was refilled.

Sitting down again, Sara asked, "What was Jack like when you met him?"

"Pretty much the same as he is now." She smiled. "Maybe a little thinner. He used to complain about being hungry."

"He still does that."

"But in those days I think he was really broke."

"Did he…" Sara shifted so that her legs weren't wedged as tightly underneath her. "Did he take a lot of photos of…"

"Of pregnant women? I don't know." Sitara took a gulp of wine. "I doubt it. I'm sorry, Sara. I should have warned you."

"No, he could have done that himself."

Sara thought back to the evening when she'd first discovered Jack's photos. "*See anyone you know?*" he'd asked. For many years, she realized now, she'd treated photographs irreverently, assuming they were only valuable if they were for sale. Though she had twice apologized to him, and he had twice accepted, the memory still made her squirm.

Hearing Sitara's head bang gently against the wall, Sara looked up. "What are you thinking?" she asked.

"That I like to drink."

Sara smiled. "Really?"

"I was wondering what will happen to my father when Parvati dies. They're like a lemon and its rind. Without her, he'll have nothing to wrap himself around."

"I suppose," Sara said, swirling the wine in her glass, "you could move back here."

Sitara shook her head.

"Maybe he'll surprise you. I bet he's more resilient than you think. He probably has friends who will help him make the adjustment." Sara wanted to reach out and rub Sitara's back. She knew a lot could change when tension was released from tight shoulders.

"Actually, I've been thinking," Sitara said slowly, "of inviting him to Halifax."

"I was wondering if you might do that."

In the severe light of the hotel room, Sara watched her friend caress the strings of old beads on her wrist. She knew that sandalwood darkened with time and moisture. She had worn a bracelet made of it once too. Reaching over, she turned off the overhead light, leaving only a bedside lamp to guide them.

"Tell me about India," Sitara said in the muted light.

"It's beautiful. I could bring you photographs."

"No, I want to go there. I want you to show me what you know."

Squeezing the pillow that was tucked under her arms, Sara said, "I wasn't there very long." The idea of experiencing India with Sitara was intoxicating, but it made her nervous too. She had no personal stories or spiritual enlightenment to share. On her three-week visit, she had passed through the country more than breathed it in. There was nothing she could say that Sitara couldn't have gained from birth, or from the glossy pages of a well-researched travel brochure. "I'm not sure how much help I could be. I don't really know anything about the —"

"We'll learn together," she said. "More wine?"

"No, thanks." Sara was feeling drunk enough already.

After sharing breakfast in a noisy coffee shop, Sitara led the way back to her parents' apartment building. Riding in the elevator, she said, "I had a dream where you were standing in a lotus flower, dressed in a sari, with your face masked by a screen of incense."

"If you couldn't see my face, then how do you know it was me?"

As the elevator door opened, Sitara pointed to her forehead. "In the dream," she said, "I had an extra eye."

Following in the wake of Sitara's morning confidence, Sara was impressed by her ability to rebound. *Like a tree with strong roots, it would take a lot to tip her,* she thought.

"Good morning," Raj said, as they opened the door. "I am happy to see you again. Your mother has been asking for you, Sitara." Sara smiled as she watched a proud father embrace his only daughter. He was six or seven inches shorter than she was, and his face was buried in her shoulder. "She will not take tea or water," he said. "I have tried."

"I'll go see her."

As Sitara moved down the hall, Raj asked Sara, "How was the hotel?"

"Bland and impersonal, like all great hotels, but I slept well and used lots of their hot water."

"You are smart." He smiled. "I am always too shy of making the bathroom dirty, after someone has worked so hard to make it clean. Come," he said, "I want to show you something."

Unwrapping a length of blue embroidered silk, Raj produced a small, brown photo album with a cover printed in gold script. As he took his place on the sofa, he invited Sara to sit next to him.

"Since you are a photographer," he said, "I thought you might like to see these." Opening the first page, he said, "This is my family."

Sara leaned in to see the tiny, wrinkled baby that Sitara had once been.

"Two days old," he said, and then turning the page, he added, "six months and one year."

Even though the curtains on the large living room window were open, the sky was dark and overcast, and Sara was having trouble seeing. Standing up, she flicked a switch behind the sofa, but nothing happened.

"I have been an electrician my whole life," Raj said, "but still I have not fixed that. Here. This will help." He switched on the white, pleated floor lamp that he used for reading. "Better?"

"Much better, thank you."

Turning the page he said, "These are school pictures. Grades one to twelve, except that grade nine is missing. That year, she was sick for photo day."

The change from baby to little girl was sudden. "Are there none in between?" she asked.

"No."

In some, Sitara's long hair was tucked behind her, in others it was arranged carefully around her shoulders, but in all of them a single gold stud rose from her face like a thorn. Not until the last photo did it seem at home in the hollow of her nose where Sara was used to seeing it.

"She looks like you in that one," Sara said.

"No," Raj smiled, "she inherited her face from her mother — as well as her brains, I believe. I am not sure what she inherited from me."

"Her kindness," Sara said, "and her empathy. And possibly her good taste in curry."

Raj laughed quietly. "What you made last night was very good — too many onions, perhaps, but very good." As he opened the next page of the book, he revealed a black and white photo of him and Parvati. "This was the night we met," he said. "We were at a party and a cousin of Parvati's had a camera."

"I can tell you were happy."

"Yes," Raj said. "For a long time, we were young and happy."

Sara watched as he touched the photo with his hand. She was observing the years in the wrinkles of his skin when his daughter came out of the bedroom.

"Bapa," Sitara said, without seeing Sara at all, "I think you should come with me now."

Rising quickly, Raj left the book on Sara's lap and followed Sitara down the hall.

After she heard the door to Parvati's room latch, Sara went into the kitchen and turned on the hot water. With her hands in the small stainless steel sink, she scrubbed until every dish was clean.

click
Crouched down, with bare feet planted firmly in the soil, a woman uses one of her two hands to wash in the Ganges river. With the other she reaches towards the camera, beckoning to the photographer.